TARNISHED BADGE

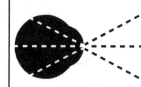

This Large Print Book carries the
Seal of Approval of N.A.V.H.

TARNISHED BADGE

PRESTON LEWIS

WHEELER PUBLISHING
A part of Gale, a Cengage Company

Farmington Hills, Mich • San Francisco • New York • Waterville, Maine
Meriden, Conn • Mason, Ohio • Chicago

Copyright © 1990 by Preston Lewis.
Wheeler Publishing, a part of Gale, a Cengage Company.

ALL RIGHTS RESERVED
Wheeler Publishing Large Print Western.
The text of this Large Print edition is unabridged.
Other aspects of the book may vary from the original edition.
Set in 16 pt. Plantin.

LIBRARY OF CONGRESS CIP DATA ON FILE.
CATALOGUING IN PUBLICATION FOR THIS BOOK
IS AVAILABLE FROM THE LIBRARY OF CONGRESS

ISBN-13: 978-1-4328-6696-9 (softcover alk. paper)

Published in 2019 by arrangement with Preston Lewis

Printed in the United States of America
1 2 3 4 5 6 7 23 22 21 20 19

*For Jeanne Williams,
who provided me the idea for this story
and so much more.*

■ ■ ■ ■

PART ONE

■ ■ ■ ■

CHAPTER 1

Drawing back gently on the reins, Ty Stoddard twisted his lean frame in the saddle and reached for the stock of his Winchester. His fingers slipped around the oiled wood of the second-best medicine a man could prescribe for rustlers. A length of hemp attached to a stout cottonwood limb was best, but Stoddard rode alone.

From down the arroyo, Stoddard could hear bleating calves answered by bellowing cows, most likely Stoddard cattle, Diamond S cattle. He eased the Winchester '73 out of the saddle boot and levered a cartridge into the chamber, staring up the draw where scraggly brush was splattered on either side of the cattle-trampled trail. The bushes hid their spindly skeletons under a gown of new spring leaves, a glossy green in the bright sun. On the gentle breeze brushing against his face rode wispy white flotsam casting itself adrift from the cottonwood tree which had shouldered its way into the bend where the runoff pooled after rains. Narrow shadows from the midday sun clung to the arroyo's red sandstone walls, broken and scattered from years of runoff.

Beyond the bend in the arroyo, Ty Stoddard expected to find Diamond S cattle. And trouble.

Since midmorning, he had tracked the sign from the prairie land above down into the Canadian River breaks. From the tracks, he figured three men herded the cattle, three men he planned to get the drop on. Stoddard ignored the alternative, though the admonition of Trent Jackson kept troubling him. Jackson happened to be Oldham County sheriff as well as Stoddard's brother-in-law.

The rustlers had been running the sheriff ragged, but Trent had warned Stoddard to come for the law if he happened across their trail. Maybe Trent was just looking out for kin or, being a rancher, maybe he just wanted the satisfaction of catching the rustlers himself. Most likely, Ty figured, Trent had his eye on November and the good it might do his reelection bid. The sheriff's badge was to Trent Jackson what the Diamond S was to Ty Stoddard, a prideful possession that brooked no challenge.

Just a year older than sister Molly, now Trent Jackson's wife, Ty had carried a man's load of work on the Diamond S since he was twelve. That was fifteen years ago, and in the two years since his mother's death Ty, more than his pa, had held the ranch together with the sinew of his own muscle and watered it with the sweat of his own brow.

And just around the bend were men intent on destroying the Diamond S. Stealing cattle was as good as taking food out of his mouth and money out of his pocket. Ty felt the anger knotting his muscles and clabbering his stomach. Common sense had dictated he should ride for Trent and his deputy, but anger had driven him this far. Alone.

Stoddard studied the arroyo, his brown eyes taking in the two crows perched atop the cottonwood tree, guarding the trail he must take. He would flush the crows when he advanced, so he gave them a few minutes to leave on their own. They stared back suspiciously, one spreading his wings to fly, then settling back onto the branch when his partner failed to move.

The soft breeze drifted with the cottonwood seed toward him, cool against the sweat staining the blue-striped percale of his pullover shirt. He wore a wool vest, the yellow string of his tobacco pouch hanging from one pocket, the gold chain of his grandpa's watch drooping from the other to a vest button. The vest hid his suspenders except the loops which hooked to buttons on his canvas ducking britches. His seven-dollar, tailor-made boots, fine in their time, were scuffed and worn from working cattle. Stoddard cradled the Winchester in the crook of his left arm and patted the Colt .44 at his waist with his right hand.

From beneath the wide brim of his sweat-splotched Texas-cut hat, his brown eyes fixed on the crows that cawed their taunts at him. The same sun that had darkened the leather of his face had lightened his moustache until it was the muddy yellow of baled hay. From beneath his hat fell tufts of hair, like straw spilling out of a scarecrow. Stoddard spent little time on luxuries like a haircut when nothing was to be gained by it, like a wife. What women were available — and Oldham County offered few — failed to turn Stoddard's head and, anyway, his pa was more butcher than barber with the scissors.

Like his frame, his face was narrow and his nose thin, hawklike. His high cheekbones accentuated the narrowness of his eyes and his hard jaw angled down to a determined chin. The red kerchief knotted in back hid a thick neck which gave way to narrow but muscular shoulders, strengthened by years of riding, roping and branding. What fat there may have been on his body was only passing through on the way to muscle. His lanky frame, barely a hundred and seventy pounds stretched out over a six-foot-two frame, had convinced an occasional cowboy he could be whipped by bare hands, but Stoddard's agility of foot and fist had shown bigger men to an early bedtime. Though he had settled disputes by fists previously, Ty had never before taken the law into his own hands. Occasionally, he had shot at young Comanche and Kiowa bucks slipping from the reservations to raid the Diamond S, land that had once been theirs. But usually those fights had come suddenly, and with other men at his side, so that Ty had had little time to get nervous. Now, though, he could not ignore the clabber in his stomach.

Up ahead, the crows still mocked him and his fears. Time was wasting. The longer Ty waited, the greater the chance the rustlers might discover him. He nudged his roan ahead, his muscles tightening in anticipation, his index finger slipping over the trigger, his left hand giving his mount easy rein.

13

As his barrel-chested gelding stepped easily ahead, the two crows lifted from the cottonwood, squawking their contempt as they flew toward the rustlers. Stoddard swallowed hard, worrying that they had given him away. He stared hard down the arroyo walls, looking for the unknown hidden in the thin shadows. The roan's ears flicked forward at the squeal of a calf, and then the gelding snorted and shook its head, its satiny mane loosing a wisp of trail dust. Moments later Stoddard's nostrils caught a whiff of burning wood and his eyes focused on a faint plume of gray smoke.

Damn them! Ty's hand tightened around the carbine. They were wasting little time in altering the Diamond S into a Diamond 8, a brand that had been showing up for sale around Fort Sumner in New Mexico Territory to the west of Oldham County.

Ty clenched his jaw, his knees squeezing into the gelding's ribs. Tossing its head and whinnying, the roan quickened its pace toward the bend in the arroyo. A chill raced up Stoddard's spine. Then the roan cleared the bend and trotted into the open. Ty lifted his carbine. There they were, three of them, stooped over a calf, two holding him down, the third altering the marking with a red-hot running iron.

Beyond them in a makeshift corral of pickets and rope mingled some forty cattle, the Diamond S brand visible on their rumps. Ty smiled. He had the rustlers. Their horses were picketed too far away for escape. Without alarming the thieves, he rode to within twenty yards of them just as the men, their backs to him, released the calf.

Stoddard pulled the carbine stock tight against his shoulder, aiming at the middle man, a squat fellow wearing a faded red sombrero and holding the running iron.

"Don't move," Stoddard shouted, and the three men flinched, then went stiff in their tracks. "Lift your arms where I can see them." They were slow to respond. "I mean business; now reach."

The branding iron fell to the ground. Without turning around, all three raised their hands above their shoulders. They whispered among themselves, judging how to make their play. Ty decided to take Sombrero first. His finger tightened against the trigger, but he couldn't squeeze off the shot. There was something evil about back-shooting a man, even a rustler.

Stoddard opened his mouth to issue his next command, but the words never came out. A powerful blow crashed into his back beneath the right shoulder blade, a sudden prick and then an explosion in his chest.

It happened so fast that the report of the rifle from behind seemed a minute late in reaching his buzzing ears. He felt his own carbine tumble from his shoulder. Beneath him the roan lurched forward. Stoddard's eyes focused briefly on the saddled horses jerking nervously at their picket pins. Four, not three, saddled mounts watched him gallop by.

Stoddard's eyes went cloudy and the world seemed to tumble around him for an instant. Then he slammed into the ground, his head exploding with a thousand lights that bounced off his brain. His mouth was suddenly dry, though he could taste the blood in his throat and feel it dripping out of his nose. His chest throbbed with spasms of white-hot pain and he wanted to rub away the hurt, but his arms and hands, entwined with his body, would not move. He wanted to scream, but his voice was silent. He wanted to move, but his body was limp and would not respond.

His agonizing senses seemed to be failing him or, even worse, playing tricks on him. From somewhere came a tapping, then three low, raspy whistles. He thought someone mentioned his name, and then through murky eyes he saw four dark forms standing like quivering demons over him. He hurt so, and yet he heard laughter, laughter that ended instantly in the thunder of pain shooting through his chest as if one of those demons had kicked him with a boot. As one of the demons bent over him, Stoddard again heard the tapping noise followed by three low whistles, and felt the demon patting at his vest pocket. Stoddard thought the demon lifted his watch, but he could not be sure of anything now, except that he was cold and the world was turning dark.

CHAPTER 2

The touch came as soft as a butterfly's breath upon his eyelids.

Though his head throbbed with pain and his chest pulsed with a dull ache, the gentle touch made him forget his discomfort. His eyelids quivered and he heard a giggle, not the harsh laugh of the demons he last remembered. Soft flesh danced over his eyelids and lashes again. He shook his head. The giggle exploded into a laugh.

Ty Stoddard pried open his eyelids. His blurred vision slowly focused on two of the bluest little orbs he had ever seen. A small face was poised not six inches from his nose, and he could feel the warm breath. Ten tiny fingers explored his face while his eyes watered at the square of bright light on the wall opposite him. Gradually, his eyes adjusted to the glare and he recognized the wide blue eyes of Delia Jackson. He wanted to laugh, but his parched throat prevented him. Then as Delia's fingers passed over his mouth, he nipped at them with his lips.

Delia squealed with delight and Ty Stoddard shared her pleasure. It was good to be alive.

From the next room, Stoddard heard a clang, followed closely by the worried voice of Molly Jackson.

"Delia, Delia Jackson," Molly yelled, "you get away from your uncle. How many times must I tell you he's very sick?"

Stoddard winked at Delia and she squealed this time.

"Delia, you're almost four now, I know you understand. Leave Ty alone and come help me in the kitchen," Molly yelled, the tread of her feet falling crisply on the plank floor.

Stoddard realized he was laid up in Molly's and Trent's featherbed, resting on his side, his back to the kitchen door. Behind him, he heard Molly sweep into the bedroom and round the end of the bed. When she came into view, her hand was uplifted to swipe at Delia's bottom.

Delia scooted away from the bed and her mother's reach as Molly bent over to swat her.

"Don't Molly," Ty said, his voice coming out a limp whisper that grated at his throat like a dried corncob.

Molly's hand stopped halfway toward the seat of Delia's skirt. Her face was lined with worry and her coal-black hair was mussed as if it had last met a brush days ago. Then both hands flew to her mouth and she fell on her knees beside the bed. Stoddard saw the tears fill her eyes to the brim and then spill down her flushed cheeks.

"Oh, Ty," she cried, dropping her hands toward his cheeks, pausing an instant as if she had thought better of it, and then letting them brush across the stubble on his jaw. "You're alive, you're alive. God's heard our prayers." She leaned over him and kissed him on the forehead, then lifted her hands from his face, her mouth falling open as if she might have hurt him.

He smiled, nodding into the blue eyes that had passed from her into Delia's generation. They were his mother's eyes, too, and Stoddard saw in Molly's drawn face a visage of his mother as she was before she turned sick. He reached for Molly's hand and squeezed it.

Then Molly fell to pieces, sobbing so that Delia took fright and cried along with her. "Oh, Ty," Molly managed between sobs, "I've been so worried. Trent brought you home, draped across your horse. He thought you were . . ." she struggled with the word, which finally exploded out in a loud sob, ". . . dead." It took her a moment to recover and continue. "I thought so, too, you looked so awful, but when we pulled you down, you groaned, so low I almost didn't hear you. We got you into bed and Trent rode to Tascosa for the doctor. Doctor said you'd likely die. Three days, Ty, three days, you've been here and not until now did I believe you would live."

Molly turned from Ty toward Delia. "I'm sorry, honey, I didn't know you were taking such good care of your uncle." Delia took a tentative step toward her mother, then rushed into her outstretched arms. "We're gonna be okay, Delia, everything's gonna be okay, now that Uncle Ty's better."

Delia sniffled. "I made him better."

"Yes, you did, honey, you really did. Won't Grandpa be happy to know his son's okay? And Trent — he was so worried, not realizing you were still alive when he brought you in. Said he came within an inch of burying you in the breaks, but figured you'd want to lie by Momma on the place."

"Water, Molly, water," Stoddard whispered. "Please!"

Molly clutched at her throat. "Oh, forgive me, Ty, for talking instead of thinking." She scurried from the bed and into the kitchen, Delia trailing meekly in her wake.

Ty rolled over onto his back, grimacing at the pain stabbing at his shoulder. Gritting his teeth against the searing throb, he lifted himself enough to prop his head up on the pillows beside him before a blinding flash of light exploded before his eyes from the molten lead rushing along the bullet's course in his shoulder. The room spun around before his eyes and the dizziness in his head would have made him sick at his stomach, had anything been there to lose.

The pain brought back the horror of the shooting. The demons standing over him, the tapping noise and then the low whistles like a ghost's call — it all came back to him, a ghastly reminder he was lucky to be alive.

Then, before he understood what was happening, he felt the mattress give and a soft hand sliding under his head and lifting it. Next, his nose sensed the fragrant water, sweet and near. His lips welcomed the touch of a tin cup and the thrill of cool water rushing into his throat, washing away the residue of death's horrible kiss. The water quenched his thirst, but his body still craved sleep. He floated off into a dream of a land covered with stirrup-high grass, grazed by fat cattle, watered by generous skies and coursed with creeks that always ran full of cool, sweet water. And nowhere in his dream did rustlers ride across the magnificent land.

Aroused from his sleep by a misplaced noise, Ty opened his eyes. The day was dying outside and Trent Jackson stood nearby, flaring a match to the burner of a hand lamp. Suddenly Ty felt uncomfortable, not so much from the pain as from the awkwardness of occupying Trent's and Molly's bed. A man had a right to his wife in his own bed. Damn those rustlers for what they had done to him! Damn them for kicking Trent and Molly out of their bed! The lamp's yellow pallor seeped across the room as Trent shook away the flame at the match tip.

"Evening, Sheriff," Ty rasped, then failed at a laugh.

Trent twisted around, his narrow smile unable to mask the concern in his eyes. The lamplight gleamed off the badge pinned on his vest. "You should've come for me, Ty. That's what I get forty dollars a month for."

Ty nodded. Forty dollars a month! That's what got him to take on the sheriff's job to begin with. Forty dollars a month! Making a success of a ranch was hard enough without taking on the county's problems as well. A sheriff had to deal only with rustlers, petty crimes and tax collections. A rancher had to deal with cattle. And, cattle suffered from heel flies this time of year, screwworms when it got warmer, and pinkeye, too. There were calves to be branded and castrated, cows to be pulled out of the bogs where they'd been trapped by mud in the flight from the heel flies. That was enough to keep a man and his hands busy without taking on the misery of a sheriff's job. Ty knew Trent was doing it for Molly and Delia, trying to give them a few comforts foreign to most hardscrabble Panhandle women, but a man could spread himself thinner than dew in a drought if he took on too much. Ty and his father had tried to talk Trent out of it, but they were rebuffed straight out. No bones about it, Trent Jackson was going to work his ranch and enforce the law in Oldham County, even if it killed him. Ty and Trent shared few traits, but a streak of stubbornness was one of the exceptions.

The badge notwithstanding, Trent Jackson lacked the look of a lawman. He stood a good six feet tall, his build solid but showing in equal parts a strength for handling hard ranch chores and a weakness for too many helpings of Molly Jackson's good cooking. His face was ruddy, round and pleasant, not menacing like that of his deputy, Dewey Slater, and his hairline was receding. He smiled occasionally, but seldom for very long, as if something were perpetually on his mind. Ty doubted he would have taken to Trent Jackson and his dour demeanor, but Molly had seen in him a good husband, which he had turned out to be, and a loving father, which no one could deny after seeing the dance in Delia's blue eyes every time he came home.

Ty twisted in the bed, grimacing at the searing pain. He caught a sharp breath and detected a pleasant aroma wafting its way from the kitchen into the bedroom. Food! His stomach was a vast chasm waiting to be filled. He felt a smile prying its way across his lips as he recognized the fragrance of hot soup and fresh cornbread. He grinned as best he could.

Trent Jackson frowned. "You should've come for me, Ty."

Ty nodded.

Trent turned toward the rocking chair and slid stiffly into the cushion seat, crossing his arms at his chest and staring over the lamp at Ty. "How many were there?"

"Four," Ty answered, trying to gauge Trent's expression, but the sheriff's face was hidden beyond the lamp's glare.

Jackson unfolded his arms and pounded

his palm with his fist. "Four, you say?" He hit the palm again. "Did you recognize any of them?"

Though he couldn't see Trent's face beyond the lamp's glare, Ty felt his hard gaze and shook his head. "The three I saw never turned around. I never saw the one that shot me."

"What about their horses — you recognize any of them?"

"It happened too fast, Trent. I saw four horses as I went down. That's all I recall."

"Damn the luck," Jackson said.

"Such language, Trent Jackson." Molly Jackson stood at the door, hands on her hips.

"Didn't know you was listening, Molly," Trent apologized.

"Doesn't matter whether I was or not; I'll not tolerate that kind of language in my house. If Delia picks it up, it will embarrass us both one day in town. Anyway, you don't be asking Ty so many questions. He needs his strength to get better."

Trent pushed himself up from the rocker and stretched his arms. "I had to ask. I figured you'd want me to catch the dry-gulcher that plugged your brother."

Molly wiped her hands on her apron, then pointed a finger at her husband. "Not as much as I want him to get well."

Her voice was rising like the wind before an approaching storm, and Ty could sense the anger. Trent apparently did, too, for he marched around the bed toward the kitchen, stopping beside Molly and kissing her on the forehead.

"I'm pleased you're improving, Ty," Trent said, as much for Molly's benefit as for Ty's.

Ty had the uneasy feeling in his stomach that Trent was relieved he could not identify the rustlers. Ty couldn't believe Trent was afraid. Possibly it was all the spring work that needed to be done. Possibly it was merely relief that it wasn't Oldham County folks that had done it. When people were losing cattle, suspicions sometimes focused on neighbors, making a sheriff's job tougher. Trent must have a lot on his mind between maintaining the ranch and the law.

Before Ty realized it, Molly was sitting on the bed beside him. "Feel up to some soup and cornbread, Ty? You need to eat."

Ty nodded and settled into his pillow as Molly abandoned him briefly for the kitchen. He could hear her filling bowls at the table, telling Trent to help Delia with her supper. Then Molly returned, carrying a bowl of soup and placing it on the lamp table. She retreated to the kitchen and came back with a platter of cornbread and a glass of water.

She propped two pillows under Ty's head and sat on the mattress edge. Taking the bowl and a spoon from the table, she hummed a gospel hymn Ty remembered as one of his mother's favorites. It brought back sad memories until the first spoon of soup passed his lips. It was hot and good and filling, and Ty had two bowls before Molly refused him more. Then, to top off the meal, she brought him a final piece of cornbread, covered with cane syrup.

It was the first of many meals Ty ate in Molly's bed. For two weeks, he recuperated without leaving the soft mattress, except on washday, when his sister helped him carefully into the rocking chair while she changed sheets. The pain of the gunshot gradually diminished, but his muscles ached from the stiffness of inactivity. By the end of the second week, Ty was finally strong enough to admit to himself he had almost died. Until then, acknowledging that fact might have weakened his resolve to live and undercut his craving to find his bushwhacker.

Except for a copy of *Ivanhoe* he read twice, he had little to do except mend. Delia would bring her rag doll in some days and play on the floor, doting over "Kay-Lee" as much as Molly fretted over her. Delia would scold Kay-Lee for making too much noise whenever Ty shut his eyelids. And sometimes Delia would bring Kay-Lee to the bed and prop her on the pillow beside Ty, repeating for her uncle's benefit Kay-Lee's imagined conversation. Ty enjoyed the closeness of Delia, her blue eyes so deep and innocent, her nose a wriggling button, her skin still unblemished by age or sun, her hair so silky fine.

"You're a fine girl, Delia," Ty would say.

And Delia would always pick up her doll to answer. "And so is Kay-Lee."

But Delia would eventually tire of the room, or Molly would shoo her out so Ty could rest. Then Delia would pick up Kay-Lee and carry her through the common door between her parents' room and her own. That would leave Ty with *Ivanhoe* and a lot of time to stare at the walls, until he could describe from memory every crack in the plaster, or the daily course of every morning and afternoon shadow. Molly had enough chores besides looking after him, so that most of her visits were short and purposeful. When she did take time to converse, she seemed restrained, worried about something unspoken. At first, Ty thought it was about him, but even after he improved and his voice returned, she was still withdrawn. Maybe it was the shock of pulling her brother back from the dead, or the worry about Trent facing the same lonely fate from rustlers.

When Ty felt the strength, and when he could no longer stand his imprisonment in Molly's and Trent's bed, he worked his way to the edge of the mattress, pushed himself up gently and allowed his bare feet to touch the floor. The wooden floor was cool and invigorating. From the kitchen, he could hear Molly preparing another meal. If he had learned one thing while confined to bed, it was that the carcass of one meal was barely removed before another one had to he skinned. Carefully, Ty eased away from the bed, his knees mushy, his back stiff. He straightened slowly and for an instant was dizzy, but he gathered his equilibrium before taking a step to the chest in the corner. There Molly had left his britches after she had washed them and there, too, she had put one of Trent's shirts. As he slipped his legs into the stiff cleanness of the britches, Ty realized these were the clothes that had been laid out for his burial. A man could meet his maker in worse, but it gave Ty an eerie feeling as he stuck his arms into Trent's shirt, baggy around him, a sign of Trent's broader girth. Ty buttoned it easily in spite of the bandages wrapped around his chest and over his shoulder. Ty checked for his pocket watch, but it wasn't with the clothes. Then he moved tentatively toward the kitchen door, gaining confidence and strength with each step.

Ty stood in the open door of the kitchen. Delia, playing at the table with Kay-Lee, saw him first, her eyes lighting up and her mouth dropping open, but Ty touched his lips to signal silence. Bending over the oven, Molly pulled out a pan of fresh-baked bread. The aroma was as invigorating as standing on his own two feet again. Molly dumped the bread on a clean cloth, then dropped the pan on the stove. As she reached to close the oven door, Ty spoke.

"Need help, Molly?"

The oven door clanged shut and Molly twisted around, startled. "Ty, you shouldn't be up." She stepped toward him, motioning him back to bed.

"A man's gotta get up some time, and now's as good as any for me," he said, moving toward the table and the nearest chair. "Sooner I'm up and around, sooner I can go home."

Molly bit her lip. "I'm worried for you and

Pa. And I'm worried about Trent." She moved to the table and fell into the rawhide-bottom chair. "The rustlers, the bushwhackers, the election! Trent's doing the best he can, doing too much for one man, and yet there's talk among some about voting him out of office. He's a proud man, Ty! Too proud to walk away from the job like I begged him to, and too proud to stand losing a vote. Now he's blaming himself for you getting shot." Molly shook her head, her shoulders drooping with the burden of a sheriff's wife.

"It's hard on us all, Molly, and I'm the only one to blame for letting myself get shot. Try not to worry."

She answered with a cynical laugh. "Me not worry about my husband's well-being? That'll be the same day you stop worrying about the Diamond S. The Panhandle's full of worry. If it's not drought, it's flash floods. If it's not wilting hot, it's bone-chilling cold. If it's not your enemies against you, it's your friends." Molly glanced at Delia and smiled. "It's okay, honey; Momma's all right, but why don't you go to your room and give Kay-Lee a nap."

Delia nodded, slipped from her chair and retreated.

Ty reached across the table for Molly's

hand, taking her trembling fingers in his. "Once we stop these rustlers, this land'll make us rich."

"If it don't kill us first," Molly interrupted.

"But Molly, it's a land worth dying for."

"Maybe if you're a man, but not if you're a woman with one child and another one on the way."

For an instant, Molly's words didn't sink in. When they did, Ty laughed. "Here I've been worrying about recovering in your bed."

Molly flushed pink with embarrassment.

His own cheeks reddening, Ty sputtered, "I mean . . . oh, that's not what I meant." He shrugged and squeezed her hand again. "Molly, I'm glad for you and Trent. Anyone else know?"

"Just Trent. I figure word'll get around come Saturday week."

"What's so special about Saturday week, Molly?"

Molly's pale lips smiled weakly. "Trent plans to have a gathering of ranch folks from around these parts. He wants to let folks know then. I'd just as soon let you and Pa know and let word get around that way, but Trent thinks throwing a fine table for folks would help him with the election. Ty, I'd just as soon he lose that election."

Ty released Molly's hand, then rubbed the stubble on his cheeks. "Politics don't set too well with me; guess I'm like Pa. But the social will be fun, let you see the other womenfolks, give you a chance to get your mind off things."

"It'll be plenty of work for me and our hands. We're down to two men now, Bill Witherspoon and Tom Higgins. Trent had to let the other two go."

Ty scratched his head. It made no sense for Trent to let men go when he was stretched thin as it was. And Witherspoon and Higgins were second-rate cowhands, compared to Grant Phipps and Sammy Baker. Trent was a hard man to figure; his insight into others seemed skewed. Like his hiring Dewey Slater as a deputy, releasing Phipps and Baker was a bad decision.

Molly's face suddenly brightened and she bounced up from her chair and ran into the front room before Ty knew what was happening. "I almost forgot, Ty," she called from the front room. "I've got something for you."

Ty hoped it was his pocket watch. It had belonged to his grandfather, his namesake. It had not been among his belongings when Ty had dressed. Ty could not recollect whether it had been taken from him after the shooting. All he remembered was a tapping noise followed by three low whistles.

Molly came back into the room, a fold of cloth in her hand.

He knew disappointment was written over his face, but he smiled as he held out his hand. "What is it?"

"You looked like somebody kicked your dog. This was supposed to be a surprise." Molly shook the fold of cloth and it blossomed into an orange-and-white-checked kerchief. "A peddler came by one day while you were asleep. I thought you might like this when you got better. It's better-looking than most I've seen you wear."

Taking the kerchief from her outstretched hand, Ty smiled, then wrapped it around his neck. "I'm mighty proud you thought of me. I was expecting my pocket watch, though."

"Grandfather's watch? The Waltham with the gold eagle on the case?"

Ty nodded.

Molly's hand flew to her mouth. "You lost it?"

"It was stolen from me after I was shot."

"Oh, Ty, that was all Momma had of grandfather's."

Gritting his teeth, Ty nodded. "I'll get it

back one day, somehow. God help the man that's got it."

CHAPTER 3

Ty and his father rested in straightback chairs on Trent Jackson's porch, their bellies bloated with second helpings of the sheriff's feast. Ty fiddled with the makings of a cigarette and his father let out his belt a notch. Their smiles were as full as their bellies, because Trent Jackson had put on quite a table spread. His hands had slaughtered two beeves, then cooked them over a pit fire for half a day. Pans of beef were still stacked on three makeshift tables, along with bowls of beans, potatoes, canned tomatoes and each woman's kitchen specialty. Platters were covered with bread, cakes, cookies and pies. The last of the women and children were heaping their plates, and still the aroma of so much food carried lightly on the gentle breeze.

Cattlemen from all over the county and several folks from Tascosa had ventured out to Jackson's place for the meal and spring's first social. Ty didn't care much for the crowds, but was glad to be with his father. He leaned the chair back against the limestone block walls of Trent Jackson's house.

"You ate pretty well for a one-armed man," Pa Stoddard said, pointing at his bandaged right arm, "even if Molly did have to cut your meat for you." His father laughed.

"I knew not to ask you. You never came to see me when I was shot," Ty needled his father.

"Hell, Ty, your sister wouldn't let me, saying you didn't need any company, just time to recuperate," Pa Stoddard replied. "She figured I'd send you home and put you back to rounding up and branding calves."

"You would have," Ty replied.

John Stoddard nodded. "When there's work to be done, there's nothing but men and excuses. Only one gets the job done." Pa Stoddard, as everyone called him, had reared his son to work hard and depend on himself first, family second and no one else third. He had never been a gregarious man, so he shunned dependence on outsiders, a philosophy that grew not so much from an inherent dislike for mankind as from a habit of settling in areas where he had no one else to depend on. And he was barely able to accept an outsider like Trent Jackson, even as a son-in-law. Ty had sensed in his father a particular uneasiness about Trent Jackson, most likely because Jackson was more at ease throwing one of these socials than Pa Stoddard was in attending one.

His father's brown eyes were steady, though his hand had a slight tremor to it now. Ty had noticed the tremor at his mother's funeral, thinking it part of the grief, but the tremor had outlasted the burial. After his wife's death, Pa Stoddard lacked the enthusiasm for life he had once had. It was hard to weigh the influence of a woman over her man, but after her death Ty realized it had been great.

Pa Stoddard doffed his hat and ran his rough hand through his thinning hair. "I don't know, Ty, where the cattle business is going. Money's tight and the spring calf crop just wasn't what I was expecting. Don't know whether to blame winter or the rustlers. We were hit again, Ty, since you got shot up."

Ty grunted his disgust. "A man works hard all his life to improve himself and his family and there's always someone there to steal it from him. It's time we did something."

"Hell," his father answered, "we got the

sheriff of Oldham County for an in-law." His words floated in sarcasm.

Ty shook his head. "Trent might make a good sheriff or a good rancher, not both at once."

Pa Stoddard straightened in his chair and pointed to Trent, making the rounds among his guests. "He works people like we do cattle. He's nothing but a politician." He spit the word out as if it were phlegm. "And no politician is on the square, in my books."

"That's a hell of a thing to say about your son-in-law," Ty answered, surprised by his father's strong words.

"Molly picked him for her husband," Pa Stoddard said. "I didn't pick him for a son-in-law."

Ty, who had been nurtured back to health by Jackson hospitality, felt obliged to defend Trent. "Fact is, he works hard as we do, even if he is spreading himself thin. And he's doing it for Molly. She could've done worse, in my books."

"Like Dewey Slater," Pa Stoddard answered. "Deputy Dewey Slater. If Trent thought this gathering would gain him good will, he should never have let Dewey Slater attend."

Ty's gaze fell on Dewey Slater, standing by himself at the corral. He was rattlesnake-

40

thin, with the black eyes of a predator. His angular nose pointed to a sliver of a black moustache over narrow lips always decorated with a corncob pipe and never with a smile. His teeth were stained from years of drinking bad water and his two left incisors were missing, some said the result of a rifle butt to the mouth. When he spoke, his deep voice came out raspy and menacing. By the way he wore them, his two fondest possessions were his badge and his Colt .44, worn butt forward on his left hip for his favored cross-draw. His boots were scruffy, his denim pants worn and his shirt faded, but his badge was shiny and new and his Colt was well oiled in an expensive and equally well-oiled holster. He seemed to watch the gathering with contempt, more comfortable smoking his pipe in solitary than in conversing with the others.

"Slater's a hard case," Ty said, "but if he makes us uneasy, figure what he must do to the rustlers."

"Not much," Pa Stoddard said, staring at Slater, then shaking his head in disgust. "Rustling seems to have picked up since Trent took over as sheriff. That's why he's throwing this grub pile — to win back votes he's lost or about to."

Ty smiled and leaned forward in his chair.

"I suspect there's more to it than that. Trent's a shrewd one," — Ty nodded in the direction of Dewey Slater — "except when it comes to judging character."

"And cowhands," Pa Stoddard said. "I heard he let go Grant Phipps and Sammy Baker. They were better hands than Bill Witherspoon and Tom Higgins — everybody knows that — but he kept them instead."

"Pa, you always said not to criticize the trail a man takes until you've ridden in his saddle," Ty challenged his father.

"I've been wrong before, Ty," Pa Stoddard answered, and then stared silently toward Tascosa road. "Speak of the devil," he said, pointing toward town. "Two riders! I do believe it's Phipps and Baker."

Phipps was a big man who seemed to dwarf his horse, and Baker was equally distinct from a distance because he carried his left shoulder, banged up in a throw into a fence by a bronc, lower than his right.

"You've good eyes for a grouchy old rancher, Pa. Wonder what brings them this way? Bet it wasn't an invitation."

Before his father could answer, Ty heard a commotion around the food tables. It was Trent Jackson, trying to get folks' attention. Apparently, he had not noticed Phipps and

Baker. Slowly the murmuring of the adults gradually diminished, though the horseplay of the kids took longer to silence. Ty watched as folks began to gather around Jackson, who climbed on a wooden bench by one of the food tables. Ty watched with envy Trent's commanding presence. The sheriff lifted his hand for more silence and everyone seemed to obey and offer him their rapt attention — everyone, that is, except Dewey Slater. The deputy had spotted the riders and stood akimbo to meet them by the corral.

"Think we need to join them?" Ty offered.

But Pa Stoddard waved the suggestion aside. "He'll be talking politics, so he'll be talking loud."

Ty snickered and settled deeper into his seat, alternating glances between Trent Jackson and the approaching riders. Phipps and Baker were good men, unlikely to cause trouble, though something must be perplexing them to ride in on a gathering like this. Ty was less confident of Dewey Slater's manners.

As Trent Jackson waited for total silence, Ty studied with envy the sheriff's ability to stand before people and not feel as if he were about to be executed by their stares. As for himself, Ty knew he'd rather ride before a hundred bushwhackers than stand before five people and make a talk.

Jackson lifted his hand to his hat and removed it, holding it with both hands in front of his belt buckle. A smile creased his face, so natural and so unlike any smile Trent could offer one-on-one that Ty was amazed at his composure. Trent was as comfortable before a crowd as a cowhand is in the saddle.

"Friends and neighbors," Jackson started, "I welcome you to my ranch and hope my hospitality has met with your approval. It has been a long winter and now that spring is here, it was overdue for us to get together and enjoy each other's company."

Out by the corral, Phipps and Baker approached Dewey Slater, who had planted himself in their course. His hands on his hips, Slater squared himself as if he expected trouble.

Jackson, enamored of the attention of the crowd, remained oblivious to the approaching riders. "Now, some among you figure that there's more to this than just Trent Jackson's hospitality. And you're right."

The men nodded their heads, as if telling their wives or fellow ranchers they were wise to the sheriff's ploy.

"Now," Jackson continued, "some of you

44

have figured, with an election coming up in the fall and me being up for reelection as sheriff of Oldham County, that I just might want to influence your vote." Jackson paused, scanning the circle of faces before him. "Well, of course I want to influence your vote. Only a fool wouldn't, and I'm no fool."

Everyone laughed, and Ty with them, but the grin on Jackson's face slid away into a frown when he saw Phipps and Baker visiting with Slater out by the corral. For a moment, Jackson lost his thought as the laughter died away. After an unnatural pause, Jackson smiled again, but not with the same confidence as before.

"Though I'd certainly like to have your vote, that's not the reason I've thrown this get-together. Instead, I have an important announcement." Jackson paused for effect and for a quick glance at Baker and Phipps, who had ridden around Slater and headed toward the crowd.

"I invited you here to announce that Molly is with child," he said. A moment of silence was shattered by the applause of the crowd. "Come October," he shouted over the celebration, "I'll be a father again." The smile was genuine now, and the women were scurrying toward Molly to offer their

45

congratulations and their advice. "Now, men," Jackson said, returning his hat to his head, "the women have something to talk about. I'd like to meet with all you ranchers in the barn in five minutes to discuss matters of concern to us all."

Ty admired Jackson's finesse. For a man who didn't plan to bargain for votes, Jackson had announced his wife's pregnancy with the same result.

"No way to tell your neighbors your wife's pregnant," Pa Stoddard said, all the time eyeing Jackson.

After shaking several hands, Jackson stepped down from his box and retreated toward Dewey Slater, watching Phipps and Baker all the way. The two cowhands nudged their horses toward the house.

Grant Phipps and Sammy Baker nodded at the Stoddards as they neared the porch. "Afternoon, Mr. Stoddard, Ty," Phipps offered. Phipps was a bear of a man with huge hands and a full beard which gave him a grizzled appearance. Because of his size, he was hell on horses and on storebought clothes, which seldom fit. Despite his rough appearance, he was a decent type, and as caring for a motherless calf as he would be for an orphan.

"Sorry about your jobs, fellows," Pa Stoddard replied. "What brings you back?"

"Money," Sammy Baker said, trying to square his uneven shoulders as best he could. His voice was high and squeaky, making him sound nervous, but his eyes were as clear and as void of deception as a cloudless sky. Cowhands didn't have much except their reputation for hard work and honesty, and both Baker and Phipps withstood the toughest scrutiny.

"The back pay we're due," Phipps said.

"You didn't get your pay when you were cut loose?" Pa Stoddard spoke in amazement.

Baker and Phipps nodded meekly, as if it embarrassed them to accuse another man of not living up to his end of a deal. "We were promised pay before now, but nothing's come of it," Phipps said. "We figured if we showed up at Jackson's shindig while he's trying to buy votes for the election, it might help him square up with us."

Ty saw Trent break away from Dewey Slater and stride toward Phipps and Baker. Trent advanced with anger in his eyes and malice in his step.

Phipps sensed Jackson's approach and twisted in his saddle. "We're back, boss," Phipps said, "to get our pay."

Jackson forced a smile. "Good to see you,

boys," he said, without sincerity.

"We want our money," Baker said. "It won't sound too good for your election chances if word gets out you don't pay your debts."

"I pay my debts," Jackson answered, turning to Pa Stoddard for affirmation, but his father-in-law did not twitch a muscle to agree or disagree.

Phipps shook his head, then spit a brown stream of tobacco juice on the ground by the porch step. Before speaking, he twisted around in his saddle toward the corral and stared at Dewey Slater. "We're asking only for what's due us! Seventy-five dollars each for three months' work." Turning back to Jackson, he cocked his head, then licked his lips of the tobacco residue. "Keep that crockhead Slater away from us. He's no cause to get involved. This ain't a matter for the law, Sheriff."

Jackson's hands knotted into fists and he took a half step toward Phipps's horse. The animal shied away. Glancing at Pa Stoddard, Jackson stopped dead and caught a big breath. "Money's been tight; you boys know that."

Baker grabbed his hat and waved it in a grand arc toward the tables. "Money wouldn't seem to be too tight, you putting on a big spread like this for all the ranch-ers."

Gritting his teeth, Jackson silently gauged his former hands, then looked at Pa Stod-dard. "See me in town at the courthouse Monday. After the bank opens, you'll get your due," Jackson answered, the hint of a threat in his inflection.

"That's all we're asking, Trent, that's all we're asking," Baker said.

Jackson cleared his throat and slapped his hands together. "Now you boys get off my place. You've no more business here, now or ever again."

A finger of tobacco juice shot out of Phipps's mouth, landing on the hardpacked ground, but splattering on the porch step. "A few years ago, you wouldn't of had a place without us to do your work, honest work. We wouldn't work for a man who's let his ambitions eat his gratitude. We'll see you Monday morning in Tascosa, Trent."

Phipps and Baker jerked the reins on their mounts and the horses spun around, then trotted away toward the corral, breaking into a canter when they reached Slater.

Wordlessly, Jackson and the Stoddards watched them ride away. The jabbering of the women still congratulating Molly on be-ing with child seemed alien to the tension

49

at the porch. Jackson brushed his forehead with his hand. Though his lips contorted into a forced smile, his eyes were hard and unforgiving when he turned around to face Pa Stoddard and Ty.

"I'll settle it come Monday; you have my word on it."

Pa Stoddard crossed his arms over his chest. "They're the ones that need your word, not us."

Jackson's shoulders drooped a moment; then he caught a deep breath. "I should've taken care of it before now, but there's been so much on my mind, with Ty's shooting and the rustling."

Only cold silence answered, and Jackson toed at the ground, scraping with his boot enough dirt to bury Phipps's tobacco splatterings.

Ty glanced at his father, taking in his set jaw, his narrow eyes. It was an expression he had seen a thousand times, as a kid and now as a man, when he had done something that hadn't met his father's expectations. But Pa Stoddard said nothing more, and the silence between the two men seemed to stretch the seconds into hours.

"I've asked the men to join me at the barn," Jackson said, looking from Pa Stoddard to Ty, "while the women are still fussing over Molly. They'll think us fellows've got a jug of whiskey, and that's just fine. What I want to talk about is men's business. Ty and Mr. Stoddard, I hope you'll all join us."

Jackson took a tentative step toward his guests, then stopped and looked back over his shoulder. "I want you there. It's important for the future of Oldham County."

CHAPTER 4

A silence hung over the porch as if it were a funeral parlor. Ty felt his face flush with embarrassment for Trent Jackson. A man was entitled to an honest mistake, but letting Phipps and Baker go without pay was more than an oversight. Trent was stretched too thin on time as well as income. Ty tapped his fingers on the porch railing, feeling a tingle of pain all the way up in his shoulder and his still raw wound. There was a touch of pain in his heart, too, for Molly, knowing how terrible she'd feel if word got out that Trent was behind in paying his debts. Ty knew he owed Molly and Trent for his recovery and for their patience as he regained his strength. He was glad only family had heard the exchange between Trent and his two former hands, because they could keep it among themselves.

As he thought, little Delia danced up toward the house, holding her doll, Kay-

Lee, with one hand and the arm of a freckle-faced neighbor girl with the other. Trent was doing everything for her, the little one on the way, and Molly, Ty figured, and maybe a man was entitled to an occasional mistake.

"Hi!" Delia said, her shy blue eyes avoiding the direct stare of her grandfather and uncle. "Momma says we need to give Kay-Lee a nap. We don't have to take a nap, just stay on the bed and make sure Kay-Lee goes to sleep."

The two girls hopped up the two steps to the porch and passed the silent men, stopping at the door.

"Momma says I'm gonna have a new baby to play with," Delia said, "but I still love my Kay-Lee. Don't you?" Grabbing her doll by the neck, Delia shook Kay-Lee's head and mumbled some gibberish for Kay-Lee's baby talk. Then Delia disappeared into the house with her red-haired friend.

"She's a charmer, isn't she," Ty said.

"Takes after her mother," Pa Stoddard answered.

The Stoddards stared out over the Jackson place, taking in the women still gathered around Molly and the men heading by twos and threes out to the corral. Jackson had spent money on the place, maybe a hundred and fifty dollars too much, considering the demands of Phipps and Baker. While the place lacked the luxuries of the bigger conglomerate ranches that were shouldering their way into the Panhandle, it stood first among the medium-size ranches, particularly the home place.

The house, with its thick block limestone walls and high ceilings, was cool in the summer, though a bit devilish to heat in winter. A smaller limestone building beyond the corral served as the bunkhouse for the hands, and nearby was a stone smokehouse. The picket corral, big enough to handle twenty head of livestock, backed up against a whitewashed barn made of cut lumber hauled in from Dodge City, Kansas, the nearest source of supplies for Tascosa and most of the Panhandle.

The buildings stood some hundred yards from the edge of the two-mile-wide chasm cut over thousands of years by the Canadian River, which ran shallow, wide, and muddy all the way into Indian Territory. South of the place, a steep trail, worn over the years by the rainwater and the hooves of buffalo on the prowl for water, ran from the canyon rim to the river. The canyon sheltered the southern approach, but the house, like a mighty castle, had an imposing view of everything from the north, east and west.

Ty knew, by the jealous talk, that some Oldham County residents begrudged Trent Jackson his place, but they couldn't say he hadn't worked for it. And some of those same people weren't too proud to come to eat his food when it was offered. By now most of the men had gathered at the corral and Jackson strutted among them, shaking hands, slapping them on the back and occasionally glancing toward the porch and the Stoddards.

"Trent's sweated long enough," Pa Stoddard said. "Let's go hear him out."

The Stoddards stepped off the porch and marched toward the corral. Ty felt proud to walk with his father. It had always exhilarated him when they tackled a chore together, because it seemed there was nothing they couldn't do. As he walked step for step with his father, he studied Trent Jackson, whose smile had more lift to it, now that his in-laws were joining the crowd. Ty couldn't get over how different Trent seemed one-on-one from when he was in a crowd.

Ty's concentration was broken by a man angling toward them from the corral. Dewey Slater! Maybe lawmen should have a hard edge to them, but Slater had a vicious streak; he was the kind of man who would bully a stumble-drunk cowboy or kick a sick dog. Maybe Trent figured it was better to have him on the side of the law rather than against it, where Slater might naturally gravitate if left on his own.

Puffing on his corncob pipe with each step, Slater headed straight for Ty. As he drew nearer, Slater spoke with all the sincerity of a perjurer: "We're lucky to have you with us, and, from what the doctor said, you're lucky to be here. Another inch to left and you'd likely be dead." He stretched out his hand for Ty's.

Out of instinct, Ty lifted his good hand halfway to Slater's, then stopped. Before he could lower it, Slater grabbed and pumped it, and slapped Ty's bad shoulder with his free hand. Ty wince as pain coursed through his veins, then gritted his teeth to disguise his discomfort.

Slater released Ty's hand. "Any idea who did it?" His voice had a cocky tone. "I'd have a score to settle, if you did." Slater took the corncob pipe out of his mouth and, with a puff, sent a serpent of smoke crawling out the hole left by his two missing teeth.

Ty shrugged. "A man doesn't generally get a good look at a backshooter."

"A boy may let himself get shot in the back. A man doesn't!" Slater shook his pipe-stem at Ty's nose. "Next time, come get a man to help, so you don't get yourself killed!" Slater slipped the pipe back between his lips with a growl.

Slater's words burned more painfully than the aggravating throb in his wounded shoulder. Slater had a knack for cutting to the quick. That was why he was so unpopular among county folks, and why Trent Jackson might have a tough time getting reelected sheriff in the fall. Ty's brain spun like the wheels on a runaway wagon, to come up with a satisfactory retort, but he lacked Slater's talent at insult. Wordlessly, Ty brushed past the deputy and caught up with his father at the corral gate.

Trent Jackson unhooked the gate and opened it enough for the Stoddards. Ever the politician, he shook the hand of each and motioned for them to join the others by the barn door. Ty glanced over his shoulder, relieved to spot Slater marching around the corral like a sentry.

By the barn door, a dozen Oldham County ranchers stood in a herd, milling like the horses at the other end of the corral. Their hats pulled low over their eyes, they watched Trent Jackson's approach. They were solid stock to a man, all dependable and guileless, none lazy, all kindred of the Oldham

County ranching nobility.

Zack Miller had taken up ranching in Oldham County about the same time as Pa Stoddard, making them the first two white ranchers in the area. The issue of which of them was the first concerned neither, as they had always been more worried about carving their ranches out of a wild land, and then keeping them together in a civilized country. As a son of the South, Miller's speech was as sticky as Georgia humidity. He wore a planter's hat, and some said it represented more than just his preference in haberdashery. He was reputed to have been a big slave owner and landholder on the outskirts of Atlanta before the War Between the States. Although most men in Oldham County wore a sidearm, Miller carried a rolled bullwhip over his shoulder, an instrument rumor said he had used to keep his slaves in line. Though he stood half a foot under six feet, that coiled bullwhip commanded the same respect as a buzzing rattlesnake, and bigger men generally gave him plenty of room.

His attire as fastidious as his Southern manners, Miller stood as stiff as his starched linen shirt, paper collar and cuffs, and as straight as the crease in his wool pants. The five diamonds — one for each wife he had outlived, some said — in the stickpin half hidden in the folds of his red silk tie were as clear and hard as his gray eyes. Miller nodded as the Stoddards approached.

"You know what this is about, Stoddard?" Miller asked.

Pa Stoddard shrugged.

"Probably more politicking," Grady "Red" Stewart answered. "Jackson's worried he won't get reelected. And with good reason!"

Stewart had a habit of expressing what was on other men's minds. He cocked his head and folded the fingers of his left hand into his palm, then with his right thumb pressed each knuckle until it popped. He scratched the full red beard that grew out of control from his chin to his ears then petered out atop his head into a poor crop that was combed straight forward in thin red furrows. His ruddy complexion and red, watery eyes suggested a fondness for good whiskey. Liquor tightened his tongue, and some, like Pa Stoddard and Miller, found him more tolerable after a few drinks, when he was more likely to keep his thoughts to himself. Stewart viewed himself as an innovator, and had been the first in the county to bring in shorthorn cattle to supplant the longhorns. The others still poked fun at his "dude" cattle, but their laughs were not nearly so loud now. Out of boredom, Stewart drew a wrinkled kerchief from his coat pocket, caught his nostrils and exploded his nose into it.

The Mason brothers, Gus and Lamar, snickered as Stewart wiped his nose and whiskers of the debris. They ran the Mirror M ranch together. In fact, they had done just about everything together — marrying twin sisters in the same ceremony, building their ranch houses side by side, having kids in pairs. One couldn't take a fever without the other one feeling poor, or even take a leak without the other feeling the urge, so folks said. Coincidence or not, the Masons took a lot of teasing about their similarities, and they took it well. They were good, solid family men with seven kids apiece, and whatever wildness had once been in their lanky frames had been gently removed by the twin sisters.

Bob Vandiver, owner of the Double Deuce Ranch won in a poker game with the lowest pair possible, stood in the shade of the barn, eyeing Jackson. Vandiver was well liked by folks, generally because he pitched in when others needed help and didn't ask many favors in return. A tall, handsome man with a sharply chiseled face, Vandiver was a widower at age thirty.

Rounding out the major ranchers were Stan Ballard, who ran the Lazy B Ranch; Mart Bigsby, sole son and heir of a late Texas congressman and now operator of the Bird Wing Ranch; and Walt Storm, owner of the Lightning Bolt Ranch. There were others, but what these men and Pa Stoddard decided, the rest would go along with.

Trent Jackson marched past the men and unlatched the barn door. "Why don't we step inside. Dewey'll see that we're not bothered," the sheriff said, nodding toward his deputy outside the corral. He swung the door open and motioned for the others to enter. Smelling of fodder and manure, the barn was dark and cool, the open door letting in too little light.

"Why the secrecy?" Miller asked, absently fingering the diamond stickpin in his silk tie.

Jackson moved to a grain bin and lifted the lid, then pulled a couple of bottles of liquor from inside. "The women figure we'll be taking a little nip anyway, so why disappoint them?" Jackson hoisted the whiskey bottles by their thin necks. "Anyone care for a drink?"

Stewart shouldered his way past the others. "Don't mind if I do," he said, grabbing a bottle with one hand and in one smooth motion uncorking it and planting it against his lips.

"Anyone else?" Jackson offered the bottle around, and both Mason brothers reached for it together. The other ranchers nodded and laughed as Gus Mason wound up with it.

"Gentlemen," Jackson started, "we've a rustling problem to straighten out in Oldham County."

Miller cleared the phlegm from his throat with a hack and then spit at a pile of manure. "We know that. It's your job to be doing something about it."

"You're right, but Oldham County is a lot of territory for me and a deputy to cover. Even the Panhandle Stock Growers Assocation can't buy enough men to look out for our interests against rustlers. We've got to give the rustlers a dose of stronger medicine." In the dim light, Jackson's gray eyes were hard to decipher.

Stewart paused in his suckling the bottle. "You mean turn vigilante?" Around him others nodded at the question.

"Regulators," Jackson said.

"Vigilante, regulator, it's all the same," Miller said. "Why not just deputize the lot of us when you need help, keep it within the law?"

Jackson swiped his hat from his head and stepped toward Miller. "Fear! There's not a one of us that hasn't worried about being backshot like Ty. I found him, brought him in for dead and burying. I'm no coward, but I can't say I've slept good at nights knowing I was likely to be dry-gulched if I protected my cattle or did my job as sheriff. I figure it's time we put a little fear in their lives. I can't scare them away within the law, but I can outside the law. We've gotta do something before more of us wind up lame like Ty, or worse."

The men grunted, a couple looking toward Ty and nodding.

Ty's face heated with embarrassment. He felt like a foolish kid again when he realized he was the youngest one standing in the barn. The men with him had plenty of grit in their craws, but they were proud and independent men who seldom would confess to a problem that they could not resolve alone.

Stewart brushed his hand against his wild beard and kissed the bottle again.

Vandiver stepped into the circle of men, his gaze bouncing from Pa Stoddard to Miller and back. "Mr. Stoddard and Mr. Miller have been around the longest. What do you two say?"

Pa Stoddard looked beyond Miller at his son-in-law, as if gauging Jackson's manhood. "I've lost my share of cattle and my headcount is down this spring from where it should be. I almost lost a son to boot. I'm tired of losing what's mine."

Miller twisted his shoulders around and studied Vandiver more than the sheriff. "I'm in, too." Slowly, his gaze went from man to man and the whip rolled around his shoulder slid down his left arm into his hand. "I'm in, but I'll kill any man that ever mentions my name in the same breath with the regulators. I'd expect the same from any of you."

CHAPTER 5

The sun peeked from the eastern horizon, a sliver at first, and then an orange ball that painted the sky with pastels of pink, orange and blue. The morning came on silent feet, disturbed only by the call of a mother quail keeping watch over her scurrying offspring, and by Trent Jackson as he harnessed the wagon team and saddled his and Ty's horses. The cool morning air was damp with the heavy dew that coated the grass in robes of sparkling diamonds.

Ty Stoddard stepped out onto the porch, stretching his good arm and wriggling the stiffness out of the right arm still in a sling. He breathed in the invigorating morning and studied the sun's painting on the sky's canvas. It was a great day to be going back to the Diamond S, though it did embarrass him that Molly had prohibited him from helping her husband saddle the horses and hitch the team. Molly was as protective as the mother quail he watched shepherding her brood through the grass. He had planned to ride home with his pa after the social on Saturday, but Molly, her arms folded across her breast, had forbidden it in no uncertain terms. Must be the maternal instinct boiling in her blood from the little one on the way. Even so, it was hard to argue with the woman who had brought him back from death's chasm. And, too, Ty had been exhausted after the social.

Jackson had business in Tascosa, so he had told Molly, and Ty knew that part, if not all of that business, was to pay Grant Phipps and Sammy Baker the wages that were theirs. But since the Diamond S was the other side of Tascosa, Molly had insisted that Ty ride with them in the wagon to town and then go the rest of the way on his own, if he felt up to it. Ty would have preferred to ride his roan the whole way, but Molly would have none of it. She alternated the last few days between stubbornness and tears, the symptoms of pregnancy when little else showed. Ty didn't care to deal with either.

As Ty straightened the new orange kerchief, Molly's gift, around his neck, he watched Jackson jump into the platform spring wagon, pop the reins against the two matched grays, and aim the wagon for the porch. The wagon's rattling trace chains, creaking harness leather and moaning axles broke nature's morning spell, but the noise seemed in concert with Jackson's brooding. The sheriff had been sullen this morning, not saying much at the breakfast table and quickly gobbling up his bacon and biscuits and gulping down two tins of coffee. Ty figured his brooding had to do with Phipps's and Baker's confrontation at the social. Nothing particularly threatening about the encounter, just the galling embarrassment of having his debt brought up in front of family. Maybe Molly's insistence that Ty ride with them into Tascosa this morning was particularly galling since Ty's presence was a piercing reminder of his shame.

Jackson swung the wagon around in front of the porch and pulled up hard on the reins. He tied the reins to the brake and jumped down from the spring seat, landing stiffly by the porch. "I've saddled your horse," Jackson said, without looking at Ty. "You gonna let Molly keep you from riding him into town?"

Shrugging, Ty grinned. "I'd rather sit in the wagon like an old woman than have Molly get teary-eyed on me again, or worse, turn stubborn as a mule."

As he spoke, he heard the door open behind him. "Stubborn as a mule! Well, Tyrus Bartholomew Stoddard, talking that way about me is unbecoming." Molly stepped out of the house carrying a basket in one hand and a stoppered jug filled with water in the other.

Delia emerged from behind the curtain of her mother's gingham skirt, sleepy-eyed and dragging Kay-Lee. Seeing her father, she started toward him, stumbling down the porch into his outstretched arms.

"How's my favorite girl?" The iciness that had tipped his words suddenly melted at Delia's giggle.

"Will the ride be long, Papa?" Delia asked. "Kay-Lee's tired and sleepy."

Jackson lifted her into the wagon seat. "You just wait here. I bet Momma will make a pallet for you and Kay-Lee in the back so she can get some rest."

Molly handed her husband the basket and jug. "I've got the quilts by the door." As she disappeared inside the house, Jackson placed the load in the wagon, then bounded up onto the porch. Something about Delia always invigorated Jackson, clearing away whatever natural moodiness clouded his outlook, Ty thought. Another child would be welcome in the Jackson home. When

Molly stepped back out onto the porch, Jackson was at the door waiting for her. He took the quilts from her, then leaned down and kissed her gently on the forehead. It was a wordless kiss of reassurance that asked forgiveness for little things unmentioned.

Jackson gave Molly his arm and escorted her from the porch to the wagon. After placing the quilts in the back, he assisted his wife into the wagon, where she began unfolding the quilts in the wagonbed and smoothing out a resting place for Delia and her doll. When she finished, she put Delia on the pallet and covered her and Kay-Lee. As she straightened her shawl, Ty grabbed the wagon seat and pulled himself up, realizing how awkward he must look with just one good arm. Molly snickered.

"Stubborn as a mule," Ty announced, and Molly laughed again.

"I'm gonna miss you around here, Ty," she said. "You've been good company, and Trent's gone so much of the time." Her hand slipped over his left hand and she squeezed it tightly. "With the election, he'll be away even more between now and fall. It'll be lonely."

"Guess I'll have to get shot more often," Ty said.

"Oh, Ty, you're just like Pa!" She jerked her hand from his. "Acting foolish when someone gets serious."

Ty shrugged and reached to untie the reins, his flesh prickling with embarrassment. "I appreciate all you did, Molly."

Molly grabbed the reins from Ty. "I'm driving, and you're gonna sit and accept my help a little longer, even if your pride makes you uncomfortable."

Jackson rode up and tied Ty's roan to the wagon tailgate. "You two ride on. I've got instructions for Bill Witherspoon and Tom Higgins to handle while I'm away. I'll catch up with you down the road."

Molly snapped the reins and the wagon lurched forward. As Jackson rode down to the bunkhouse, Ty wondered why Higgins and Witherspoon weren't already up and at work. It was past dawn, their horses were still in the corral, and no smoke was coming out of their stovepipe. Ty shrugged. He shouldn't second-guess Jackson, because the sheriff was doing as well as any other rancher in Oldham County and, some thought, better.

The six miles to Tascosa rolled away quickly, the trail skirting the edge of the Canadian River canyon. Beneath them the canyon changed personality as the sun rose and the long shadows retreated into the draws, and the river glistened like a gold necklace. Jackson caught up with them shortly, but rode ahead, leaving Ty and Molly to talk about old times, the new one on the way, and all the gossip from the Saturday social.

Overhead the sun continued its climb, the pastels of early morning fading away into a faint blue sky without a cloud, and the dawn cool drowning in the flood of sunlight. A couple of miles from Tascosa the trail merged with the road from Dodge City, Kansas. The road, the principal supply route for the Panhandle, was scarred and rutted from heavy loads and peppered with the manure of oxen and mules. As the matched grays trotted, their hooves kicked up clouds of dust and the wagon wheels churned up tiny dust devils.

The road twisted north away from the canyon lip and then back toward it, leading down a gentle slope that fanned out into the river's wide cut. At the bottom of the gentle slope, Tascosa had sprouted up beside Tascosa Creek, which offered drink to the some four hundred citizens and then emptied into the Canadian River farther south. Some fifty permanent buildings and half again as many tents and small shanties, many to the south of Tascosa in "Hogtown," a cowboy retreat with a reputation no better than that of the women who inhabited it, had sprung up to meet the area's needs, both for sustenance and sin.

Delia awoke as the wagon clambered down the sloping trail toward town. Gathering Kay-Lee while she wiped the sleep from her eyes, she climbed from the wagonbed into her mother's lap. Molly passed the reins to Ty and he sighed. He didn't care to ride into Tascosa with Molly handling the reins, even if he had but one strong arm.

The trail leveled off at the steepled schoolhouse at town's edge. Just ahead stood the two-story stone courthouse and jail. Like many structures built with taxes, it was a bit too fancy, Ty thought, with its tin roof, its tall glass windows and shutters and its waist-high white picket fence. Nonetheless, he had to admit it was the best-looking building in town.

At the hitching post beside the courthouse, Ty spotted Phipps and Baker beside their horses, waiting. About the same time Ty saw them, so did Jackson. He twisted around in his saddle, checking whether Ty had noticed, then yanked the bridle on his gelding and started back for the wagon, his face drawn and without the hint of a smile.

"I've business at the courthouse," he told Molly. "Go ahead and visit the stores, but watch what you spend. I'll catch up with you after lunch." He galloped toward the courthouse.

"Bye, Papa," called Delia, but Jackson did not respond.

By the time the wagon reached the courthouse, Jackson had escorted Phipps and Baker inside. If Molly saw her husband's former hands, she said nothing, being preoccupied with brushing Delia's hair and tying a yellow bow atop her head.

Ty herded the team past the courthouse and at the end of the next block turned the team onto Main Street. Some twenty structures stared at each other across the street, a few with gaudy false fronts, but most with faces as unpretentious as their owners.

The clang of hot metal caught between heavy hammer and anvil rang down the street like a sick bell. Ty glanced at Abe Polk's blacksmith and stable and saw Polk's stocky form outlined in the orange glow of the hearth. As the only blacksmith in town, Polk was a busy man who had won the respect of county ranchers by refusing to make running irons for every cowboy in the county. Those running irons were too often used for altering honest men's brands, and

Polk wanted no part of that. Everyone in Oldham County town knew where Polk stood on lawlessness.

Opposite the Burleson store, Ty pulled back on the reins and the team stopped, tossed their heads and blew. It was nearing nine o'clock, Ty figured, though he couldn't be certain without a watch. Morning was the best time of day in Tascosa because the town was gentle. Except for Polk's constant but honest and productive clatter, the town stood tranquil, the saloons quietly recuperating from the night before, the lusts of yesterday spent and today's desires still budding. Delia asked to get out of the wagon to run along the boardwalk in front of the Burleson store. Molly obliged, easing her daughter by her hands over the side until she touched ground. Giggling as she jumped onto the rough planks, Delia charged back and forth in front of the store.

"She's a doll," Ty said to Molly. "Reminds me of you."

Molly flushed. "I hope she takes to the new one well."

Before Ty could answer, the glass panes rattled as the door to Burleson's store swung open. "Open for business," he called, glancing at the wagon, then smiling as Delia darted inside, her doll, Kay-Lee, in tow. "Go

74

right in," he said, then snickered to himself. Tobe Burleson was a hefty man who had eaten too many crackers from his cracker barrel. His appetite, like his store, was the biggest in Oldham County. He had a deep laugh that erupted regularly from his broad girth. He nodded to Ty, then smiled weakly at Molly, as if it were forced. It confounded Ty, because Burleson had made a reputation as the friendliest merchant in Tascosa. It could be that Burleson still suffered indigestion from all the food he had put away at the social.

Ty stretched the stiffness out of his joints and stood up, yawning. Then he jumped out of the wagon onto the street, stumbling for a step, the team dancing nervously against the tied reins for a moment.

"Agile as a deer." Molly laughed.

When Ty turned around to help Molly from the wagon, he realized Burleson had disappeared into the store. Molly stepped lightly from the wagon and caught a deep breath once she was on the ground. She looked pale, and Ty held her hand as he studied her. "I'm okay, just light-headed for a moment. It's usual for a woman with child."

Ty nodded, but studied her carefully as he accompanied her onto the boardwalk and into Burleson's store. The smell of newness tickled their noses as they moved among the tables stacked with merchandise. Molly headed for the clothes and bolts of cloth stacked on a table near the front window. After circling the saddles and shaking his head with envy, Ty ambled toward the gun counter where Burleson waited.

"Glad to see you're about now, Ty. We were sure worried for a while."

"Thanks, Tobe. I'm glad to have my feet under me again and to be heading home," Ty answered, studying the guns under the glass case. "Some good-looking pieces there, but guess I'll have to pass for now on one. I could use a couple cartons of .44 slugs."

"Planning on using them, are you?"

"Rustlers won't get the drop on me again," he answered.

Delia passed by, talking to Kay-Lee and heading for the back counter where the candy jars stood full and inviting.

"I need a watch, a dependable one that won't set me back a lot, Tobe."

The storekeeper smiled and ushered Ty on down the counter. Stopping at a glass-enclosed case, Burleson pulled out a couple of gold timepieces and displayed them in his palm.

"Good-looking, but too expensive, Tobe.

What about the stem-winder," Ty said, pointing to a timepiece displayed in the back corner.

Burleson exchanged the two gold watches for a silver one and offered it to Ty. "Six dollars and eighty-five cents. I'll throw in a good strong chain for a quarter more."

Ty shook the watch in his palm, satisfied with its weight, then wound it and placed it against his ear. Satisfied with the steady tick, he nodded. "I'll take it."

"You paying cash today?"

"No, sir, add it to the Diamond S bill and we'll pay at the end of the month," Ty added.

"Always a pleasure to add it to an account that is paid as regular as sunrise," Tobe said, frowning in Molly's direction.

Delia was pestering her mother for some rock candy. Molly, comparing materials on a couple of different bolts of cloth, nodded. "In a moment, Delia, in a moment."

Ty hooked the chain to his watch, slipped it over a button and put the new timepiece in his vest pocket. As he caught his reflection in a countertop mirror, Molly walked up, a bolt of material in one hand and a wad of cloth in the other.

"Oh, Ty, look what I found!" She held up a tiny woolen gown with matching white hood trimmed with red ribbons. "These will be just right for a winter baby, help keep her warm."

"Her?" Ty smiled. "You mean, him!"

"Tyrus Bartholomew Stoddard, you are just like Trent, thinking it's just gotta be a boy." Molly strolled away in mock anger. "Either is fine as long as it's healthy," she said with a smile.

Retreating to the back counter, Molly placed the gown and bolt of material beside the candy jars. "Mr. Burleson, I'd like a pound of peppermint candies for Delia and three yards of this gingham material."

"You paying cash, Mrs. Jackson?" Burleson asked.

"No, just add it to my account."

Burleson swallowed hard, then sighed. "I wish I could do that, Mrs. Jackson, but I can't."

"You don't want my business?"

"Sure I want it; you know that, but your account hasn't been paid off in three months, and it's too much money for me to be adding to it."

Ty could see Molly's face redden at Burleson's words. "I didn't know."

"Sorry I'm the one to tell you, Mrs. Jackson."

"Momma, I want candy!" Delia tugged at

78

Molly's dress.

Ty strode to the back counter and grabbed Delia, who giggled. "I'll get you some candy. Tobe, add the candy, this baby gown and the gingham to the Diamond S account."

Molly shook her head. "No, Ty, it's not your place to do this."

He shook his head. "Why not? It's a gift. I'd be dead without you and all the care you gave me."

Molly shrugged. "Thank you, Ty. Delia, let's you and I go out and wait in the wagon. Thank you, Mr. Burleson," she said, with little enthusiasm, and retreated toward the front door.

Burleson's brow furrowed as he wiped a smudge off the glass display case. After the door shut behind Molly and Delia, Burleson's green eyes locked on Ty. "Sorry, Ty, but the bill's already ninety-six dollars and some change. I guess you might say the social didn't set well with me Saturday, Trent Jackson spending so much money to impress people and him owing me almost a hundred dollars."

"I can't excuse a man for not paying his debts, Tobe. I just hope it's an oversight with all that's been on his mind," Ty said, but he knew better.

"Maybe so, Ty, maybe so. Let me cut this cloth for Molly and get the peppermints for Delia." Burleson finished the business quickly. Ty noticed the merchant had put a pound and a quarter of peppermint in, but was charging for only a pound.

"Just add it on to the Diamond S account — that extra quarter pound of candy as well, Tobe."

Burleson grinned sheepishly. "That's on me, for Delia."

"Thanks, Tobe. I'll see you next trip." Ty took his cartridges and Molly's goods and marched down the aisle, Burleson scurrying ahead of him to open the door.

"You be careful, Ty, and don't go chasing rustlers alone next time," the burly merchant said as he passed.

Outside in the bright sunlight, Molly and Delia sat in the wagon. Molly had covered her head with a bonnet, as much to shield her from the embarrassment as from the sun, Ty thought.

Down the street rode Dewey Slater on his dun. The deputy, leaving a trail of smoke from his corncob pipe, nodded weakly as he rode past. He was riding west out of town, and Ty wondered what type of mischief he was up to.

As Ty handed the goods to Molly, he

heard two familiar voices behind him. He turned and watched Sammy Baker and Grant Phipps dismount and tie their horses to the hitching post.

"Morning, Ty." Baker glanced over his bad left shoulder.

Phipps nodded as well, and started to speak until he realized Molly was watching. Wiping his beard, he motioned for Ty to join them. As Ty reached them, Phipps stuck his hand out and grabbed Ty's. "We got paid. Thank your pa for his word with Trent."

"Pa'd appreciate that, but he didn't talk to Trent."

"Pa Stoddard don't have to say anything to have words with someone," Baker said. "His silence says more than a lot of folks' speeches."

Ty clasped Baker's callused hand and shook it firmly. "Wish we had some work to offer you, but times are tough between the rustlers and the poor calf crop.

"You got two good cowhands anyway," Baker said.

"We figure it's time to clear out, see some new territory," Phipps added.

Ty suspected there was more to it, but it was futile to attempt to pry it from them.

"Yeah, Sammy has had his eye on a red

81

shirt in Burleson's that he thinks'll fit. I don't think it's big enough, but he sure likes it."

"Then we've gotta repay the boss at the Equity Bar. A couple nights ago, he loaned us a bottle until we could get our money," Phipps added. "Then we're heading for New Mexico Territory. Ty, you think your pa would mind if we cut across your place? It'll save us a couple hours."

"Heck no, Grant. Fact, I'd ride with you, but I thought I'd treat Molly and Delia to lunch for all the meals they fixed me while I was mending."

"We're obliged, Ty, and good luck to you," Baker said.

"Same to you boys."

CHAPTER 6

Molly toyed with the cracked-wheat pudding in the porcelain bowl ringed with brightly painted daisies. Molly's mood was anything but bright, and Ty wondered if he shouldn't have ridden on home instead of treating Molly and Delia to lunch. Harvey Worley's was the best restaurant in town, but Burleson's refusal to extend more credit to the Jacksons had burned like a hot brand into Molly's pride. Ty couldn't blame her any, but it sure threw a trough of water on their lunch. Even Delia realized something had turned sour for her mother, and she sat silently rocking Kay-Lee in her arms.

Ever since taking her seat by the window, Molly had avoided Ty's eyes, looking down at the checkered oilcloth, worn from countless bought meals and small tips. She had scarcely touched the beef loaf, potato cakes and spiced apple brought hot from the oven by Worley, all smile and bushy white eyebrows. With the food cold and scarcely touched, Worley had cleared the plate from before her and marched away with a frown.

Uncomfortable himself, Ty had watched Main Street come to life as if the sun's warmth had melted people from their homes for another day. As he ate, Ty had seen Grant Phipps and Sammy Baker ride by and hitch their animals in front of the Equity Saloon. They were inside long enough to have a final drink in Tascosa and to repay the barkeep for the bottle he'd given them on their word. Good men they were, to repay their debt.

Why wasn't Trent Jackson as prompt in meeting his debts? Maybe there was some reason for it, but likely Ty would never know. He just knew he was damned uncomfortable sitting with his sister, and he wished she would either take a bite or put the spoon down on the table instead of excavating holes in her pudding. Then he could pay Harvey and ride toward the Diamond S, Stoddard land. Any man who ran cattle loved his place, or he was in the wrong business. Ranching was in Ty's blood, and doing it right took too much of a man's energy, time and affection. He could never feel comfortable tending his ranch part of the time and a job the rest of the time, like

Jackson. Sometimes, Ty even wondered if he could find time for a wife — not that prospects were likely around Tascosa — and still run a ranch.

Finally, Molly took her spoon from the pudding and placed it beside the bowl. Then she gently straightened it, as if she were setting the table. "Thank you, Ty," she said, her eyes catching his straight on for a moment, then glancing away. "The ride and the baby took a lot out of me."

Reaching across the table, he placed his hand over hers and squeezed. "I know," he said.

She nodded, then pulled her hand from his grasp, as if she felt unworthy of his touch. "You best be going, so you get home plenty before dark."

Ty knew he could ride home and back two times before dark, but he didn't argue. He was as anxious to get home as a calf is to get the hot iron off his flank at branding time. Motioning for Harvey Worley, Ty pushed his chair back from the table.

Worley scooted over to the table, his white eyebrows hanging low like pale storm clouds over his eyes, perpetually watery from too much time over a hot cookstove.

"Add this to Pa's bill? I'm low on . . ."

"No!" Worley said, crossing his arms over

his chest.

Ty felt a sinking in his stomach. "Diamond S credit no good?"

Molly sniffled for an instant, but Ty couldn't tell if she were about to cry or not, so he avoided staring at her.

Worley cleared his throat. "The Stoddards have been good, dependable customers through the years, and if I cook something that Molly can't eat, then you shan't pay."

Ty laughed. "She's with child, Harvey, with child. Delia's gonna have a brother or sister by the end of the year. She can't even stand her own cooking these days."

Worley's arms unraveled and he clapped his hands, his eyebrows dancing gaily over his eyes. "Congratulations, Molly. I know you and the sheriff must be proud."

Molly glanced up and nodded at Worley. The corner of her lips lifted, but enough for only a sliver of a smile. "Yes, thank you."

"She's not feeling well, now, Harvey, so we'll be going. Just add it to Pa's account," Ty said, standing and helping Molly out of her chair.

Delia hopped down, banging Kay-Lee's head against the chair back. Realizing what she had done, Delia hugged the doll tight against her shoulder.

Taking Molly's arm, Ty herded Delia

before them out the door. Just as they stepped off the boardwalk and into the street, Ty heard a shout from down the street.

"Molly! Molly!" Trent called, waving a paper in his hands, "I've good news for you!"

Ty felt Molly's arm stiffen in his grasp, and she tossed her head back as he remembered her doing as a little girl when she was mad. She stared coldly at her husband as he walked up and handed her a letter and envelope.

"Read for yourself," he said, nodding at Ty. "Where you been, the Equity Saloon?" he kidded.

"No, Trent," Molly answered, her words as cold as a blue norther. "We stopped first at Burleson's."

The merriment strangled in Jackson's throat. He coughed. "The letter's from Wilma. She's coming to stay with you until the baby comes. Wilma's my sister," Jackson explained to Ty.

Molly turned the sheet of paper over and read the back side, only the creaks and rattles of a passing wagon breaking the cold silence. She handed the letter back to her husband.

"You keep it," he said, as she pressed it

into his hand.

"I best be going," Ty interrupted. "I'm anxious to get home. Thanks for all you did, both of you."

Ty bent down and picked up Delia from behind her mother's long skirt. "You be a good girl and take care of Kay-Lee." He kissed the doll atop the head and then kissed Delia's cheek as she giggled.

"Goodbye, Ty. Don't let Pa overwork you," Molly instructed.

After placing Delia on the ground, he hugged Molly. "Things are seldom as bad as they seem," he whispered in her ear. Releasing his sister, he turned around and offered Trent his hand. "Take good care of my girls and yourself with all your sheriffing."

Jackson nodded. "And don't you go chasing rustlers alone anymore."

Ty pulled his hat down and stepped to the wagon, untying his barrel-chested roan from the tailgate. With just one good arm, he swung awkwardly into the saddle and touched the animal's flank. As the roan turned toward the Diamond S, he heard Molly's scolding voice behind him.

"Never in my life have I been so embarrassed, Trent Jackson."

Ty raked his spurs over the roan's flank

and Molly's words were lost in the hoof-beats.

Soon the trail west had taken him out of the canyon and out of sight of Tascosa. He pushed his roan to a canter and watched the countryside. Before him spread the gentle swells of a vast land, greening under the sun's gathering warmth. He relished the breeze massaging his face and the freedom of riding a good horse toward home. At first his shoulder twitched with a dull ache, but the exhilaration of nearing Diamond S land soon eased the discomfort. In good time, he touched Diamond S land when the trail crossed the wash made by Sand Creek. A couple of miles farther stood the Diamond S headquarters, in the vee made by the joining of Antelope and Pedarosa creeks.

The Diamond S extended from Sand Creek, past the ranch house, toward New Mexico Territory. The Canadian River cut across the bottom third of the place. While his gelding watered in Sand Creek, Ty studied the muddied tracks of two mounts that had passed before him, likely within the hour. It must be the trail of Grant Phipps and Sammy Baker. He wished them luck on their way to New Mexico Territory, and wondered why it was always the best men that never seemed to get a fair shake.

After Sand Creek, Ty gave his gelding free rein, and the strong horse bolted ahead. As Ty rode, he tried to sort out the details of the shooting. All he remembered, though, was that tapping, then the whistling noise. For the first time, it struck him as strange that the rustlers had taken the Diamond S cattle east. By going straight west, they would have been in New Mexico Territory sooner. But maybe that deception was how the rustlers kept from getting caught. They moved east, screened by the depths of the Canadian River breaks, then altered the brands in the box canyon Ty had found. Once that chore was finished, perhaps they left the canyon to the south and made a wide circle around Oldham County, going to Fort Sumner or even White Oaks and Lincoln in the territory. There the stolen cattle were likely sold to the contractors who supplied the forts or the Indian agencies. It was the damndest thing that the sheriff would've found him closer to the Jackson place than to the Diamond S.

For all the figuring he had done, Ty had come up with few answers by the time the land sloped away to Antelope Creek and the Diamond S home. He pulled up his roan and jerked his cigarette fixings from his vest pocket. Slowly, awkwardly, he rolled a cigarette in his left hand, then slipped the smoke between his lips. He took a last match from his tin and flicked it to life with his thumbnail. Touching the match to the cigarette tip, he took a deep drag and smiled at the whitewashed batten-board house, the unpainted barn and the old dugout that had been the Stoddard home until the new house was finished four years ago. The smile drooped when he saw Momma's plot, a rough wooden marker standing where a fine granite marker would go once it arrived from Dodge City.

Smoke was rising from the stovepipe and two familiar horses were hitched in front of the house. Phipps and Baker had stopped to offer their goodbyes to Pa. Ty finished his cigarette and crushed its remnants between his fingers, then nudged the roan forward, going slowly now and enjoying the security of a place he had wondered if he would ever see again.

"Pa," he called, drawing up to the house, its windows open and the curtains slipping out in the breeze.

"Come on in," he heard his father's voice calling from inside. "We've got company."

Ty slid out of the saddle and tied the roan to the hitching post beside the visitors' mounts. Stepping up onto the porch, he scraped the bottom of his boots off as Momma had always demanded, rain or shine, then opened the door. The parlor was empty, but Ty heard a clatter of pots and pans in the kitchen. His nose twitched at the smell of something burning, and he knew his father was trying to put some food together for Phipps and Baker.

As he entered the kitchen, he saw his father pulling a pan of blackened sourdough biscuits out of the oven. "I hope you boys like your bread well-done."

"You sure those are done?" Phipps wrinkled his nose, then brushed his hand across the front of the red bib shirt he'd purchased at Burleson's store.

"Ouch!" Stoddard yelled. "That pan's hot." The pan clanked onto the stove, bouncing between a skillet of sliced steaks and a pot of canned tomatoes.

"Take a seat, Ty," Baker said, his teeth bare from a broad smile, "before your pa maims you."

"Keep standing," Phipps countered. "If you take a seat, he may poison you."

Ty took off his hat and hung it on a peg by the back door, then grabbed four tin plates and forks from a wooden counter along the wall and dropped them on the table in front of Phipps. The plates clattered and Phipps flinched. "Sorry, Grant," Ty said. "Your shirt blinded me."

Baker slapped his knee. "It's so bright, I see my shadow every time I come within three feet of it."

"You fellows are just jealous of a man so finely attired."

Pa Stoddard dropped the pan of biscuits on the table, but no one made a move to take the first stone. "It's early for supper, Ty, but I figured you might be hungry after your ride, and with company, I went ahead and fixed a meal, such as it is. Grant and Sammy want to get a little farther down the trail today. They're anxious to get into the territory."

Stoddard stepped to the stove and returned with the pot of tomatoes and the beefsteaks. "Take a plate there and I'll fork you up some meat."

"You'll need a chisel for those biscuits." Baker laughed.

"Or dynamite," Phipps added.

Stoddard slapped a slice of beef on each plate. "Tools are out in the barn if you need any for supper. It's a good thing you boys are going on to New Mexico tonight. I don't know that my hospitality could stand many more insults."

Phipps stuck his fork in a biscuit and pried

93

it free from its neighbors. He took the fork straight from the pan to his mouth and crunched into the black ball, his mouth crackling as he chewed. "Not bad, once you get past the shell." He laughed and dug into his steak.

As the pan of tomatoes made its way around the table, Pa Stoddard put the coffeepot on the table beside four tin cups. "Wish I could offer you boys a job instead of my lame cooking, but I've got two good hands and Ty. That's all I can pay, and I can't cut any of them loose to take you on. Wish it were different."

Baker shoved a hunk of boiled tomato into his mouth. "We appreciate that, but we just feel more comfortable out of Oldham County now."

"You see, Trent Jackson was involved in too much politics to our liking," Baker said. "Little things, mostly, but he just wasn't our kind."

"You saying he wasn't honest?" Pa Stoddard took his seat and stared hard at Baker.

"We're just saying," Phipps interrupted, "he wasn't our kind."

CHAPTER 7

Dawn came with a tremor worming its way through his muscles. Ty stretched under the sheet, then patted a yawn at his lips and rubbed the stubble growing on his cheeks. Molly had helped him shave his whiskers and trim his moustache every other day during his stay with her. Now, Ty was on his own. As the light gathered strength after chasing away the night, Ty tossed back the covers and pushed himself up. He stared at his right arm, clinging to him in its sling. Wriggling his fingers, he pushed his arm against the sling's binding. Ty caught his breath, not so much from the pain as from the effort to produce movement. His arm burned with numbness and no longer seemed a part of him. Gently, he untied the sling and unwrapped the bindings until they fell away and his arm collapsed into his lap. Clenching his teeth and grunting, he tried to lift his arm. It quivered, then rose slowly, like a serpent. He exhaled slowly, then took a deep breath and gritted his teeth as he struggled to lift the arm further. But it fell into his lap like a limp rag. Ty brushed his hand against his forehead. He had broken into a cold sweat.

Damn arm! Damn rustlers!

Ty picked up the bindings, planning to fix the sling, then tossed them on the floor. The arm would never get better if he didn't try to use it.

From the kitchen, Ty could hear his father wrestling wood from the woodbox to the stove, then clanging the coffeepot over the fire. Ty hadn't remembered Pa Stoddard's cooking being so bad as yesterday's meal with Baker and Phipps, but then Ty had just spent most of a month eating Molly's cooking, which was as good as his momma's cooking had been.

Standing up, Ty found his britches and struggled into them, popping the suspenders over his shoulders. The cool floor prickled his feet as he stepped to the washbasin and picked up the hand mirror. Maybe a beard wouldn't look too bad. He returned the mirror to the table and poured the cool water into the white porcelain washbasin. Bending over the basin, he splashed water over his face, then rubbed his eyes. As he raised his head, water dripped from his face into the bowl. With his left hand, he manipulated his right into the basin. He just shook his head as he tried to wash his hands. The arm would heal eventually, and with it he would kill the man who had ambushed him.

He toweled off his hand, then pulled on his shirt and slid into his boots. That was easy compared to managing his gunbelt with one hand. Lifting his holster belt from the chair by his bed, Ty moved toward the kitchen. Despite his arm, he felt better from a night in his own bed. Something about a man's own bed provided special recuperative powers. Ty wondered how many nights it would take before his arm could return to normal.

His father was bent over the stove when Ty entered the kitchen. Ty prayed his father wasn't cooking more biscuits.

"How you doing this morning, Ty? Must be okay, as much noise as I heard in your room."

"This arm's left me no better off than a steer with a herd of heifers. Fact, maybe worse off, since the steer doesn't have anything flopping around to get in his way."

Stoddard poured his son a cup of hot coffee and set it on the table. Ty took a seat.

"I don't fix much breakfast anymore, just

drink some coffee and eat anything that wasn't eaten last night for supper. Biscuits weren't worth a damn, and there was no meat left."

"Coffee'll do fine." Ty swallowed the strong liquid and stared out the window at the bunkhouse. "Where are the hands?"

"Finishing off the branding. We need to rework the canyon, see if we missed any there, Ty. We're down maybe two hundred head from where we should be for no worse a winter than we had."

"Rustlers?"

"No other explanation, Ty."

"Damn! What I can't figure is why they took our cattle east instead of heading straight for the border."

"It don't make sense, son, but you wouldn't think twice about men riding east with cattle. You'd expect them to be heading for New Mexico Territory." Stoddard swallowed a mouthful of coffee, his brow furrowing with his thoughts. "If I was stealing cattle, I'd get them to the canyon to screen my ride west. We've been looking, but we've found no sign that we can identify as men herding cattle through our place to New Mexico."

"I spent a lot of time figuring when I was

laid up at Molly's place. Nothing made sense."

The men studied their coffee a while, finished off one cup, then another.

"What do you say we ride into the canyon, scour it over, see if we find any rustler sign or cattle I figure I'm missing, Ty?"

Ty finished a last sip of coffee, then nodded. "I'm ready to get out and do whatever work this flimsy arm'll let me do."

They rose in unison, the father's features evident in the son, the old man slightly stooped but possessing the same narrow build, thick neck and muscular shoulders. They made their way outside, Ty carrying his gunbelt over his shoulder, his father picking up rifles for them both.

Ty trailed behind his pa, enjoying his first morning in weeks on the Diamond S. Something about standing on family land made a man feel prouder, more alive than when his boots left tracks on another man's land.

In the corral, his roan trotted around, tossing his head and kicking up wisps of dust. The gelding was as eager as Ty to get away from the home place and work off some stored energy.

Pa Stoddard roped Ty's gelding, saddled him, then caught himself a mount for saddling. As each horse was done, Ty picked up one of the rifles and shoved it in the saddle boot. His pa was about to mount when Ty waved him over. "I need help putting my gunbelt on." Ty let the belt slide down his arm, then caught it in his hand.

"Well, I'll be, Ty, I never thought about that, you still having one good hand; but, by damn, it does take two to buckle a gunbelt on." He took the gunbelt and wrapped it around Ty, then buckled it in front.

Ty had felt more helpless in recent weeks, but no more foolish than now.

They mounted and rode south, following an old cow trail from the house along Pedarosa Creek. Pa Stoddard took the lead and Ty rode in his wake. His must have ridden thousands of miles in his life, following his father. Now he respected the old man more than ever. As a kid, he hadn't understood the magnitude of his father's accomplishments, taking a piece of unclaimed prairie land, shaping it into a ranch, stocking it with cattle, taking whatever the unpredictable Panhandle weather threw his way and holding his own against rustlers and occasional Comanche braves who swept out of Indian Territory to relive a lost way of life.

Carving the ranch out of raw land had been a man's job, and his father had irrigated the Diamond S with the sweat of his own brow. Overseeing the ranch now didn't seem nearly the challenge.

Along the creek grew clumps of wildflowers waving in the breeze as the riders passed. Overhead a hawk circled silently on invisible air currents rising with the warmth of the morning sun. The gentle slope turned steep and the horses heeled back against the incline. Ty felt his right arm bumping against his side. He tried to lift it and it rose, as if by some alien magic, to the saddle horn, then went limp on him. Ty smiled and let his breath out with a slow whistle. He would fight that arm until he could use it again.

Before him, the Canadian River sparkled like a shimmering serpent across the Panhandle. The river was broad and shallow in most places, though men who had been around earlier recalled it as narrower and deeper than it was now. They remembered a time when a man worried about swimming his horse through it, more than getting bogged down in the quicksands that gathered along the banks. Nobody could figure why the river had changed, though some suggested that cattle had overgrazed the perimeter and erosion had filled the main channel until the river broadened its banks. Still, it was water, and water in the Panhandle, in all of West Texas, was a valuable commodity.

When the trail reached the level ground that bordered the river, Ty reined up beside his father. "You expect to find many cattle through here?"

Pa Stoddard shrugged. "We didn't lose that many to winter, so we've either've missed a couple hundred, haven't run across their carcasses, or let rustlers get away with them."

"You think that's possible?"

"Ty, I've spent many a night since your shooting, pondering, and it don't add up. Some of our beef's been appearing in New Mexico Territory. So's a lot of other people's. That's to be expected. But our calf crop's down like most other folks' around here. Somebody's been branding them for their own. That's got a lot of other folks to thinking, too. It may be that one of our neighbors is doing the stealing."

"Any suspicions, Pa?"

"Plenty, but that's all I've got — suspicions."

Ty watched a blacktailed jackrabbit scurry from a nearby clump of brush and run twenty yards before sitting down with head and ears erect to watch the passing riders.

"Think the regulators will help?"

"I doubt it, son. What if it is one of the regulators that's behind all this? We're worse off now than we were! We didn't know what to expect, but neither did the rustlers. Bad thing about it is that it may turn neighbor against neighbor, before all's said and done."

"Do you think one day we'll rid the country of rustlers?"

"Barbed wire's helping keep cattle on their home ranch, so likely we'll end the wide-spread rustling. But if it's not rustling, something else will be a problem for us. God didn't intend for cattlemen to become rich — not in the Texas Panhandle. But I've got more than I deserved, and I'll be leaving you and Molly more than I got from my pa."

They crossed the river at a gravel bed, pausing midstream to let their horses drink. The crossing was the best for miles, and many riders took advantage of it and Pa Stoddard's good will. Ty stood in his stirrups. "Which direction from here?"

Pa Stoddard pointed west along the river, where the broken country turned brushy and offered a thousand places for cattle to hide in twos and threes, but not by the hundreds. As Ty shook his head and started to sink back into the saddle, his eyes spotted movement down the trail where it began to climb back out of the canyon. He blinked and stared again. Were his eyes playing tricks on him? No, there was movement, a couple of horses grazing.

"Horses, Pa, horses on down the trail." Ty kicked the roan's flank with his spurs and went splashing through the water.

Pa Stoddard shook his reins and his gelding followed Ty's. "You sure?" he called.

As they rode out of the riverbed, Ty could make out the animals much better. "Yeah!"

Both men spurred their mounts to a gallop. As they drew nearer, the two grazing horses lifted their heads to watch. Ty felt a queasiness in his gut. The horses belonged to Phipps and Baker. They tossed their heads, but didn't run. Ty saw they were hobbled. He studied the territory beyond the horses, and then saw a sight that made him sick. Two forms were sprawled on the ground twenty yards off the trail.

"Pa, over here," he yelled, even though his father was just behind him.

Suddenly, Ty was reining up on his roan and jumping out of the saddle. He dashed to the form wearing the bright red shirt, now stained by a dark red blotch on the back. Grabbing Grant Phipps's cold arm, he pulled the big man over on his back, as if quick action might help. The contorted lips and white glassy eyes told him he was too late. Pa Stoddard toed at Sammy Baker, there being little else he could do for a dead man.

Ty twisted around for a response from his father. There was none — just clenched fists and a frown. The two dead men were sprawled on the ground beside their saddles and their bedrolls. They had made a cold camp and already there was a musty odor about their bodies. Phipps's bedroll was askew, as if he had been spreading it out when he was shot, perhaps from some of the rocks just up the trail along the canyon wall. He had been shot first; his gun was still in its holster. Baker must have had a slim chance to survive; his gun was beside him on the ground. Ty picked it up and broke it open. Two empty hulls were in the cylinder.

The pants pockets of both men were turned inside out. They had been robbed of the last pay they would ever receive.

CHAPTER 8

In the twilight, Tascosa melded into the land. Except for the lights in solitary windows and in a line along Main Street, the town was easy to overlook. Ty twisted in the saddle and stared behind him, first at the sun, a dying wick on the horizon, then at his father, his face grim and gray in the dim twilight, and finally at the horses carrying Phipps and Baker.

Death made an awkward riding companion, and Ty stared at Tascosa. The evening was warm and smelled of spring, but he was chilled with the reminder that he, too, had been brought out of the canyon strapped over a jumpy mount. Molly had saved him. No one would save Phipps and Baker.

Pa Stoddard had brooded the entire trip, but Ty noticed his father's hand flinch toward his revolver when the horses flushed a covey of quail. Their eyes locked when Stoddard's hand released the pistol butt.

Stoddard read his son's mind. "I'm spooked, you bet! I've survived many an enemy over the years," the old man said, "but at least I knew who the enemies were."

They circled Tascosa to avoid attracting a crowd and the thousand questions to which they had no answers. Then they aimed at the courthouse and the solitary light which burned in the sheriff's ground-floor office. But people noticed and gawked, pointing at the two trailing horses and their grim cargo, then scurrying away to tell others.

Ty wished it were darker so Phipps and Baker, in death, could have a little privacy. Death lost its dignity when propped up for display. Phipps and Baker, both good men, deserved a better fate than becoming a spectacle for all of Tascosa. Maybe he and Pa should have buried them on the Stoddard place. Phipps and Baker would've preferred that to a hole in Boot Hill, where petty crooks, slow gunmen and unlucky card cheats were buried. Those sorts weren't the equals of honest men like Phipps and Baker.

Ty pointed his roan to the courthouse hitching post. From the corner of his eye, he could see a crowd approaching. He just shook his head. He would be curious, too, he supposed, but it grated on him that

107

Phipps and Baker had become a sideshow.

The Stoddards drew their mounts up by the courthouse fence. Ty jumped to the ground and tied the reins around the hitching post. His father tossed him the reins to the two pack animals. Not a word was said until Pa Stoddard stepped out of his saddle.

Then the crowd closed around them and showered them with questions.

"Who is it?" one asked.

"You finally get a pair of rustlers?" called another.

After Pa Stoddard tied his horse, he opened the gate in the picket fence and stepped toward the courthouse door. The corner office, the one with the light on, was the sheriff's office. "Hope Trent's here, Pa."

"Way our luck's been going, I figure Dewey Slater'll be the only one here."

Behind them, the crowd had moved in on the horses. "This one's Grant Phipps," yelled one man.

"Sammy Baker's the other one," came an answering shout, and the crowd broke into a wave of murmurs.

Just as Pa Stoddard was to grab the doorknob, the courthouse door swung open.

"What's the commotion?" Dewey Slater called.

"Remind me not to get in a poker game

while I'm in town, or we'll likely lose the Diamond S, Ty."

"What are you talking about, Stoddard?" Deputy Slater demanded.

"Where's Trent, Slater?"

"Home, I reckon. I'm in charge now, so tell me what's the commotion."

"Grant Phipps and Sammy Baker were ambushed," Pa Stoddard said. "Found them on our place this morning."

Slater pushed his way between the Stoddards and strode toward the horses. "You two go inside and stay there til I get back," he commanded as he reached the gate and stepped out among the crowd. "Get back, clear the way; the law's here, you folks understand?" Slater shoved his way to the horses and then spread his arms. "Give me some room here. Give me some room."

Then Slater's voice was lost in the commotion. The Stoddards stepped inside, the door creaking on dry hinges as Ty pulled it shut. "Looks like the county could buy a little oil instead of wasting money on picket fences around this place."

The hallway was dark except for a rectangle of light around the thick door to the sheriff's office. Pa Stoddard shoved the door open. It, too, screeched open on thirsty hinges. They stepped inside to be engulfed by a stifling heat. Pa Stoddard pointed to the potbelly stove in the corner. "Slater built more fire than he needs for coffee." The old man strode past the desk and wrinkled his nose at Slater's smoldering pipe and its pungency. "He must smoke turds," he said, stepping beside the stove and lifting the blackened coffeepot. "Plenty for us." He took a couple of tin cups off hooks on the wall and filled each.

Ty stood at the barred window, watching the crowd lift the remains from the horses and carry them through the gate. They propped the bodies up against the picket fence. Someone had fetched the doctor and several others brought lanterns. Ty could stand no more. Clenching his fists, he spun around from the window.

Pa Stoddard was beside him, offering him a cup of coffee.

Ty grabbed the cup. "I'll want something stronger after this."

The old man nodded as he walked around the room, working the stiffness from the long ride out of his legs. He circled the desk a couple of times, paused at the gunrack and then studied the wanted posters tacked to the wall. On the desk a pistol was broken apart next to a can of gun oil and a pair of soft rags spotted with black oil smudges.

Finishing his coffee, Ty left the cup on the desk and slumped into a nearby chair. He fought his right hand into his lap as his father poured himself another cup of coffee. No sooner had Ty bent over and studied the floor than Slater burst through the office door.

"Phipps and Baker didn't fare as well as you did, Ty." His words seemed laden with a perverse pleasure. He pointed his index finger at Pa Stoddard. "Maybe you best explain a little, Mr. Stoddard, about how you came to bring two dead men to town."

"We found 'em on our place, just across the Canadian on the trail to Fort Sumner. They'd been shot and robbed," Stoddard said, then gulped down a mouthful of coffee. He slammed the cup on the stove.

"Robbed, Stoddard? How do you know they were robbed?"

Ty stood up. "Their pockets were turned out when we found them. No money on them anywhere, and we know they left here with near a hundred and fifty dollars between them."

Slater stepped behind the desk and picked up his pipe, jamming it between the gap in his teeth. He studied it a moment, tapped the smoldering tobacco down with his thumb, then sucked on it until the tobacco glowed. He sank into the worn desk chair, facing Stoddard, then propped his feet on the corner of the desk. His gaze was hard, even through the smoky veil.

"You seem to know a lot about the money they was carrying. You count it after you shot them?"

Stoddard stepped toward the desk and reached across it for Slater, but froze with his hands outstretched. The old man backed away and Ty saw a pistol in Slater's hand. "That was a foolish thing to try, old man. I don't care if you are Trent Jackson's father-in-law. I'd plug you as soon as I would a thief. You go easy, or I'll throw you in jail for their murder."

Ty wished for two good hands and a chance to use them on Dewey Slater. No weapons, just fists.

"You old-timers don't run this county, the law does," Slater lectured.

Pa Stoddard's hands knotted into fists and he leaned forward across the desk. "Us old-timers maintained order here. You ain't done that yet, Slater."

"I follow Trent's orders, Stoddard. We'll take care of the bad elements, once word gets out about the regulators."

Ty's throat tightened. Slater was not one he cared to have know anything about the regulators. It would only lead to trouble.

Slater lowered the gun, his beady eyes never blinking. "We can send a message to the rustlers right now," Slater said, pulling his feet from the desk and leaning toward Stoddard. "All we've got to do is tell folks you caught Phipps and Baker altering your brands."

Pa Stoddard struck the desk with his fists. "Phipps and Baker were honest men, and we won't muddy their names."

"It might help save you cattle, even save the Diamond S, if your losses are as bad as I heard."

Stoddard straightened, his lip curling with contempt. "Those two men don't have a thing now, except their good name. I'll not take that from them, and neither will you!" Stoddard spun around. "Let's go, Ty."

Slater sprang from his chair. "I didn't say you could leave just yet."

"You try and stop us!" Ty challenged.

"An old-timer and a one-armed man won't be hard to stop when the time comes."

"If you ever try," Pa Stoddard said, "you won't live to talk about it, Slater."

Stoddard and Ty stomped from the office, their tempers burning hotter than the fire in Slater's stove. They heard a string of profanities mixed with their names as they strode outside. The bodies had been carried away, but the folks still mingled around the horses: As the Stoddards stepped past the picket gate, the crowd was drawn to them like metal filings to a magnet.

"What happened?" called one of them.

"Where'd you find them?" yelled another.

Stoddard pushed his way through them. "Ask the damned deputy!" Both father and son mounted quickly, silently, and nudged their horses through the crowd, then galloped away. "We'll take the night at the Exchange House," Pa Stoddard called.

They approached the hotel from behind and tied their horses in back, then walked quickly to the front door, pushing it open and agitating the bell which hung there to announce visitors. Ben Russell sat at the desk, reading a paper in the yellow glow of a desk lamp. He looked up and smiled to see a couple of regulars with good credit.

"Good to see you, Mr. Stoddard," said Russell, all smiles.

Stoddard just shook his head and waved the greeting away. "We brought Grant Phipps and Sammy Baker in dead. They were ambushed on our place and robbed."

"Damn." Russell sighed. "This whole county's going to hell."

"And no matter what you hear, Phipps

and Baker weren't rustling any cattle."

"I wouldn't expected that of them, anyway," the clerk answered.

"That damned Deputy Slater may tell folks we shot them rustling cattle, but he'll be lying on both counts."

Russell pushed them the register and a pen. "Your regular room's open; you want a room for both of you?"

Stoddard nodded. "We'll share, tonight. If anybody comes asking questions, Ben, play dumb."

"Before bed, Pa, I want a drink."

The old man nodded. "We'll step down to the Equity and have a shot."

They walked outside, the bell ringing behind them, and down the street to the Equity, a squat adobe building with dingy windows palled with light. They walked quickly and were inside before anybody recognized them. The bar ran along the side wall; a painting of a young woman with veiled charms hung behind the barkeep who stepped up to serve them.

"What'll it be?" he asked, then recognized the Stoddards.

"The same brand as the bottle you loaned to Phipps and Baker," Pa Stoddard said.

The barkeep nodded. "I just heard."

"We don't want to talk about it. Just give

us a bottle and a couple of shot glasses," Pa Stoddard said. "We'll take a seat at the corner table out of the way."

Bottle in hand, Ty moved through the tables and the stares, to the corner. His father paid, then followed. The glasses clinked as the old man set them on the table. He uncorked the bottle and poured a drink for himself and Ty. Picking up his glass, Ty held its amber contents up to the smoky lamplight, studying it a moment, then put the glass to his lips and tossed the whiskey down his throat, which tingled as the liquor seeped to his stomach. Two more glasses followed the first, and Ty began to feel the effects of the liquor, but it didn't erase the memory of the blood-splattered bodies by the trail.

A half-drunk customer stumbled toward the Stoddard table. "You boys ain't being too talkative about what you seen."

Ty rose slowly from his seat and jerked his thumb toward the door. "Let's go, Pa; I've had enough." He grabbed the bottle.

Marching out of the saloon side by side, the Stoddards retraced their steps to the Exchange. Stars dotted night's dark veil, and the street was splotched with light escaping from dusty windows.

Pa Stoddard shoved open the hotel door,

the bell jingling at the disturbance. Both men marched past Ben Russell toward their room. "Our horses are out back, Ben," Stoddard called. "See that they are attended."

"Sure, Mr. Stoddard, be glad to," the clerk answered.

The slamming of the hall door answered the clerk. In their dark room, both men removed their hats, unhooked their gunbelts and hung them over a bedpost, then pulled off their boots, Stoddard helping Ty with that. They worked in the dark, then shared the bottle, both taking healthy swigs of whiskey. They collapsed into bed still dressed, and drifted quickly into sleep.

When Ty awoke, it was morning. His father stood by the window, glancing over his shoulder at the bed as he heard Ty stir. "We'll wait until Burleson's opens and settle my account, take a meal at Harvey Worley's, then head back to the ranch. Sleep a little more if you like."

Ty sat up, shaking his head from the lingering effect of the whiskey. "I'm fine." Ty struggled his way into his boots, then picked up his gunbelt and waited for his father's help. The old man obliged. Ty doused water against his face at the washbasin, then studied himself in the cracked mirror on the wall. His face was drawn and his eyes were red and troubled, like Oldham County.

"I brought plenty of cash from the ranch," Pa Stoddard said. "I'm gonna pay Russell for the room and for taking care of our horses last night. I'll meet you up front."

As Ty nodded, a pain from last night's liquor rattled around in his brain. He brushed his hand through his hair and grabbed his hat. He was eager to leave town and get back to the Diamond S.

The hallway was still dark from the shadowy remnants of night. Ty went to the front window and watched the street as his father settled things with Russell.

"That'll cover last night, with enough extra to have our horses saddled and ready in an hour," the old man said.

"Sure thing, Mr. Stoddard."

From the Exchange, they marched to Harvey Worley's eatery and took a breakfast of eggs, steak and fluffy biscuits with plenty of apricot preserves and hot coffee. They were finishing up when Dewey Slater walked in, slamming the door behind him. Ty saw Harvey Worley grimace, take a deep breath and move over to the window where the deputy seated himself.

"Just coffee," Slater said.

Ty felt an anger rising in him, and the

food suddenly tasted bitter. His father seemed to sense Ty's impatience to leave. Stoddard motioned for Harvey Worley as he delivered a cup of steaming coffee to the deputy. Worley retreated quickly from Slater's table. "Yes, sir, Mr. Stoddard?"

"We're ready to leave. Total what we owe you for today and anything else we've run up our bill on," Pa Stoddard said.

Worley nodded, his bushy white eyebrows lifting with the prospect of pay. He returned shortly, showing Stoddard a bill for eleven dollars and thirty-two cents.

Stoddard stood up and pulled a roll of bills from his pocket. He counted out twelve dollars and told Worley to keep the change. "Let's go, son!"

Ty stood up in range of Slater's threatening gaze. The two men marched past the deputy's table.

"Well, well, if it isn't the Stoddards!" the deputy taunted them.

Both men ignored Slater and headed out the door. "That bastard's getting me where I hate to come into town," Stoddard said. "Let's settle up at Burleson's and get back to the ranch."

"What about Phipps and Baker?" Ty asked.

"Not much we can do for them now. Their

horses and saddles ought to bring enough for a decent box and funeral, if Slater don't steal that. I'll leave a note for Trent with Burleson to make sure of that."

They walked down Main Street, the low sun and long shadows telling them it would be a while before Burleson opened up. Spotting Ben Russell leading their horses toward the Exchange, Ty whistled, his roan tossing its head at the noise and Russell glaring at the culprit until he realized it was the Stoddards. "Here, Ben, we'll take them off your hands."

Russell grinned and headed in their direction. "I figured you'd be a little longer at breakfast."

"Dewey Slater ruined our appetite," Pa Stoddard answered.

"Yeah, I know what you mean. No offense, but Trent Jackson's disappointed me by hiring him as deputy."

"Us, too!" Ty answered, taking the saddle reins. "Hey, there's Burleson heading for the store. We'll catch him and get out of town. See you next trip, Ben!'

The Stoddards mounted and rode toward Burleson's, reining up outside the store just as the owner was putting the key in the lock.

"We know you've a while before opening, but allow us to settle up with you and leave a letter for Trent."

Burleson nodded. "Sure, boys, come on in. I heard the news about Phipps and Baker. Two good men!" Burleson shoved the door open for them to enter. Closing the door behind him, he locked it, then lit a lamp to chase away the morning's lingering shadows.

Pa Stoddard took a pencil and paper and wrote out a message to Trent. Burleson, meanwhile, looked over his ledger book and the Diamond S account. Ty patrolled the store as his father sealed the letter to Trent. Burleson took it and announced thirty-seven dollars and fifty-three cents was due from the Diamond S. Just as Stoddard stuck his hand in his pants pocket, Ty saw a shadow from the street fall through the window. He glanced that way and his gaze froze.

Dewey Slater was standing there, watching.

Pa Stoddard and Burleson exchanged the money, then talked for a couple of minutes about the Phipps and Baker killing. Ty knew his Pa had seen Slater and was just making idle conversation until the deputy went away. When Slater failed to move on, Pa Stoddard said his goodbye to Burleson and marched over to Ty. "I guess the son of a bitch has taken root out there."

"He's waiting on us," Ty offered.

"If we didn't have work at the ranch, we'd wait him out."

"I appreciate your business because you square your account regularly," Burleson said, as he stepped to the door, pulling the key from his pocket. Ty fell in line behind his father, then emerged outside onto the boardwalk.

Slater waited, taking the corncob pipe out of his mouth, holding it by the bowl, pointing the stem at the Stoddards. "Odd to me that two men were robbed of a hundred and fifty dollars one day, and the next, you're in town paying off your debts."

Pa Stoddard's fists knotted. "You plan on doing anything about it, make your move. Otherwise, get out of our way."

Slater retreated a step and tapped the pipe in his hand to relieve it of used tobacco. "Not this time, but you remember the law's watching you."

The Stoddards stepped off the boardwalk to their horses, mounted and turned toward the Diamond S. Ty felt a chill run up his spine when he turned his back to Slater. He raked his spurs across the roan's flank and galloped out of Tascosa.

CHAPTER 9

With a thundercloud festering in the western sky, the air smelled of impending danger. Thunder rolled from the purple clouds in rumbling threats and the wind came in gusts, like the breath of a labored but dangerous prizefighter. When Ty's barrel-chested gelding tossed his head and whinnied, Ty leaned forward in the saddle and stroked the roan's neck with his right hand. His hand remained weak, but the feeling was returning to his arm.

Beside Ty rode his father, on a piebald gelding. Neither his father nor his piebald seemed to notice the approaching storm.

"Looks like a downpour," Ty said.

His father just shrugged. Pa Stoddard had ridden wordlessly from the Diamond S along the Canadian River. Now they were east of Tascosa, still following the river toward Big Tree, a local landmark where a giant cottonwood had shouldered its way out of the soil and clung to a river bend. There was no bigger tree nor bigger circle of shade in all of Oldham County than at Big Tree.

Ahead Ty could make out the giant tree and a handful of men on horses. The sheriff had asked Pa Stoddard and Ty to be at the meeting, but the old man had made no promise to his son-in-law. Only when Zack Miller extended the same invitation did the elder Stoddard accept. He was bound, by respect for his fellow Oldham County pioneer, to attend. The two pioneer ranchers had squatted out by the Diamond S corral, discussing the matter, Miller fingering the butt of his bullwhip, Pa Stoddard nodding occasionally, but mostly listening. Ty had not been invited to their discussion. When Miller had finally ridden away, Pa Stoddard said nothing except that Ty was to be ready to ride the next afternoon in time to reach Big Tree by four o'clock.

Up ahead Ty could make out Zack Miller in his planter's hat and Red Stewart with his bushy beard, but there were others around the cottonwood as well, including one Ty recognized as Trent Jackson, by his chestnut mount and the set of the sheriff. Trent trotted out to greet his in-laws, doffing his hat and nodding at Pa Stoddard.

"Glad you could make it," Jackson said over the distant thunder. "You, too, Ty! How's the arm?"

Ty lifted his arm in an anemic arc. "Some better."

"Mighty pleased to hear it! Molly'll be pleased, too."

Ty grinned. "After we're done, I might run up to see her."

"She'd like that, Ty," Trent replied, as he wiped his brow with the patched sleeve of his shirt, then replaced his hat. Reining his chestnut around in step with the Stoddard mounts, Trent nodded toward the tree. "They're waiting."

Neither Ty nor his father answered. They just rode, Ty studying the sheriff, taking in his stiff saddle posture, watching the fingers of his right hand tap nervously on his thigh. Trent's frame was leaner and his face more drawn than usual, as if Molly had cooked too little or pestered him too much about his debts. Maybe it was the election, even if it was still five months away. While no one else had yet filed for office, many ranchers were talking about supporting someone to run against Trent Jackson, someone who would let Dewey Slater go.

A couple of the horsemen nudged their mounts out from under the tree. Riding toward the Stoddards, Red Stewart pulled his watch from his vest pocket and studied the time with his watery eyes. "Early you ain't; late you ain't, either," Stewart said, replacing his watch and scratching his beard. "You Stoddards stay on schedule better than a horny train conductor."

Zack Miller followed behind, tipping his planter's hat at Pa Stoddard and grunting at Ty.

Ty could make out the others, now. Both Gus and Lamar Mason were there, as well as Bob Vandiver, Stan Ballard, Mart Bigsby and Walt Storm.

The cottonwood tree rustled in a stiff gust of wind that carried the scent of rain. A bolt of lightning cut through the thunderhead, and shortly afterward thunder rumbled over the gathering.

"Let's get on with it," Stewart commanded. "If that cloud's a goose drowner, I want to be on high ground."

The others mumbled their greetings to the Stoddards and nodded their agreement with Stewart. Leather creaked as they twisted in their saddles toward Trent Jackson.

The sheriff stood in his stirrups, then settled into his seat, resting his hands on the saddlehorn. His gaze went from man to man around the circle, stopping at Pa Stoddard, as if his message was meant most of all for his father-in-law. "There's not a man here I don't trust," Jackson started.

Before he could complete his sentence, Zack Miller lifted the curled bullwhip and pointed its butt at the sheriff. "We know that, Trent, and most of us figure you're ready for us to start riding as vigilantes to help you with the job you was elected to do."

"It ain't been easy," Jackson said, leaning forward.

"We've all lost cattle," Stewart interjected. "We're ready to put an end to it."

Miller nodded. "You call 'em regulators, I call 'em vigilantes. We've defended our property before and we'll do it again. But we've talked it over and none of us want to ride with Dewey Slater. If he knows what we are up to, count us out." Miller shook the bullwhip at the sheriff.

The other ranchers nodded and Ty shared their contempt for the deputy.

"Slater'll be in the dark on all of this," Jackson promised. "I figure it's me and those of us gathered here, all of us honorable men."

The ranchers stared with narrowed eyes and tight lips at the sheriff. Ty figured they had agreed on Zack Miller as spokesman, since he was the only one equal to Pa Stoddard. Red Stewart would say what he wanted to regardless of any agreement, but that was just Red's way. The others would follow Zack Miller, as a herd would follow the dominant bull. But all of them seemed to be weighing Jackson's word.

"Fact is," Miller continued, "a deputy that would suggest Pa Stoddard and Ty killed and robbed Baker and Phipps is likely to be more against us than for us."

Jackson's face clouded and his hands tightened around the saddlehorn. "Slater's a hard man. We all know that, but deputies are hard to find! Any of you like to hire on for what the county pays?"

"We just as well," Stewart laughed, "if we're going to start night riding."

Miller waved the bullwhip at Stewart. "This is serious business, Red. Leave us keep it that way." Miller turned to Pa Stoddard. "You in or out, Stoddard?"

Stoddard pursed his lips and nodded, a clap of distant thunder accompanying his decision. "It's time we ended it, as long as Slater's out."

Jackson nodded again. "Slater'll have no part in this."

Miller waved his whip at the sheriff. "A

few things need to be understood by everyone. Any man who names one of us to an outsider will be killed. We'll draw straws to see who does the killing. If you don't like that, ride on out now."

No one moved, except for nods of agreement.

"As much trouble's we've had catching the rustlers, it could be some of our own people," Miller said. "If they're my hands, it's my job to shuck their cobs. If it's your men, it's your job. Anyone that can't stomach it, needs to leave. We've all hired mistakes before, so we should correct them ourselves."

Again, just nods from the other ranchers.

"No one is asked to join us unless all of us here have agreed upon it. No town folk will be asked to ride with us. They're not losing their livelihood like we are, and they've too much opportunity to let the word out. When we ride as vigilantes, we ride with no less than five of us. If the sheriff's along, fine, but we can take care of our interests without him when we need to. Is this agreeable to everyone?"

Trent Jackson nodded first. "It's all reasonable."

"And when we're called to ride," Miller called out, "we drop everything and ride.

Nothing — not wives, not family, not ranching — nothing can come between us and the job to be done."

From a bulging pocket Red Stewart pulled out his kerchief and draped it over his nose. He blew a benediction over Miller's words, then dabbed at his nose. Beneath his chafed nose his beard split into a grin. "Hell, Zack, why don't you put all that in writing and we can file it down at the courthouse?"

Miller's fist turned white around the butt of his bullwhip, and his face reddened.

Stewart shoved the soiled cloth back into his distended pocket. "We know what has to be done. You ain't our pappy."

Miller spat at the ground, then drew the sleeve of his shirt across his lips, his eyes fixing hard on Stewart. "I'm a cautious man, Red, and don't leave much to chance."

Red's eyes held Miller's gaze, the grin slowly draining from his face until his lips were hidden again by his beard. "I've had as much success as you, and damn sure had more fun by leaving more to chance."

Pa Stoddard nudged his horse between the two men. "If we talk ourselves to death, rustlers won't have any worries. Rain's a'coming, so we best get to high ground."

For a moment, Stewart's and Miller's eyes remained locked on each other. Around them the others grunted their agreement with Pa Stoddard. Stewart twisted his head toward the cloud towering over the west and now blocking out the sun. Then he glanced at Miller. "Reckon the rain'll cool us down, Zack?"

A slight grin pried at Miller's lips and his grip loosened on the butt of the bullwhip. "You don't think without talking."

"And you don't talk without thinking," Red shot back. "Beats all that we get along so well."

Both men laughed, along with the others, Trent Jackson the hardest among them. Trent seemed more confident since the ranchers had agreed to turn vigilante. His frame had lost its stiffness and he sat easily in the saddle, even though the storm was nearing and the other men were edgy in their saddles. "When the time comes to ride, I'll spread the word," the sheriff said.

A brilliant flash of lightning was punctuated by a crashing thunder. The intermittent breeze had turned into a steady wind that carried the sweet aroma of rain.

"Save your breath, Sheriff," Red Stewart shouted over the thunder. "It's time to skedaddle, boys." He jerked the reins on his horse and whistled, the chestnut pounding down the trail toward home.

Quickly, the Mason brothers, Stan Ballard, Mart Bigsby and Walt Storm were riding after Stewart, racing the wind for home.

"I'll ride home with you, Trent," Ty said, his roan tossing its head, ready to run. "I'd like to see Molly."

Trent shook his head, his face clouding for a moment. "I've work in town. Be tomorrow before I make it home."

Ty suspected Trent was having trouble at home, but he had to take him at his word. "Mind if I ride on over, howdy her?"

"She'd like that," Trent said softly, a puzzled look furrowing his brow as he gazed at Pa Stoddard, Zack Miller and Bob Vandiver.

The three had maneuvered their mounts about fifty feet away and sat there talking, all with their backs to Ty and Trent. Ty asked Trent if he had any messages for Molly, but the sheriff didn't hear the question. He just stared at the trio, curiosity etched in his brow and in the corner of his eye. When the three finished their talk, Miller and Vandiver galloped away and Pa Stoddard turned his piebald toward Ty and Trent.

"I need a word with you, Ty," the old man said, his stare coldly on Trent.

Ty knew by the set of his father's jaw that

this word was meant to be a private conversation.

Trent seemed not to understand for a minute, his horse blowing and stamping nervously at the approaching storm.

"We'll see you in good time, Trent," Pa Stoddard said, nodding rather formally at his son-in-law.

Then the unstated message seemed to sink in. A shade of anger darkened the sheriff's face, as if he would forever be the outsider. "Sure thing," the sheriff growled. "You're welcome to stay at my place like Ty. Molly'd be glad to see you." His eyes were as gray and as hard as aged ice. "I've business in town for the night, if it makes any difference in your decision."

"Heading home, Trent, once I'm finished with Ty," Stoddard replied, his voice rising with impatience as he looked at the mean cloud.

"You be careful, then," Trent answered, jerking the reins of his chestnut around toward town and touching his heel to the animal's flank. Rider and mount bolted toward Tascosa.

The world seemed to rumble with another clap of thunder and the pounding hoofbeats of the sheriff's horse. Then the noises evaporated and there was a moment of unnatural silence.

"Weren't you a little hard on him, Pa?" Ty sidled his roan up beside his father's piebald.

"There's a lot of things in this world I can't figure. Trent Jackson's one of 'em. Politics is another. Mix the two, and I'm as perplexed as a two-headed calf at dinnertime."

"What's politics got to do with this?"

Pa Stoddard stroked his cheek. "Plenty. You know Zack Miller's not one to have an idle conversation. He and Bob Vandiver got me aside for a purpose. Zack said it was nothing personal, but the ranchers had gotten together and decided they'd run Vandiver for sheriff."

Ty let out a low whistle. "What'd you tell 'em?"

"Most likely . . ." The rancher started, then paused, looking around him as if the land had ears. "That most likely, I'd vote for Vandiver."

Ty caught his breath, then shook his head. "How can you vote against family?" He was surprised at the anger in his voice, but unsure if it were directed at his father or at Trent.

His father, too, seemed startled. The old man cocked his head, his eyes turning defiant. "Trent's not family!"

Ty felt his left hand knotting into a fist around the reins. "How can you say that?"

"Molly's family; so's the girl and the young'un on the way, but they need a husband and a father. Weren't for politics, Trent might be better at both!" Stoddard's words were bedrock hard.

"He's doing it for Molly and his children," Ty shot back, his words lifting in anger.

"He's doing it for himself, Ty. You mark my words on that."

Ty lifted his weak hand and pointed a finger at his father's face. "You're wrong, Pa." His hand shook and Ty was uncertain if the tremor came from the weakness or the danger of challenging his father so directly.

His father jerked the reins on the piebald and turned away. "Say hello to Molly for me, and I'll see you tomorrow night back on the Diamond S." He slapped his mount on the flank and galloped away toward the approaching storm, pulling his hat down low over his forehead.

Ty stared until his father had disappeared into the blowing wind. He untied from his neck the orange-and-white bandana Delia had given him and pulled it over his hat, knotting it under his chin to keep his hat in place. A bolt of lightning coursed a jagged path through the sky and the thunder followed quickly behind it. The storm was getting too close. Ty yelled and raked his spurs across the gelding's flank, and the surprised roan dashed away from Big Tree, down the canyon and toward the trail that led to the Jackson place. Ty let the roan run and the land seemed to pass by in a blur, Ty thinking more about the election and the hard feelings between his father and Trent Jackson. Ty wondered if it meant anything that he was riding away from the same storm his father was riding into.

The gelding enjoyed free rein and the chance to outdistance the storm. The land was now in a great shadow, and the gelding trembled after each crash of thunder. The roan seemed to fly. Only when the roan slowed did Ty emerge from his thoughts. The gelding was climbing the trail to the rim of the canyon and to Molly's home. The storm seemed not quite so near as when he had turned the roan loose at Big Tree, but the purple clouds still boiled like a giant cauldron overflowing with wind and rain.

Topping the rim, the gelding increased his stride until Ty eased back on the reins. No sense in throwing a fright into Molly. The gelding's hoofbeats were lost in the cloud's windy breath, which sent ripples through the thick grass. Up ahead he saw Molly's stone house, the fine home she deserved. On the clothesline between the house and corral, sheets and Trent's clothes snapped in the great gusts of wind. Ty glanced over his shoulder, gauging the storm's approach. The cloud stabbed the earth with a dagger of lightning and the whole sky grumbled.

Molly must have forgotten the clothes. He couldn't blame her, though, with all that must be on her mind. Just as he touched his heel to the roan's flank, the back door of the house was flung open and a flurry of skirt, blouse and bonnet dashed for the clothes. So unlike Molly to wear a bonnet, especially on a day like this, Ty thought, then nodded. She was pregnant. That changed women — not just their appearance, but their thinking, as well. At the clothesline, she worked with more determination than speed. At her rate, the rain would catch up with her before she finished. At the back corner of the house, Ty jumped off the roan, quickly tied the reins to a porch post and dashed to help.

So absorbed was she at removing the pants and shirts that she hadn't heard his approach. She pulled the clothespins from one shirt and then another, then jerked some workpants free and bent over to stuff the clothes in the basket.

Remembering how much it had annoyed her as a kid for him to swat her with his hat, he slipped it free from under the bandana just as big drops of rain began to dot the hardpacked ground beneath the clothesline. Ty's hand swooped from his head toward Molly. The hat landed solidly on her rear.

She squealed, her voice a higher pitch than Ty remembered.

"Surprise!" Ty laughed over the wind.

She spun around from the basket, her eyes bewildered for a brief instant, her arms reaching for the next sheet on the line, the bonnet shielding her face for but a fleeting instant.

Ty gulped, feeling the hot flush of embarrassment upon his cheeks.

This woman was not Molly.

CHAPTER 10

Ty stumbled for words, his outstretched hand frozen with his embarrassment. "You're not Molly."

"And you're not helping." She turned and dropped another sheet into the basket.

Ty tugged his hat down over his head, glancing at the cloud. He could hear the roar of approaching rain as it pummeled the thirsty earth. He jumped at a wild sheet billowing out with the breeze like an anchored clipper's frustrated sail. He caught the sheet, jerking it loose from a pair of clothespins, then lost his grip. The sheet whipped away from the line, snapped taut against two pins that still held, and whipped back into his face. For an instant, he thought he heard a delicate giggle. His arms clawed at the sheet, which suddenly leaped from his face.

This woman, whoever she was, gathered the stubborn sheet in to her breast. "Grab the basket and run," she shouted, then dashed for the house.

For a moment, Ty held in his mind the lingering image of her face. Striking green eyes, a complexion the pale white of fresh cream, a teasing smile. As large raindrops struck his hat brim, he snatched the basket and ran after this woman.

Whoever she was, she wasn't from Oldham County. Whoever she was, he must apologize for his rudeness. He both dreaded and relished that opportunity.

As the rain began to pour, she reached the porch and jumped under the overhang, startling his roan tied at the corner. With the sheet all wadded up before her blouse, she spun toward Ty.

"Here," Ty called at the porch, "I've got to get my horse out of the rain." He shoved the basket into her arms. As she took it, his gaze locked on her green eyes.

"Well, get going," she scolded, "before your horse drowns."

Ty darted for his roan. In his wake, he heard her laughter as delicate as the clink of fine crystal. He jerked the knot from the reins, then clambered up into the wet saddle as he turned the roan toward the barn. At the fence, Ty bent over in his saddle, unlatched the gate, pushed it open. The roan danced inside the corral, spooking a pony that had been standing in the open barn door. The pony dashed by the roan, then circled the pen, eyeing the open gate. Ty whistled at the pony and grabbed his hat, slapping it against his leg. The pony darted for the gate, then changed course when Ty yelled. The pony splashed through the accumulating puddles. Ty latched the gate and rode the roan into the barn. Perturbed at these trespassers, the pony dipped and tossed its head as it galloped around the corral.

Inside, Ty dismounted and unsaddled the roan, tossing the gear on a rail. Then he led the gelding to a stall and removed the bridle. From a stack of hay he pulled a pitchfork, carried two loads to the horse's trough, and, from a bin on the back wall, added a scoop of dried corn. Ty heard mice scurry for the kernels of corn that had fallen from the scoop. Overhead, the rain attacked the wooden shingles and the barn leaked in a dozen places, but not so badly for a barn. Returning the scoop to the corn bin, Ty wished the rain would end so he could meet this woman. Though the rain fell in a fury, the dangerous lightning seemed a bit distant and thunder rumbled down the canyon along the river. Rain was funny in the

Panhandle. Mostly it didn't come. But when it came, it came with the fury of a caged cougar broken free. And the more furious the rain, the shorter its duration.

Ty eased over to the barn door and stood in the cool draft, watching the pony splattering a trail around the pen. Slowly, the downpour subsided and the few raindrops drifted rather than exploded from the cloud. Ty stroked his jaw with his left hand. His cheeks were rough with two days' whisker growth, and he wished he had shaved before coming to Molly's, but then he had only expected to find Molly and Delia and possibly Trent. And his clothes — they were work clothes, dirty from riding the pastures, trying to turn up cattle that had disappeared. Ty knew he made a shoddy presence, but short of entering the house naked, he figured he had no alternative. When the rain subsided, Ty strode out of the barn, through the corral and toward the house. And toward this woman!

Steam rose from the ground and the atmosphere was close, like the collar around his neck. He stepped up on the back porch, scraping the mud off his boots on the step. The door swung open and Ty smiled as Molly emerged, her arms outstretched for a hug. Sheepishly, Ty offered her his right hand.

"Ty, a handshake instead of a hug?" Molly questioned. Then it seemed to strike her. It was his bad arm, the one that had been so useless after the ambush. Her grin widened by degrees. She grabbed his hand and shook it vigorously.

Bending forward, he kissed her cheek. "You look fine, Molly," he said, standing back and studying her. A bulge showed in her stomach and she radiated the maternal pride of an expectant mother.

Delia burst out of the door, dragging her doll, Kay-Lee.

Ty grabbed Delia and hoisted her into the air. "How's my favorite niece and favorite doll?" Ty tickled her ribs and Delia giggled, then pointed to the corral.

"See Delia's horse?"

Turning to look, Ty kissed her cheek. "That's your pony? Well, I'm glad. I figured your father had lost his senses keeping an animal no bigger than that for ranch work."

"I like Delia's horse, Rainbow. Papa says I can ride him."

He let Delia slide from his arms to the porch. "Guess you're old enough to start riding, Delia."

A frown carved across her lips, Molly

stood with arms crossed and head shaking. "It was her father's idea, not mine. She's too young to be riding a pony."

"You gonna invite me in or not, Molly?" Ty took off his hat and stamped his boots on the porch a final time.

Molly's smile reappeared, like the sun now slipping through breaks in the clouds, and she pushed the door open, herding Delia in before her. "Yes, I'm inviting you in, and I've someone to introduce you to, though I hear you've already met."

Ty felt his face heat with embarrassment from the awkward moment by the clothesline. He stepped into a kitchen hot from a strong fire in the stove.

By the table, folding clothes, stood the woman. She smiled. Without her bonnet, Ty liked what he saw even better. Her auburn hair cascaded in ringlets over her forehead and ears. There was a smile in her green eyes and on her delicate lips. There was something familiar about the set of her head when she lifted her hand toward his.

"Ty," Molly said, "I'd like to introduce you to Wilma Jackson, Trent's sister."

Trent's sister, of course! Now Ty remembered. She was coming to stay with Molly until the baby came. He took her hand, relishing the softness of her fingers as they touched his. "I must apologize. I figured to give Molly a surprise. Guess I surprised myself more."

A lilting laugh escaped from her delicate throat. "I shall not forget our first meeting, Mr. Stoddard."

"She's had so many forgettable meetings, Ty. Why, most of Oldham County's single male population has come by our place to visit since Wilma arrived. She's quite popular."

"I can see why!" Ty grinned and released her hand. He thought he detected a blush on her cheeks, but she turned back to the clothes. It tickled him to embarrass her, finally.

"Oh, Wilma's been a great help, doing the hard work," Molly said. "I don't know how I could've made it without her, Trent being gone so much."

Ty thought he detected disappointment in her words, but he could not be sure. He slid into a chair by the table and Molly sat opposite him.

"Trouble isn't dying down, Ty, is it?" Molly stared at her lap, as if she were afraid to look up. "More cattle missing, and Trent's gone half the time chasing rustlers or ghosts. He never catches up with them, and I don't know if I'd want him to, because he might get hurt."

"Molly tells me they hurt you, Mr. Stoddard," Wilma said.

"I got careless." Ty said nothing more, ashamed of his lapse in judgment.

Wilma seemed to understand and changed the subject. They talked for more than an hour, the three of them, on small matters like the weather and what news they had picked up on occasional visits to town or from the young men visiting Wilma.

Wilma finished folding clothes and carried them into another room. She returned with a suggestion. "Why don't you two visit in the parlor? I'll get supper going."

"She's gonna spoil me, Ty." Molly said, easing up from her chair. "And she's a good cook, too!"

Ty escorted Molly into the front room. She checked on Delia, playing with her doll in her own room, then claimed the rocking chair. Ty pulled a cane-bottom chair beside hers and settled into it, leaning back on its hind legs.

"I've been anxious for you to visit, Ty, and to meet Wilma. She's a fine woman with good sense. She'd make a good wife."

Ty leaned forward in his chair and the front legs came down hard against the plank floor. "I just met her! Sounds like I'm too late."

Molly nodded. "There's several, including Dewey Slater."

Ty felt a knot in his stomach. She seemed too delicate, too fine for the deputy. "What did she say?"

"Yes! She told him yes."

The knot tightened in his stomach. He wasn't interested in a woman who would court a man like Slater.

"But you know how Slater is, always trying to be a tough one," Molly continued. "She saw him ride away from here, beating his horse with his quirt. She changed her mind quickly, saying she wouldn't court a man that treated his horse that way. He wouldn't respect much else if he didn't respect his horse."

Ty's stomach improved, quickly. "Glad to hear that."

Molly nodded. "Through Trent she sent word back to Dewey that she'd changed her mind. That ended that."

"Slater ruins everything he touches," Ty said, not really thinking about the implications until the words were out of his mouth and too late to call back. His eyes looked instantly at his sister and her face was pale, worry trapped behind her eyes.

"Has he ruined my husband?" she asked, her voice trembling like her hand as she lifted it to wipe at her moist eyes. "I was hoping he wouldn't run for sheriff again, but he's still set on it. Then I hoped somebody would run against him so he'd lose, but he can't take that. I don't know what I can take anymore."

Ty shook his head. "Everybody's on edge, Molly. I've never seen folks so jumpy, but we're gonna fight back and we're gonna win. It may take a while. . . ."

"And cost some more lives," Molly said softly, as if she feared it could be one of her family.

"It could. Nothing's without risk, Molly; you know that."

"Talk's going around that Trent can't be trusted to pay his debts." There was dejection in her voice. "He won't discuss it with me, says it's man's business. There's more talk, too, Ty, that Trent's cows all have twins. Everybody else's herds dwindled over the winter, but not ours. I've heard Trent tell we're up a couple hundred head from the fall."

Ty took Molly's hand. "You shouldn't worry about what talk you hear. Likely it's all politics, and anyway, you know Trent better than any of us."

Molly sobbed. "I thought I did, but I'm not so sure anymore. But if you were a rustler, you wouldn't steal cattle from the sheriff's ranch, would you? You'd fear getting caught, wouldn't you?"

Delia stepped tentatively into the parlor, standing by the door and staring at her mother. She held Kay-Lee tightly against her chest with both arms.

Molly sniveled and dabbed at her eyes with a kerchief that had appeared from her sleeve. "I'm okay honey," she told Delia. "Mommas cry, too, sometimes, when they are sad or tired."

Nodding, Delia stepped toward her mother. "I'm sad, too. Papa's not home much anymore." She dropped Kay-Lee and ran to her mother with her arms out.

Molly bent in her rocking chair to hug her daughter. "Momma's sad, too, when Papa's not around. He'll be here tomorrow."

Delia's face brightened with an idea. "I should go ride Rainbow and find Papa."

Molly shook her head. "No! You stay away from your horse until Papa's here to help you. You need to learn to ride better so you won't get hurt. Do I hear Kay-Lee calling?"

Glancing over her shoulder, Delia saw her doll on the floor where she had dropped her. Worming her way out of her mother's arms, Delia stumbled toward Kay-Lee, mumbling something, then picked the doll up and carried it back into her room.

The moment with Delia seemed to alter Molly's mind. She dabbed at her eyes a final time, then smiled with a poignancy that bared her soul and her vulnerability. She loved her husband and hated his faults and the harsh words of others against him.

Then Molly talked of the old days and the tough times when they were kids, as if she were reassuring herself that these hardships, too, would pass with time. This was the Molly that Ty always remembered, the one whose soul was a cauldron of joy, always seeing the humor in life, always looking at the best side of a troublesome coin. They talked for most of an hour and all the time Ty was hungering to sit down at the kitchen table. He was famished, sure, but he was interested in visiting with Wilma and complimenting her cooking, no matter how good or how bad.

The aroma of black-eyed peas boiling and cornbread baking tickled his nose and his eagerness to sit with Wilma Jackson. When she called, Ty shot up from the chair, and he wondered if his zeal had caught Molly's attention. He glanced full into Molly's face and detected a hint of delight behind her gentle smile. He took Molly into the kitchen on his arm, Delia following.

Wilma smiled and with a wave of her hand invited them to take a seat. "It's nothing fancy, but it'll fill your stomach."

"Looks fine," Ty said, taking in the squares of cornbread, the bowl of black-eyed peas, a platter of boiled potatoes and a dish of cooked onions. After helping Molly into her chair, Ty slid into his, Delia clambering onto the pillows in the chair beside Ty. Ty felt an awkward moment when Molly asked him to say grace. He thought it out, figuring he couldn't refuse the request, but neither could he say words eloquently enough to impress Wilma. He offered thanks meekly, then filled his plate.

"Wilma's been such a help, I don't know how I would've managed without her," Molly said, as she dabbed small helpings onto her plate.

"Remember, you're eating for two, Molly," Wilma chided, then turned to Ty. "I hope you find dinner to your liking, Mr. Stoddard."

Ty ate with pleasure. Wilma was indeed a good cook, an observation he repeated several times, until both Wilma and Molly laughed. Ty ate his full, then topped that with a couple of helpings of dried-apple cobbler. When they were done, Wilma lit a lamp in the kitchen and shooed Ty and Molly into the front room again while she cleaned up. Molly put Delia to bed and made excuses to keep Ty company, but Ty could see the exhaustion in her drawn face and sent her to bed. He retreated into the kitchen and picked up a dish towel.

"My, my, Mr. Stoddard, aren't you the handiest thing," she teased. "First you help me get the clothes off the line; now you plan to dry dishes."

"I like the company." He picked up a plate, his right hand still weak, but he was determined not to let it show. He worked quickly, taking plates and bowls from the rinse pan and stacking them on the table when he was done. He had gotten plenty of experience doing dishes since his mother had died, but never had he enjoyed it more than now. He was close enough to smell the sweetness of Wilma's hair and the faint scent of lilac. They talked, mostly about the people she had met in Oldham County, about Trent and Molly and, for brief moments, about themselves. And when they were finished in the kitchen, Ty pulled his watch from his vest pocket and shook his head. It was after ten o'clock already. Though he wanted to learn more about

Wilma, he had to get up early in the morning to ride back to the Diamond S.

"Please tell Molly goodbye for me in the morning. I'll leave before daylight."

She smiled. "I shall, and I shall also tell you goodbye in the morning, after I fix your breakfast."

Ty opened his mouth to speak, but she held up her hand.

"No argument, Mr. Stoddard," she commanded, then walked from the kitchen to Molly's room and returned with an armload of quilts. "I'll make you a bed on the floor in the parlor."

"I can sleep in the barn."

She dropped the blanket and held her hand up again.

"No argument, right?" Ty laughed and she laughed with him.

After she made the bed and fetched a pillow, Wilma slipped into Delia's room and closed the door behind her.

Ty crawled onto the quilts and quickly was asleep, soundly so, until he heard noises in the kitchen and saw a thread of light framing the kitchen door. Stretching, he arose, pulled on his boots and slipped into the kitchen, the aroma of coffee and fried bacon greeting him.

Wilma was opening the oven door and

pulling out a pan of biscuits. "I thought you were gonna sleep all day." She laughed. Quickly, she filled his plate with bacon and creamed corn and biscuits and then fetched him a cup of hot coffee.

He ate quickly and quietly and when he was done, he pushed himself away from the table. "Thank you, ma'am. Best breakfast I've had in a spell."

"You're welcome, Mr. Stoddard. I hope I shall have the pleasure of your company again." She offered him her hand and they stood together.

Ty's arm tingled at her touch. "Certainly. Why, we're almost kin!" He released her hand and retreated to the back door, slipping out into the dark and to the barn.

Quickly, he saddled up, ignoring Delia's pony, which seemed unnerved by his presence. Ty led the roan out of the barn and corral, then mounted. There at the back door stood Wilma, watching. He waved and touched his spurs to the gelding's flank, and the animal dashed away toward the canyon trail. He thought he could feel the caressing touch of her gaze until he rode out of sight.

Morning was just tinging the fringes of the sky. Except for the roan's hoofbeats, the earth seemed at peace. Ty chose to follow the canyon trail back to the ranch to see whether there was much flooding or, if he admitted it to himself, whether he could pick up the signs of any rustlers. He rode a ways, and then realized something was wrong about the canyon; something didn't look right, even in dawn's dim light. He found himself at Big Tree, but something was odd; the tree seemed not nearly so tall. He smelled the odor of burnt wood and, in the gathering light, he could just make out the misshapen tree, bowing over to the world.

Lightning had struck the tree and split it right down the middle.

CHAPTER 11

Overhead, a hawk drifted on the canyon's unseen air currents. What he must be able to see from the blue sky! Ty envied the winged predator for what he could see and cursed himself for what he could not. Five times the regulators had ridden. Five times in vain. The rustlers were ghosts who seemed to know their every move. Ty twisted in his saddle and checked on his father riding behind him. Pa Stoddard had been silent, sullen. Something weighed heavily on his mind, but he didn't care to talk about it. He just followed Ty toward Big Tree, where the regulators were gathering for another sweep across a corner of Oldham County. As noon approached, Ty was glad to see Big Tree, or what was left of it, in the distance.

Each side of the once big tree curled in opposite directions. What leaves still clung to the tree had yellowed, but most had fallen away, leaving the skeleton of what had been a proud sentinel standing guard by the Canadian.

Other riders were already congregated by the cottonwood's corpse. All the regulators and the sheriff appeared to be there.

When they were within talking distance of the group, Red Stewart pulled out his silver pocket watch and shook his head. "Noon on the money. Never early and never late!"

Ty figured Red was not as interested in punctuality as he was in showing off his watch, a fine silver piece imported from Switzerland. It was a good watch indeed, but Ty would've traded a dozen of its kind for the one that had belonged to his grandfather, the one stolen by his ambushers.

The men greeted each other with grim faces. Zack Miller sat away from the others, his skeptical eyes moving from man to man, but generally coming to stare at the sheriff. His fingers tapped impatiently on the handle of his whip. Bob Vandiver seemed ill at ease as well, staring uncomfortably at the sheriff.

The strain showed in Trent Jackson's face; his lips were tight, his cheeks gaunt, and his eyes red and watery. When he spoke, his words came softly, not like a man in command, nor like a man running for reelection. All the work with the ranch and the sheriff's job was catching up with Trent.

"Men," Trent said, shifting in the saddle, "our luck's changed."

Zack hawked and spat the result on the ground.

Trent pretended to ignore the gesture. "Yesterday I found a pen in the breaks, a dozen head of cattle. Diamond S cattle."

Ty felt his right hand tighten around his reins and he nudged his roan toward Trent.

"East of here, where the canyon widens and the country gets rougher."

Like Ty, the other riders closed in around Trent, their eyes narrow, their jaws set.

"The cattle didn't pen themselves up, now did they?" Red Stewart fingered his auburn beard. "What about the rustlers — any sign?"

"Tracks" — Trent nodded — "nothing more, but they'll be back. I figure we can ride in, surround the place. If our luck holds, we just might snare us some rustlers before dawn."

Zack Miller spat again. "Only luck we've had, Sheriff, has been bad."

"It's bound to change," Trent Jackson replied, his gaunt face creased by a grin as cocky as that of a gambler holding four aces. "If you're with me, Zack, we ride now. Anybody that wants to back out, now's the time." Trent stared from man to man. No one moved. "We'll follow the river up to the gravel shallows, then split up. The cattle are in a draw a mile up from there. There's enough cover we can hide and wait 'em out."

If they were holding Diamond S cattle, Ty knew he would stay until winter to catch the thieves, and maybe settle a score with the man who had backshot him. "Let's ride," Ty said.

Trent held up his hand to stop them. "We're all in this together, as regulators?" The sheriff plucked the badge from his vest and shoved it in his britches pocket.

"Time's a wastin'," Zack Miller said.

The men rode east along the river, Trent leading the band, which advanced in a clump, in no particular order, except for Zack Miller and Pa Stoddard lagging behind. Trent Jackson glanced over his shoulder occasionally, checking on the elder ranchers. The gambler's grin was gone. The men paced their horses at a trot, saving their mounts should it come to a chase.

Ty's muscles were knotted in anticipation. His hand kept dropping to the Colt resting upon his hip. The strength had returned to his right hand, though some numbness remained, along with the memory of the ambush. That tapping noise, the low whistles! Sometimes at night they haunted him until he would wake up with a start, his body soaking with a cold sweat. Damn that son of a bitch!

At the gravel shallows, the horses splashed through the water, then weaved among the brush, post oaks, and cottonwoods scattered along the riverbank. The riders paralleled the river for a mile until Trent pointed to a cut in the canyon wall, the mouth to a blind draw. "There it is, men. One of you come with me; the rest of you fan out around it. We may be a while."

Stan Ballard reined his horse over beside Trent.

"Keep my horse, Stan, while I slip down the canyon for a look-see," Trent commanded.

The horsemen began to scatter, Ty figuring to stay close to his father, but Vandiver cut his chestnut in ahead of Ty's roan.

"Good cover among those cedars," Vandiver said, pointing to a stand of trees down the riverbank. "Good cover for two."

Nodding, Ty reined his gelding in that direction, Bob Vandiver riding alongside him. Ty saw his father and Zack Miller heading toward a pair of cottonwood trees.

Vandiver rode silently, as was his style, but his eyes seemed jittery. Ty studied the lines in Vandiver's face, wondering if he had the stomach for this regulator business or for a sheriff's job. Once in the trees, Ty glanced at the mouth of the draw. Trent was afoot now, slipping up the cut, clinging to the shadows along the wall. Stan Ballard cradled a Winchester in the crook of his elbow and held the reins of the sheriff's horse. Sliding out of his saddle, Ty tied his reins around a cedar. He pulled the makings out of his pocket and started constructing a smoke, his glance alternating between his fingers' handiwork and Vandiver's tentative look.

"Want a cigarette?" he offered, as he stuck the rolled tobacco paper in his mouth.

Dismounting, Vandiver nodded, then grabbed the fixings from Ty. He spent a minute working on the smoke, spilling too much tobacco onto the ground for Ty's taste. He tossed the pouch back to Ty, who stuffed it in his vest pocket and returned with a match. Flicking it to a flame with his thumbnail, Ty touched it to the tip of his cigarette until he drew smoke, then extended his cupped hand and flaming match toward Vandiver.

The owner of the Double Deuce ranch bent over the match, then stood up, his face disguised behind a veil of smoke. He drew hard and deep on the cigarette, so much so that the end flamed just a moment. He exhaled another cloud of smoke and took two more hard drags. No enjoyment in the way Vandiver was smoking. Tobacco had to be taken slow, not forced on the body. It didn't calm the nerves this way, and Ty figured Vandiver had a bad case of nerves.

Vandiver dropped the remainder of the cigarette and with his boot crushed it into the soil far longer than necessary to extinguish it. "Ty," he started, "I wanted to tell your pa this face-to-face, but it appears he and Zack Miller are deep in conversation of their own. I'm not fool enough to interfere with those two old buffalo bulls."

Ty studied Vandiver and enjoyed his cigarette. "I'll give Pa your message."

"Obliged, Ty," Vandiver started. "Maybe Miller's telling him now, but this morning I filed for sheriff."

Ty sucked hard on his cigarette a moment, then exhaled slowly and silently.

"Trent wasn't in town," Vandiver continued, "so he doesn't know yet, and I'd appreciate your letting him find out on his own once he gets back to town. It'll make it more comfortable on all of us."

Ty offered Vandiver his hand. "Good luck, Bob!"

Vandiver grabbed it and shook it heartily,

as if he were trying to coax water from an old handpump. "It's nothing to do with any of you Stoddards. You're men of your word and I've nothing but respect for you — Molly, too. It's just too many funny things are going on and we need a change. You be sure and tell your pa I meant to tell him myself and figured I might not get a chance if there was any excitement up the draw."

"I'll tell him. He knows a man's gotta chose the trail he rides, and he's never begrudged a man a decision as long as it was honest," Ty answered. "Trent losing the election would kinda make Molly happy, maybe pull them closer together now."

"Glad you see it that way. I just don't want any hard feelings between me and you Stoddards," Vandiver offered.

"We can't back you publicly because of Molly, Bob; you know that. But I suspect you'll pull a Stoddard vote or two in the ballot box."

The exchange seemed to take a load off Vandiver's shoulders, but Ty didn't have time to reflect on it. Vandiver pointed toward the draw. "Jackson's coming out!"

Ty realized Vandiver no longer called Jackson sheriff.

Both men gathered their reins and pulled themselves into the saddle. They turned their mounts toward the draw and stared. Jackson was mounting up, motioning with his arms to Stan Ballard. In a moment, Stan was riding at a canter toward Ty and Vandiver.

Both men rode out to meet him. As he approached, Ty could see anger in Stan's wide eyes. "We've got one. Looks like he's gonna be riding out shortly with some cattle. Trent says to get ready to cut him off once he comes out." Stan rode on to pass the word on to the others.

Ty pulled his watch from his vest pocket and studied its face. It was twenty minutes after one, and an age since the ambush. He recalled the triumph of catching them altering brands, then the ultimate disgrace of getting plugged in the back. He kept hearing that tapping noise followed by the three whistles. Chills ran down his back. He craved a chance to repay the favor, give a rustler bad memories to last a lifetime — a short lifetime. Ty slipped the watch back into his vest pocket and pulled the Winchester from his saddle scabbard. He glanced around to see Stan Ballard completing the round to all the regulators. It was just a matter of time.

Ty and Vandiver waited silently, their eyes fixed on the draw. Finally, the sound of bellowing cattle began to drift toward them. The cattle were on the move. Ty's grip tightened around his Winchester. In ones and twos, the cattle trotted out of the draw, until two dozen heifers and yearlings were leading a rustler to a surprise. Then a lone rider emerged from the gash in the canyon wall. He rode his horse easily, his attention fixed on the cattle.

Ty and Vandiver nudged their horses forward and into the clear. Around them, other regulators were emerging as well, forming a semicircle some fifty yards ahead of the rider. The cattle, headed toward Pa Stoddard and Zack Miller, then shied away, looking for an unblocked route. There was none, and the cattle began to circle. It was then that Ty noticed the Diamond S burned into their hides. He spat venom at the ground.

The lone rustler whistled, trying to break up the milling of the cattle, then glanced ahead, realizing he had company. He jerked on the reins, his horse rearing on its hind legs.

Ty lifted his carbine to his shoulder. If the rustler made a break, he would plug him.

The rustler wrestled the reins on his bay mount, then calmed the strapping animal instead of running. Ty cursed silently, wishing for one shot at the fleeing rustler's back. The rustler leaned forward in the saddle, his hand reaching toward the stock of the carbine which was visible over the saddle horn. Ty's finger tightened on the trigger, then eased off. The rustler was patting his horse on the neck, still calming him. Ty lowered his Winchester as he noticed the others gradually riding forward, closing in on the rustler like a noose around his neck. Ty touched his boot to the roan's flank and advanced.

When the regulators were within speaking distance, the rustler took off his hat and swiped with his sleeve at the sweat beading on his brow. He looked from man to man, mirroring their silent stares with a helpless gaze. "Been a misunderstanding." He sighed. His hat trembled in his hand as he put it back on.

"Not now," Trent Jackson answered, as Stan Ballard rode beside the rider, lifting his revolver from his holster and his carbine from the saddle boot.

"There's a misunderstanding," the rustler repeated, his voice quivering.

Ty studied him. He wasn't much more than a kid, maybe eighteen, nineteen. His face had soft, rounded features, not the hardened features Ty expected of a rustler.

His skin was ruddy and his hands were callused from outdoor work — or thievery.

"What's your name?" Trent asked.

"Jake Shaw, Jacob Shaw from Throckmorton County."

"What's your business up here in Oldham County?"

"Looking for work."

"Work?" Trent's voice was triumphant. "You mean cattle to steal, don't you?"

"No!" Shaw yelled. Panic tinged his voice. "I didn't steal cattle. Man promised me money to deliver these. I need work."

Trent pointed to Pa Stoddard. "You ever see him before?"

"No, sir," Shaw answered, licking his lip.

"That's Mr. Stoddard. Those are his cattle you were stealing."

"I wasn't stealing, honest. I got papers." Shaw reached into his vest pocket, his fingers digging for a sheet of paper, then fumbling to unfold it. He offered it to Trent.

The sheriff studied it a moment. "It says Jake Shaw has permission to move these Diamond S cattle over to the Rockin' R. It's signed J.T. Stoddard." Jackson offered the paper to Pa Stoddard, who studied it a moment. "That your signature?"

Stoddard shook his head. "Not even my right initials."

"But that's what the man said. You gotta believe me. Man was slender, had two missing front teeth."

Ty jerked his head toward Trent. That description wouldn't match anybody in Oldham County — except Dewey Slater, Deputy Dewey Slater.

"Sounds like Slater, Trent," Zack Miller said, and for a moment everyone's gaze turned to the sheriff.

"The man said his name was J.T. Stoddard, owner of the Diamond S." A touch of hope rose in Shaw's voice.

Trent nodded. "Dewey's been riding the county, warning every drifter off that he runs into, but he's been in Mobeetie the last two days."

"No. This morning, I swear, he told me to deliver these cattle, said if he wasn't here by one-thirty he'd catch up with me on down the trail." The panic was rising in his voice.

Pa Stoddard nudged his horse between Shaw and the sheriff, holding the note at Trent's nose. "Is this Slater's scribbling?"

Trent shook his head. "Dewey can barely scrawl his own name, and can't read too well."

"You gotta believe me, all of you." Shaw reached into his pocket. "He said if he wasn't here by one-thirty, I was to ride on."

He looked at his watch, sunlight glinting off the gold embossed eagle on its cover. "It's quarter of two. I was riding out like I was supposed to."

That gold watch! A lump caught in Ty's throat. He reined his horse hard toward Jake Shaw and jerked the watch from his hand, the chain ripping from his vest. "Damn you," he spat out, as he fingered the Waltham watch that had been his grandfather's, "where'd you get this watch?" Ty offered the watch to his father, the rage surging in him like a boiling tide.

Pa Stoddard nodded. "It's yours, Ty."

The regulators moved in closer around Jake Shaw.

"How'd you come by the watch?" Trent demanded.

"This man, Mr. Stoddard, Slater, whoever he was, I don't know, but you gotta believe me."

Ty grabbed the watch from his father. Damn, Jake Shaw. "You ever seen my face before?"

"No," called Jake Shaw. "No!"

"I reckon you haven't. Backshooters don't look for the face of their target," Ty answered.

"No, no, I've never been in Oldham County until the last two days. I didn't shoot nobody, never have," Jake pleaded, then spurred his bay, which bolted past Zack Miller and Bob Vandiver.

Jackson, Vandiver and Stan Ballard slapped their horses into mad pursuit.

Ty lifted the carbine to his shoulder, but with the watch in his hand his aim quivered. For an instant, he had the barrel sighted on Shaw's back, but the sheriff rode into his line of fire. Ty lowered the rifle, then fingered his grandfather's pocket watch, his eyes fixed on the chase.

Shaw raced along the river, slapping his long reins against his bay's neck. His mount was a good-looking, powerful steed, but lacked the balance for a run over rough terrain. Twice the bay stumbled and almost fell, each time losing valuable seconds to his pursuers.

By the time the bay had regained his stride, both the sheriff and Vandiver were galloping beside him. Shaw swatted the reins at the sheriff, who flinched, then grabbed the leather thongs. Trent held the reins long enough for Vandiver to grab the halter around the bay's head and jerk back. The bay slowed, then started, confused by the tight hold on the halter and the spurring from Shaw's heels. When Jackson shoved his pistol into Shaw's ribs, both man and horse calmed. Shaw's shoulders dropped in defeat.

Gradually, the horses halted, then turned around, Vandiver pulling the reins from Shaw's hand and leading the horse back toward the others. The sheriff followed, his gun aimed at the rustler's back.

Ty slipped his grandfather's watch into his pocket with its replacement and then slid his carbine back in the saddle boot. He realized that he was alone. Those who hadn't given chase were behind him, under the closest cottonwood tree. Red Stewart was tossing a rope over a thick limb.

Jackson and Vandiver headed their prisoner toward the tree; Ty nudged his bay toward the cottonwood tree and waited.

"No, no, you gotta believe me," Shaw kept repeating. His words quivered with desperation and his eyes teared up when he saw the noose swinging from the tree. "Get the law, let me have a trial," he begged. "Not this."

Jackson pulled his badge from his pocket and shoved it at Shaw's nose. "You're dealing with the law, and you're getting as much trial as Ty Stoddard got when you backshot him."

"I didn't backshoot nobody."

Vandiver maneuvered Shaw's bay under the cottonwood branch and held him there.

171

Zack Miller tossed a leather thong at the sheriff. Trent grabbed Shaw's hands and tied the leather around his wrists, pulling it tight against his flesh. Red Stewart draped the noose around Shaw's neck and pulled it snug until the knot was behind his ear. Stan Ballard pulled the other end of the rope until it was taut over the branch, then wrapped and knotted the loose end around the cottonwood trunk.

The sheriff motioned to Ty. "Since you're the one he shot, you can send him on his way."

Ty eased his roan toward the rustler's mount.

"Any last words?" Trent offered.

Ty felt a knot in his stomach, though it was something that had to be done.

Jake Shaw sobbed for a moment, then took a deep breath.

"Go to hell, all of you! Go to hell!"

"Keep our place warm," Red Stewart answered. "You'll get there ahead of us."

Ty raised his arm.

Jake Shaw drew a deep breath.

Leaning over in the saddle, Ty swung his arm in a tight arc at the bay's rump.

The animal bolted for freedom.

With the last breath he would ever take, Jake Shaw screamed as the horse flew from under his legs. The scream died into sudden silence as the rope bit into Shaw's neck and he was suspended over the ground, his legs thrashing to touch earth, his bound arms flailing at the lariat that was strangling him. The branch jerked with death's convulsions, and the rope made little circles as Shaw continued his fatal dance. His face turned blue and his mouth opened for a taste of the air he could never breathe. His arms fell, and then his legs lost their energy and just quivered. Like a pendulum, the rope moved back and forth from life's last exertions. And then, like the pendulum on a clock that gradually winds down, the rope was still.

Ty took no pride in the lynching. It was something that had had to be done, but it was not a deed he would soon forget. Shaw's blue, bloated face was etched in his brain like the inscription on a tombstone.

Around him, the others sat silently on their horses, staring respectfully at death's work.

Trent Jackson finally broke the quiet. "When a man starts stealing other people's cattle, it's the same as committing suicide."

Nobody answered. The men turned their horses from the ugly, yet fascinating, sight before them. Jackson galloped after Shaw's horse. Pa Stoddard, Zack Miller and a couple of others rode out to round up the Diamond S cattle which had scattered after Shaw's capture. Vandiver and the rest meandered up the draw to inspect the rustler's hiding place.

Finally, Ty rode away toward the draw. His stomach was queasy, revenge being a more bitter dose of medicine than he had expected. He could hear the men ahead, shouting and whistling, as he entered the draw. When he passed the crook in the trail that screened them from him, he could see them dragging down some crude pens the rustlers had built to hold their cattle. Now, his stomach churned. He rode back away from the others, hoping they would not see him get sick.

CHAPTER 12

Ty fingered the watch in his sweaty palm, then glanced at the time. Whenever he looked at the watch, once his proudest possession, he saw Jake Shaw's death grimace burned into its face. More than two hours until noon. Ty shoved the watch into his vest pocket. Sunday dinner just wasn't the same since his mother's death, and neither was Ty's appetite, not since he had first tasted his father's cooking or tried his own hand over the stove. So he just sat on the porch step watching the morning clouds saunter by.

From somewhere a dove cooed, softly punctuating the quiet that always accompanied Sunday. Pa Stoddard had arisen early to ride down to the river. On Sundays when the weather was good, Pa Stoddard had enjoyed riding to the Canadian with his wife and sharing nature's altar together. His father had continued those rides since his beloved wife's death, always offering some excuse to Ty, then stopping at the granite tombstone fresh from Dodge City before riding on with her memory. By the sad smile and the distant eyes, Ty knew his father missed her. It was a good thing, a faithful love, and it stayed with a man, even a tough man like his father, through good times and bad times. These were bad times with the rustling, times when a man needed a good woman, a woman he could share everything with. Everything except knowledge of a lynching!

Out in the corral, Ty's roan was trotting in circles, tossing his head and kicking at the ground, as frisky as a new colt just finding his legs and realizing their potential. Ty stood up and stretched his arms, figuring to saddle up and give the roan a good unwinding. He yawned and was about to turn for the door to fetch his boots, hat, and holster when he saw his roan suddenly stop in the corral. Its ears flicking forward, the gelding watched the trail on the eastern rise. In a moment, Ty heard the jingle of trace chains. A wagon was coming. With his hand, he shaded his eyes against the climbing sun that peaked at him from amid the scattered clouds. A wagon escorted by a rider on horseback topped the rise, heading straight for Ty.

Squinting against the glare, he recognized Trent Jackson by his set in the saddle. Surely the wagon carried Molly and Delia. And, he hoped, Wilma Jackson, as well! The wagon bounced along the trail and, over the road noises, Ty heard singing, female singing — not just one, but two voices. Wilma had come. A cloud passed before the sun and the shade crept past Ty's feet. Then he made out Wilma, handling the wagon reins. Suddenly, he felt as frisky as his roan, and raced inside the house for the washbowl. He had shaved after rising, but hadn't put on any tonic water. Grabbing the bottle, he splashed some in his palm and wiped it across his cheeks. Glancing in the mirror over the washbasin, he brushed at his hair with his fingers. By goodness, if he didn't think he might buy a haircut the next time he was in Tascosa. Pa's trims, though free, just weren't as satisfactory as they once had been. He jumped to his unmade bed, reaching for his best boots. He pulled them on, then opened the trunk at the foot of his bed and grabbed the orange-and-white kerchief Molly had bought him. He knotted it around his neck and grabbed his hat. Dingy and sweat-stained, the hat looked poorer than he'd noticed before. Danged if he didn't need a new hat the next time he was in town!

Satisfied he could do no better on such short notice, Ty slipped back outside on the porch as the Jacksons rode up. Molly and Wilma both wore Sunday dresses and big smiles. Trent, though, arrived with tight lips and narrow eyes.

"Surprise," Molly greeted. "We came a'calling and brought fixings for dinner. Thought you might like a real Sunday meal for a change."

Ty stepped down from the porch as Wilma tugged the team to a stop. Just above the wagon sideboard Ty saw Delia's doll peeking. Stepping up to the wagon, Ty slipped his hand over the side, his fingers quickly finding Delia and tickling her ribs. "How's my favorite girl in the whole world!" Delia shot up from her hiding place, all giggles and eyes, Kay-Lee held tight against her chest. Bedding was stacked in the back of the wagon, as though the Jacksons planned on staying the night, and under the wagon seat were two black kettles, a couple of covered pots and a basket with fresh bread. When Delia stood up, Ty lifted her from the wagon and placed her on the porch.

"I wanted to ride Rainbow over, but

Momma wouldn't let me," Delia confided.

"Delia, I don't want to hear any more about riding your horse. Your father and I don't agree on how much you should be allowed to ride at your age."

Trent Jackson dismounted, hitching his horse to a post. "Let's not discuss that again, Molly." His voice was curt, his gaze sharp. Trent turned to Ty. "Your father around?"

"Down by the river," Ty said, offering Molly a hand.

Molly stood up from the seat, lifted her skirt with one hand and took Ty's hand. "He misses Momma more than he lets on."

Carefully, Ty assisted Molly to the ground. His eyes met hers for an instant and he saw in them a deep burden. There was the danger of Trent's job to worry about. And, with Bob Vandiver filing for sheriff, Trent's disposition had likely worsened. The pregnancy must be hard on her, too. He was glad that Wilma was here to help. Glad for Molly. And glad for himself.

With Molly on firm ground, Ty extended his hand to Wilma. She was standing now, unfastening her bonnet, her auburn locks tumbling out in disarray, her eyes the green of new grass, her smile aimed at his. "We've no laundry for you to help with this time,

Mr. Stoddard, but we did bring Sunday dinner."

Ty blushed at her teasing.

"Yes," Molly interjected, "Wilma got up at four this morning to fix dinner for our trip."

"You shouldn't have gone to the trouble. Pa and I could've fixed you a meal you'd never forget."

"That's what we were afraid of," Molly replied.

Wilma's soft hands squeezed Ty's as she leaned forward, then stepped out of the wagon and jumped to the ground at Ty's feet. He stumbled backward a step, then caught his balance as she bumped into him, giggling as if she enjoyed his awkwardness. "Molly," she said, "you go inside and seat yourself. We'll carry dinner to the kitchen and then we can visit."

Molly opened the door for Delia, who was still pouting as only a four-year-old can. Trent walked inside without a word. Wilma showed embarrassment at his rudeness. "Trent's angered about this man Vandiver filing for sheriff," she offered. "Sometimes I think he should give it up, look after his ranch, his wife and family."

Ty lifted the two covered kettles from the wagon while Wilma took the basket. "Trent pushes himself too hard, others too, at times."

Wilma held the door open for Ty to pass and he led her into the kitchen. "Better shape than I was expecting for no woman to be around," Wilma said of the kitchen, then followed Ty back outside for the last load. He noticed that Molly and Trent ignored each other in the front room. "After this load, we can visit an hour before I start fixing things up for dinner," she said.

Her suggestion went unanswered, because Ty wasn't sure he wanted to get caught between Trent's and Molly's difficulties right now. But, he did want to be with Wilma. He carried the last load back to the kitchen and left the two pots on the table. Wilma patted him on the forearm, her silent thanks pleasing him more than words. She seemed to sense Ty's reluctance to make small talk with Trent and Molly, so she grabbed his arm, slipped hers under his and marched toward the front room. She guided him toward the sofa and sat down beside him, her hand falling across his for a moment, then retreating meekly to her lap.

An awkward silence followed for a few moments, and Ty realized he was still wearing his hat. Wilma must think him crude. He removed the hat and placed it in his lap.

"Glad you could come for a visit, all of you," he said, looking at Wilma. "It's not just a visit, Ty," Molly said, staring at Trent.

Ty saw a flash of anger in Trent's eyes.

"Trent wanted to discuss politics with Pa," Molly continued. "Have you heard that Bob Vandiver has filed for sheriff?"

Ty nodded.

"Then the lynching on our place." She sighed. "You heard about that?"

"A little," Ty answered, wondering if she could see the deceit in his eyes and the flush of his face.

"It's been a bad week," Molly said.

Delia wandered through the parlor, dragging Kay-Lee and nodding as if she agreed.

Wilma stamped her feet and Delia whirled around, then giggled and ran into the bedroom, peeking from behind the door. "Boo," Wilma whispered, and Delia covered her face and giggled again. "We're playing 'run and boo,' " Wilma explained. "We've made up lots of games. All the troubles in the county, and she's just giggles and pouts." Wilma folded her arms across her breasts. "But let's talk no more of the trouble. There's good news, too."

Trent sat sullenly in his chair, tapping his fingers against the armrest and watching out the window. Whatever he wanted to discuss with Pa Stoddard was weighing heavily on his shoulders.

"I said there's good news, too," Wilma said again, looking straight at Ty.

Ty swatted his knee with his hat. "I didn't say a thing," he answered sheepishly.

"That's what I mean. You aren't interested," Wilma chided, and turned her head. "You men are so worried over the troubles you can't think about anything else."

"I surrender," Ty answered, lifting his arms above his head.

Wilma smiled triumphantly. "The dance — haven't you heard about the dance Saturday night in town?"

This question Ty could answer truthfully. "Not a word." He lowered his hands.

"Saturday night, the whole county'll likely be there. A chance for everyone to get their minds off all the bad and have a little fun. I'm going to see all the handsome fellows."

There was a tease in her voice, and Ty thought she was playing him for an invitation to escort her, something he'd like to do mightily, but he just couldn't bring himself to ask her, not now, not in front of Molly and Trent. It would be hard enough to ask Wilma out without an audience, much less with one. Maybe he could play her along. "I might go, if I could figure someone to ask."

Ty watched her blush, then saw Molly scowling at him.

"You have so many choices, from what Molly says," Wilma replied, a note of triumph in her voice.

Now it was Ty's turn to redden. Molly must have told her he didn't take too much to courting. He never could better a female in an exchange of courting wit. When a man learned he was not a good card player, he ought to give it up then, Ty figured, but why did he have this desire now to come across witty? It was a feeling unlike any he'd ever remembered before, as if he'd eaten some loco weed for breakfast. He had been himself until he recognized Wilma in the wagon, and then there was this impulse he couldn't quite explain. Wilma had that effect on him.

Molly leaned forward in her chair, pointing out the window. "There comes Pa."

Trent Jackson bolted from his chair and strode to the door.

Wilma smiled at Molly. "I'll attend the cooking; you just visit with your pa. If I need something, I'll ask Mr. Tyrus Stoddard for help."

She was up and moving toward the kitchen before Ty could answer. He enjoyed the bounce of her auburn hair and her delicate step until she disappeared into the kitchen. Putting on his hat, Ty pushed himself up from his seat.

Molly strained against the bulge in her stomach and rose awkwardly. "Wilma likes you," she said softly. "She's turned down a couple of invites to the dance, hoping you'd ask her."

Ty felt a rush of pride that she would be interested, and a dash of embarrassment that she would share her feelings with Molly. He had to admit he didn't understand his own sister, much less other women.

Her arm in his, Ty escorted Molly out onto the porch. They stood in the shade as Pa Stoddard rode into the corral at the barn, dismounted and unsaddled his horse. Trent Jackson fidgeted a minute around his team and wagon, as if he were checking the harness leather, then strode toward the corral and Pa Stoddard. Ty had a feeling Trent wanted something from Pa Stoddard for the election. Ty watched the two men exchange greetings at the gate and wished he were with them to hear their discussion, but Molly was holding tightly onto his arm as if she were keeping him away, as if she could read the bad portents in the strained smiles of her husband and her father. Molly was the common link between two men of vastly different personalities and philosophies. For several minutes, the emotion of both men lay hidden within them as they talked. Then came the moment Ty had expected. He couldn't know what Trent's question had been, but his father shook his head emphatically, then squared around as if he expected more than just a verbal response. Trent Jackson pointed his finger at the older man, then pounded his palm with his fist. Both men gestured forcefully at each other.

Ty felt Molly lean her head against his shoulder. "I told him not to ask Pa, but he wouldn't listen, Ty! How do you make a man listen to a woman, Ty? How?"

His hand slid to hers on his arm and he patted her trembling fingers. "Most of us are too stubborn for our own good."

"Since Bob Vandiver announced for sheriff, Trent's been fretting for a chance to ask Pa to electioneer with him. I told him Pa wouldn't get involved in politics, but Trent just wouldn't believe me. I told him it'd do more harm than good, and he said I didn't care if he won or lost. I do and I don't, Ty. He can't stand to lose, and I can't stand to see him win."

Ty shrugged. He knew Trent's asking Pa for his support was as smart as wading in quicksand, but he didn't see a way out of Molly's tangle. Some problems have no solutions, as some bushes have no flowers, just thorns — and those in all sizes. Ty was still toying for an answer when he heard Wilma behind him at the door.

"Sunday dinner's almost ready," Wilma said. "Have Trent and Mr. Stoddard discussed their business, Molly?"

Molly nodded. "Neither of them'll be worth talking to over dinner, Wilma!"

"We'll manage, Molly. You will, too," Wilma added. "Call them and I'll finish getting things on the table." She retreated into the kitchen.

"I'll help Wilma," Molly said, releasing Ty's arm. "Please call them to dinner, Ty." She sighed and was gone in an instant.

Ty stepped off the porch. "Time to wash up," he called, motioning with his arm for them to join him. "Dinner's almost ready."

Both men answered with sullen stares and clenched jaws, pausing a moment for the other to make the first move. Trent finally stepped toward the house and Pa Stoddard followed in his wake. Not caring to join in their dispute, Ty went on inside, cleaned his hands at the washbasin and stepped into the kitchen, the aroma of roast, boiled potatoes and red beans greeting him. He hung his hat on a wall peg and took a seat.

Shortly, Trent and Pa Stoddard came to the table, silently taking seats at opposite sides of the table. As Molly helped Delia into her seat, Wilma put a plate of her bread on the table. Then both women sat down. For a moment, silence enveloped the table, until Delia figured she was supposed to say grace. She bowed her head and pressed her hands together beneath her chin. She thanked God for the food and asked that next trip she be allowed to ride Rainbow. When she said amen, everyone at the table smiled except for Trent Jackson.

The meal passed in silence, no one trying to close the chasm between Trent Jackson and Pa Stoddard. Eventually everyone finished, Ty only after a second helping of apple crumb cobbler. He eased himself away from the table and loosened his belt a notch. "Fine meal," he said, his gaze falling upon Wilma. "Better'n Pa's cooking any day." Leaning back in his chair, Ty pulled his watch from the vest pocket, staring at the time and seeing the death look of Jake Shaw in its face.

As he was about to insert the watch back in his pocket, Molly gasped. Her hand flew to her mouth with a napkin which could not cover the shock in her eyes and the sudden paleness draining her cheeks of color.

"You okay?" Ty asked, snapping the watch cover shut.

She nodded, shaking some color back into her cheeks.

Then Ty realized she had seen Grandfather's watch. She needed no explanation to connect Ty and the newfound watch with the hanging.

Molly exhaled deeply and tried to grin, but her smile lacked sincerity. "I lost my breath!" She stared at Ty when she spoke, her feelings masked, except for the shock in her eyes.

Knowing no excuse would explain the sudden reappearance of the missing watch, Ty sat silent as a stone.

Wilma sensed something more amiss than just the hard feelings between her brother and Pa Stoddard. "Well, men, if you'll take Molly into the front room, I'll attend to the dishes."

"Absolutely not, Wilma Jackson," Molly replied, her voice firm and unequivocal. "I'll clean the table. You were up at four this morning cooking, so we could make it here for Sunday dinner. You have Ty show you around the place and I'll attend the dishes."

Just like Molly, Ty thought, when she was upset, to insist on doing the chores. She was funny that way. When angered or upset, she would do dishes or laundry or sewing or gardening to help her work out her frustrations, resolve the problem in her own mind, and then go about her life.

"I'll let you," Wilma told Molly, then turned to Ty, "if Mr. Stoddard will agree to show me about."

"He'd be pleased," Molly answered.

Ty threw his napkin on the table. "Don't I get a say in this?"

"No!" both women answered in unison, then laughed together.

"I should be safe," Wilma giggled, "since I don't have laundry to hang."

"Give her a tour in my wagon, Ty," Trent offered, as he and Pa Stoddard rose and stretched. "Your pa and I've got a little more to discuss."

Out of the corner of his eye, Ty saw his father shake his head. "Obliged, Trent!" Ty answered, knowing that despite what Trent thought, he would never be able to change his father's mind. Ty was just glad to be leaving his father and Trent to work out their differences, if that were possible.

Ty eased up from his chair and grabbed his hat from the wall peg. Wilma stepped beside him as he reached the kitchen door, her bonnet in her hand, a smile on her lips and a sparkle in her eyes. Silently, they emerged from the house onto the porch, where Ty paused long enough to make a cigarette. Wilma stood at his side, the sleeve of her blouse brushing against his arm as he built his smoke. Her closeness pleased him and, after he had lit his cigarette, he wanted to put his arm around her, but she might think awkward things of him, so he studied the blue sky. "Pa and Momma liked to take Sunday rides by the river."

"Then that we shall do," Wilma answered, her words as encouraging as her smile.

Ty took her arm and felt the thrill of her touch as he stepped toward the wagon. With a boost from him, she took a seat on the wagon bench and scooted over to make room for him, but not all the way to the other side. Ty climbed aboard and plopped down beside her, the spring seat bouncing more than he would have liked. Untying the reins, Ty slapped them against the team's flanks and the wagon jerked and rattled away from the house, the jingling of the trace chains and the moaning of the wagon frame providing a serenade Ty enjoyed with Wilma.

Wilma edged closer to Ty, her arm slipping through his and her other hand coming to rest on his forearm. They rode without speaking, their touch the only communication that was necessary. As the trail gently inched down the incline into the canyon, all their troubles seemed lost behind them. Ty talked about the ranch and the land, its richness, its character and its promise. And Wilma responded with enthusiasm, like a woman who could share the right man's life, and enjoy it no matter the hardships. She laughed when Ty pointed out the swimming hole where he had gone skinny-dipping as a kid. And they stopped in the shade of a cottonwood tree, a favorite spot of his parents when they had kept their weekly appointment along the river.

The grass was a thick carpet beneath their feet as they strolled arm in arm beside the river, flushing a covey of quail, Wilma's grip tightening on Ty's arm. Suddenly, Ty felt stronger and protective, as if she were a trembling dove in his hand. Now was the time. "Might I meet you at the dance come Saturday?"

Her grip tightened even more around his arm. "It would pleasure me greatly. I had hoped you would ask."

Ty stopped and pointed out a cottontail hiding beneath a hackberry bush. Prying her fingers from his arm, he turned around to face her, to savor the smile on her lips and the joy in her eyes. She loosened the bonnet string around her chin and let the bonnet slide behind her neck. With his finger, he lifted her willing chin and leaned toward her face until his lips met hers. His arms slipped around her and he felt powerful and yet gentle with her in his arms, a feeling like none he could ever remember. And Wilma nestled in his arms as if there was where she belonged. Finally, reluctantly, he let his lips slide from hers and they just stood, their arms, like their lives, intertwined.

"Perhaps we should be getting back," Wilma said, a note of disappointment in her voice.

Ty nodded, then kissed her gently a final time and led her to the wagon. Soon they were headed back to the ranch house and Wilma sat tight against Ty's side. They rode without speaking, as if words could never capture the feelings that had passed between them at the river. And there was disappointment in both their eyes when they topped out of the canyon and saw the Diamond S ahead. Their private moments were over for today, but they might have a chance in the morning before the Jacksons returned to their place.

As they approached the house, Ty saw

Trent Jackson sitting alone on the porch. By the time Ty pulled the team to a stop, Jackson was there beside them. "Gather your things, Wilma; we're heading back home tonight. Be quick about it," Jackson said, his voice gruff and impatient.

Wilma turned to Ty with disappointment in her eyes. She patted his hand, then stepped out of the wagon and disappeared inside.

"Sorry you've gotta leave, Trent," Ty offered, but the sheriff didn't answer.

"Molly, get Delia," Trent called. "Let's get to moving, so we make home by dark." Trent retreated to his horse and mounted, riding up the trail toward Tascosa before drawing to a halt atop the gentle hill that overlooked the ranch.

Shortly, mother and daughter were using Ty's assistance to get into the wagon while Wilma made two trips to bring out the pots and pans she had used for lunch.

"I'm sorry, Ty," Molly said. "Pa and Trent argued fierce, and it just won't do to stay."

Ty could see in Molly's eyes the redness of tears freshly spent, and Delia was strangely still and quiet. Wilma came out of the house with her third and final load. "I enjoyed seeing you, Ty," Wilma said, using his given name for the first time. "I shall look forward to meeting you again at the dance." Standing on her toes, she gave him a gentle kiss on the lips. Then he helped her into the wagon and assisted her with the reins. She snapped the leather thongs and the wagon lurched forward and made a circle which straightened out toward Trent Jackson, who then disappeared over the hill.

When the wagon was gone, Pa stepped out onto the porch. "Trent asked me to make election visits with him. I told him I wouldn't do politics for anybody. He kept on pestering me until I told him no better job than he had done as sheriff, that I was voting for Bob Vandiver."

Ty shook his head.

Pa shrugged. "You know me, son! I'm not gonna lie to a man just to save his feelings."

CHAPTER 13

Dumping a third pail of hot water into the porcelain tub, the attendant with peach fuzz on his face heaved a hard breath and swiped his towel-wrapped hand at the sweat soaking his forehead. "I hate dance days," the boy said, running his fingers through clumps of sweat-matted hair.

Ty Stoddard mixed the fresh water with the rest, then splashed a handful in his face. "Shame you don't like dances," Ty sputtered.

"Didn't say I don't like dances — just dance day. We do two, maybe three baths a week regular. On dance days, we do a dozen or more, treating all you fellows with calico fever," Peach Fuzz said, then retreated behind the curtain of the bathing cubicle.

The room smelled of damp wood and tonic water which drifted from beyond the curtain where Ty could hear the snip of scissors and the Saturday conversation of the barber and his customers. When the thirty minutes he'd been allocated for his bath was done, Ty figured he'd get a haircut and a shave. Since he had met Wilma Jackson, Pa's free haircuts were no longer a bargain.

Ty lathered his hair with a clump of lye soap and scrubbed it hard with his nails as he remembered his mother doing on Saturday nights when he was a kid. Even if his mother were still alive, Ty doubted Pa would have accompanied him into Tascosa for the dance. Pa Stoddard, never much to socialize, was even less so without his wife, but Ty figured Pa wanted to avoid an unseemly confrontation with Trent Jackson. Pa Stoddard would not work for Jackson's reelection, but neither would he show up his son-in-law in front of other voters. So Ty had ridden into town alone, leaving his roan at the stable, then visiting the barber.

After rinsing his hair, he soaped his arms and chest, never having felt quite so clean as he did now. Figuring his time was about up, Ty reluctantly pushed himself up from the tub and stepped out onto the squishy wood floor. He picked up a clean towel left by Peach Fuzz and quickly dried, as he watched his distorted reflection in a cracked wall mirror clouded by condensation. Ty slipped into his best Sunday pants and winced at the stiffness of his new linen shirt. Sitting on the bench beside his pile of riding clothes, Ty stuck his clean feet into a pair of fresh socks and then his best boots. Standing, he buckled his gunbelt around his waist.

As Ty gathered up his riding clothes and shoved them in his warbag, Peach Fuzz stuck his head through the curtain. "Time to get out," he called, then realized the tub was empty. "Oh!"

Ty stuck his hand in his pocket and pulled out a dull nickel. "Here's for your dance day troubles," he said, flipping the coin toward the curtain.

Peach Fuzz snapped the nickel from the air, then disappeared wordlessly to heat more water for his next customer.

Grabbing his warbag and his old hat, Ty pushed his way through the curtain into the barber shop.

The customer in the chair was squinting at his trim in a hand mirror, while the barber, a wisp of a man who stood on a soda box to reach his customers and wore thick spectacles to see them, shook the cover cloth. "Next," called the barber, and one of the men sitting on the bench against the opposite wall stood up, stretched his arms and waited for his predecessor to pay.

Ty slipped into the empty spot, leaving his warbag at his feet and his hat atop it. Leaning his head against the wall, Ty felt his eyelids slip shut, and he saw Wilma Jackson's inviting smile. He dozed off until a tap on the shoulder awoke him.

"You're next." The barber stamped his foot impatiently.

Shaking the cobwebs from his head, Ty stumbled from the bench toward the barber's chair.

"You been drinking already?" the barber asked, as he climbed on his soda box to wrap the cover cloth around Ty's collar. The barber pinned the wrap tightly.

Ty thought of a noose, then of Jake Shaw and his wretched demise. He swallowed hard. "How about loosening that?"

The barber grunted and obliged. He picked up a comb and scissors and attacked Ty's hair. "Getting spruced up for the dance?" the barber asked, as snips of hair fell on Ty's shoulder. "Sure you are," the barber answered himself. "On dance days I get every man in Oldham County that has Cupid's cramp."

Like his father, Ty wasn't much for idle talk, so he let the barber chatter without response. If he didn't talk, maybe the barber would work faster so he could get on down the street and find himself a new hat for tonight.

A clatter came at the door. The door swung open, revolving all the way around on its hinges until it hit against the wall, rattling the windows. Ty and the barber flinched, both twisting their heads toward the street. It was Dewey Slater.

Slater barged inside, his pipe stuck between his teeth, his hand resting on the butt of his six-shooter. His gaze moved from man to man along the wall, then to Ty and the barber.

Ty felt his muscles tighten and his hand slide under the cover to his sidearm, his fingers resting on the gun's butt.

"Heard I'd find you here, Tyrus Stoddard." Slater's words hissed like a snake.

"You found me, Deputy. What of it?" Ty shifted in his seat so he could pull his gun if it came to that.

Slater's hand moved slowly away from his sidearm, as if he thought Ty had pulled his own gun, and toward his pipe. His fingers wrapped around the pipe bowl and pulled the stem from the gap between his teeth. He nodded and pointed the stem at Ty. "It true what I've heard about Pa Stoddard not supporting his son-in-law for sheriff?"

"Whatever you heard, Deputy, it wasn't

from Pa."

Slater advanced to the barber's chair.

Ty tugged his Colt halfway out of his holster.

Slater lifted his boot to the chair's footrest and plopped it onto the metal by Ty's boots. Bending over, the deputy held his pipe by the stem and tapped it against his boot heel. Tobacco char tumbled from the pipe onto the floor. Three times he rapped the pipe against his boot heel; then he straightened and inserted his pipe in his vest pocket.

The barber grimaced at the added mess on the floor, but did nothing except step off his stool and away from Ty.

"Word's going around you Stoddards won't support a member of your own family. That true?" Slater's voice was bloated with a challenge.

"What's family stays family with us, Slater."

"How do you stand, Stoddard? With us? If you're not with us, you're against us." Slater's face was cold, his eyes hard like a cat toying with a mouse before making the kill.

"The Stoddards don't get involved in politics. When Trent ran before, we stayed out of it except at the ballot box. We'll do no different this time."

Slater licked his lips, his flitting tongue snakelike. "I figured you'd be too yellow to answer a straight question, Ty."

Ty leaned forward in his chair. The four customers on the bench stood up and retreated to the corners.

"You talk big, Slater, but you're the problem. You're the one that'll cost him the election."

Slowly, deliberately, Slater's hand moved from his vest pocket to his sidearm. "Step outside to finish our discussion."

Ty eased up from the chair.

"Hold it right there," came a voice from the door. "Nobody make a move."

Ty recognized Trent Jackson's voice.

Slater turned around, nodding at the sheriff. "Discussing a little politics with Tyrus here."

"Get out, Dewey," the sheriff commanded.

Slater stroked his chin. "You better re-member what kind of law you could have if we lose the election, Tyrus Stoddard!"

"That's enough, Dewey. Get on out of here."

The deputy backed toward the door, his beady eyes never leaving Ty. He inched past Jackson and out onto the boardwalk, then disappeared down the street.

Ty nodded toward Jackson. "Thanks, Trent!"

"Only doing my job, Ty. Something I've been trying to do since I was elected." Trent touched his hat brim, but his eyes were grim and his lips hard. The sheriff closed the door.

"See you at the dance, Trent," Ty offered.

Only the click of the door and the footfall of the sheriff's boots answered.

The barber approached his soda box meekly, mounting his perch quietly and then running the comb through Ty's hair. As his scissors started snipping away, the other customers reclaimed their posts on the benches, whispering among themselves. "Most folks take Trent for a decent man," the barber said, a tremor in his squeaky voice, "but few folks have taken a liking to Slater."

At the mention of Slater, Ty thought he felt a quiver in the barber's hand. Ty nodded, but said nothing. The less he said about his brother-in-law as sheriff, the less likely anything might drive a wedge further between them and add to Molly's agony. The haircut seemed to take forever, and then the barber wielded his straight razor carefully along Ty's whiskers, delaying the finish even longer. After the barber wiped the splotched soap from around Ty's ears and washed his face with a damp rag, he massaged tonic water on Ty's face. The barber was still dusting talc on his neck when Ty pushed himself up from the barber's chair.

Wiping his hands, the barber stumbled from his perch and coughed into his hand. "Ten cents for the shave, two bits for the haircut and another quarter for the bath. Sixty cents total," the barber said, extending his open palm.

Ty dug into his pocket, then flipped a silver dollar at the barber. He picked up his warbag and pulled his old hat down on his new haircut. "Keep the difference," he said, striding for the door and out onto the boardwalk. He eased the door shut, then stood for a moment, studying the street in both directions. He didn't want trouble, but neither was he running from Dewey Slater. Convincing himself that the deputy had moved on, Ty stepped down the street and toward Tobe Burleson's store.

The street flowed with Saturday traffic. Families in from all the ranches, bringing their daughters and sons to town for supplies and the dance. Cowboys came in by the dozens, all hoping to dance with one of those daughters, seldom admitting there weren't enough good women to go around.

There were always the saloon women, but they shared their dances and other favors only for a price too high to meet on monthly wages.

A pair of barefoot boys dashed by Ty on the boardwalk, their freckled faces a blur as they weaved among women carrying baskets away from the stores. A dog chased them, barking with each stride. It must be great to be that age, when the only worry was about Momma's punishment for misbehaving, not election politics, Ty thought. He slipped between a couple clerks emerging from the grocer's with fifty-pound sacks of flour, then threaded his way across the street among wagons, drays and riders. Pausing a moment outside Tobe Burleson's store, he could see through the windows a covey of customers wandering around the crowded aisle and lining up at the counters where Tobe and his wife scurried to keep pace. Ty hoped Tobe still had a hat or two that might replace his weatherbeaten prairie crown.

Atop the door, a bell tinkled as Ty pushed his way inside, but no one, least of all Tobe Burleson, seemed to notice. Ty held the door open as a matron with a full basket and a full bustle walked through, her nose held high. "You're welcome," Ty mouthed to her back, then shut the door.

Ty wandered among the merchandise and customers to the back counter where hat boxes were stacked on dusty shelves. He studied himself in the mirror stand on the counter as Tobe Burleson charged by and through a door in the back room. A moment later Burleson emerged, his pace slowed enough by a No. 3 pine tub that he saw Ty out of the corner of his eye. "Howdy, Ty; wish I had time to talk," he said, twisting his head Ty's way. Before Ty could answer, Burleson was past him at the far end of the counter. Burleson nodded at another request from his customer, a woman with gray-streaked brown hair and a child hanging onto her skirt, then started Ty's way, more slowly this time.

"What you need, Ty?" Burleson said, stopping for a moment to do a little figuring with his pencil.

"A new hat."

"Work or social?"

Ty felt his face flush. "Social," he answered, his voice little more than a whisper which sounded awkward still.

Burleson grinned as if he had just been let in on a secret. "Figured as much." Burleson stepped to a swinging gate at the end of the counter and motioned to Ty. "I'm snowed under. Come on around behind the counter

206

here and pick you out a hat. I'll add it to your account."

"Obliged," Ty answered, pulling his warbag through the gate.

As Ty passed, the storekeeper spoke in a low whisper. "A lot of rumors going around about you, Ty — not about you and Wilma Jackson. Serious things like murder and rustling. We need to talk at the dance."

Ty felt as if he'd been hit broadside by a runaway freight wagon. "What?" he exclaimed, the shock coming out louder than he wanted.

"Ty," Burleson began, his voice barely above a whisper, "a lot of bad rumors around about you. Some say you've been rustling; some say you hanged that fellow that was found on Jackson's place."

His fingers knotted into fists and he stood up to face Burleson. "What else?"

"Some are saying you've taken a liking to Wilma Jackson so the sheriff'll think twice about arresting the brother of his wife and the boyfriend of his sister."

Ty's gaze hardened and his stare bored through Burleson, who shifted uneasily beneath Ty's inspection.

Burleson shifted his feet and coughed into his hand. "I'm not saying anybody believes it, but that's the word that's being spread by some."

"Politics!" Ty spat the word out like bile. "I'd never figured Bob Vandiver to be spreading such nonsense just to win an election."

"That's the funny thing, Ty," Burleson answered. "It ain't Vandiver. From what I hear, it's Dewey Slater that's been doing all the talking. It don't make sense. Seems that would hurt Trent Jackson's election chances, but he's doing it anyway. Too busy to talk now, Ty," Burleson said, and then was off to fetch more goods for the woman at the counter.

His fingers tightening around the grip on the warbag, Ty felt the heat of anger racing through his blood. There was talk, he knew, about the regulators. Likely his name would be associated with that — but rustling? He dropped his warbag and stared at the boxes lining four rows of shelves. Finding a couple marked his size, he yanked them from their perch. Both boxes were Stetsons. Opening the first, he found a dark brown with a shallow crown, and quickly replaced the lid. Inside the second, he studied a tan Carlsbad-style Stetson with a seven-inch crown and a four-inch brim. He switched the hat on his head for the one in the box. The fit was a bit stiff, but it would be okay after a couple of days' wear.

Rustling! The gossip gnawed at him so much he forgot to price the hat. He reshelved the first hat, then turned to the storekeeper. "Tobe," he called, "I'll take this one."

Burleson spun around, his eyebrows arching. "The Carlsbad?" Tobe nodded. "Costs sixteen-fifty! I'll add it to the Diamond S account."

"You do that," Ty answered, grabbing his old hat from the counter and his warbag from the floor, then pushing his way past the gate and striding toward the door. He didn't wait for the woman closing in on the door with a No. 3 pine tub in her hands, but barged out just ahead of her.

He turned down the street toward the stables, his chin hanging low on his chest, his brow furrowed. The Stoddard name was a good one in Oldham County, and Ty didn't care for it being muddied by malicious tongues. But chasing gossip was like trying the catch the wind; there was no way to grab ahold of it and strangle it. He turned in at the stables, found his roan feeding on an extra scoop of oats, and left his warbag and old hat outside the stall.

The stable smelled of damp straw and horses, an odor that was stirred by the draft between the front and back doors. Ty figured he would stable his horse overnight and ride back in the morning to the Diamond S. He could picket his horse out by the dance ground, but invariably some cowboy would drink more whiskey than he could hold and start a commotion that would spook the horses. Too, if Wilma had to leave the dance earlier than he liked, he could always come back to the stable and sleep in the loft until morning.

He unhooked his gunbelt and shoved it in his warbag. Carrying a gun to a dance with Wilma Jackson just didn't seem right, even if Dewey Slater might be there.

CHAPTER 14

Ty emerged from the stables into the bright sunlight and pulled the brim of his new hat down closer over his eyes. The street bustled with activity, much of it drifting south toward the river. There, amid a stand of cottonwood trees, the dance would occur. Men were hanging lanterns from the branches and others were spreading tarps on the ground as a makeshift dance floor, to keep the dust down. Wagons were arriving and their passengers taking positions around the trees. Many folks would spend the night sleeping in or under their wagons.

Ty meandered along the street without a destination, not particularly interested in visiting with anyone. As he passed Harvey Worley's restaurant, he heard a rapid tapping on the windowglass. Glancing to his side, he stopped. Molly was rapping on the glass for his attention, while Delia held Kay-Lee to the window. Ty spotted Wilma with them, and instantly he felt like talking. He spun around on the boardwalk, startling an old man with a cane right behind him. "Pardon," he said, and stepped around the old man, who just shook his head and hobbled on. Marching inside, Ty nodded to Harvey Worley, then to Wilma.

"A very pleasant surprise," Wilma offered. "I expected not to meet you until the dance."

She always had a way of making him feel good, as if no other man in the world mattered to her. Ty hoped that was true. He took off his hat. "I had business in town, so I arrived early."

"Looks like a haircut and a new hat were part of that business," Wilma replied, her smile sincere. "You must be trying to impress someone. If it's me, you've succeeded."

Ty let his own smile answer hers.

"Well," said Molly, "you going to greet your sister or not?" Ty felt his face reddening with embarrassment as he said his hellos to Molly and Delia. He took off his hat and hung it on a wall peg behind the table and took the seat next to Wilma.

"Pa didn't come?" Molly asked. The tone of defeat in her voice said she already knew the answer.

Ty shook his head. "You know better; not with Momma gone."

"Just so many hard feelings right now, Trent may take it wrong." She shook her head and pursed her lips tight.

"I been riding Rainbow," Delia offered, and then, with Kay-Lee drawn tight against her chest, pouted when no one answered.

Ty looked around the restaurant, nodding greetings to a couple of ranchers and their families. Always busy on Saturdays, the restaurant was even more so on dance days. Gradually, Harvey Worley was working his way to their table. Ty felt reassured when Wilma's hand slipped over his on the table.

"These last several weeks've been hard on us all, but let's forget our troubles and enjoy the dance tonight," Wilma said, her voice encouraging, not chiding.

Harvey Worley approached, his smile as thick as the wad of money this crowd would bring him. Everyone agreed that the special of roast beef, candied yams, red beans and cornbread sounded the most appetizing. Worley promised to bring the meal as soon as possible, then moved on to the next table.

Molly, Wilma, and Ty visited, with Ty ever careful to steer the conversation away from politics, elections and rustling, all topics sure to plunge Molly into melancholy.

The meal finally came and went, good fare even if a bit slow in getting to them, but they had time to kill. When they were finished eating, they lingered, drawing stares from Harvey Worley, who glanced from them to the line of folks waiting at the door for a table. "Harvey's nervous we may spend the night," Ty said. "Everyone ready to leave?" Ty dug in his pocket for money to cover the meal, and left it on the table.

Ty helped Wilma, then Molly from their chairs and picked up Delia. He grabbed his hat and ushered the women out the door.

"We're staying in jail tonight," Wilma laughed, as they stepped outside on the boardwalk.

"Oh, Wilma," gasped Molly, "don't let the whole world know."

Wilma just laughed. "Trent's gonna set up a couple of places for us to sleep in his office," she explained. "Molly'll need her rest, but I'm planning on dancing as long as I can." She slipped her arm through Ty's as they walked toward the river.

Though the sun had not yet touched the horizon and the day was still bright, a couple of men were lighting lanterns in the tree branches. Musicians were arriving, the fiddler having come all the way from Mobeetie to play. The strains of their tuning notes added a gaiety to the air and Ty noticed a lift in Wilma's step. Nearing the crowd and the dance grounds, Molly gasped and Ty instantly let Delia slide from his arms to the ground. Ty followed Molly's stare and saw Trent Jackson standing opposite Bob Vandiver. The two candidates were pointing into each other's faces, arguing over something.

"Don't let them ruin the dance," Molly pleaded, to no one in particular and everyone in general.

"Infernal politics," Wilma answered.

The two candidates shook their heads, then turned away from each other, Vandiver heading into the crowd, Trent standing a moment, his fists clenched. He took a step toward the crowd, changed course when he saw his family. He strode toward them.

"Don't make trouble, Trent, please," Molly pleaded.

The sheriff gave a curt nod to Ty, then stared at his wife. "Vandiver and I agreed not to bring up politics tonight."

"Didn't look much like an agreement to me, the way you two were in each other's faces," Molly shot back.

"I did what you asked, Molly. Enjoy yourself; I've got work to do at the courthouse." Trent pulled his hat down tighter and stomped away toward the opposite end of town.

Molly turned and watched. "You've changed, Trent Jackson. You're not the man I married. Politics has done it to you."

The sheriff stopped in his tracks. Without looking back, he spoke, his voice low and menacing. "The rest of your family's against me. I should've expected you'd be against me, too." Then he stormed away, shaking his head.

Molly sobbed softly, her head buried in her hands. Delia, grabbing Molly's skirt, cried, too.

Wilma tightened her grip on Ty's arm and shook her head. "He doesn't mean it, Ty," she whispered. "The election's got him rattled so he thinks everybody's against him."

In a moment Molly regained her composure. "I'm sorry, honey," she said, stroking Delia's long hair. "Sometimes Father and I disagree, but we still love you."

Delia pressed her cheek against her mother's leg.

"You up to going and meeting folks?" Ty asked Molly. She nodded, though her eyes were still red and moist. "If I can't face them now, it'll only be harder next time."

Ty offered Molly his arm, the one that had

been injured and she had nursed back to health. The slight smile vanished from her lips when she saw Bob Vandiver approaching.

Vandiver advanced, hat in hand, his expression serious but not menacing. "Afternoon, ladies. I don't mean to bother you, but I'd like a moment with Ty."

"Sure, Mr. Vandiver," Molly answered, her voice quivering on his name.

Vandiver lowered his eyes, as if he were uncomfortable. "I don't mean to cause you any embarrassment, ma'am," he said to Molly. "No family in these parts respected more than the Stoddards, and you're still a Stoddard."

"I'm a Jackson, too, Mr. Vandiver," she replied, then stepped toward the other women gathered around the dance area.

A pained expression settled on Vandiver's face as Molly, Wilma and Delia walked away.

Vandiver replaced his hat, returning the stares of a few observers. "Let's step away from listening ears."

Side by side they headed back toward town, neither speaking until they stopped by a chicken coop at the back of a slat house.

Vandiver's lips were tight and his eyes narrow. His clenched fist tapped nervously in his open right palm. "Word's going around that you Stoddards aren't supporting Trent Jackson," Vandiver began. "I don't know who started those rumors, but I want you to know it wasn't me. You and your pa both suggested you might vote for me, but I haven't told a soul. I just wanted you to know that and to tell your pa."

Ty nodded. "I figure it's Slater. He tried to draw me into a fight at the barbershop. He's got a big mouth, a hot temper, and no sense. He as much as told the barber shop what Pa had said. He's likely the one planting all these bad seeds. I never figured you the type to start this bad talk. We'll all be glad when the election's over."

Crossing his arms over his chest, Vandiver blew out a breath of relief. "I'm playing this hand as straight as I can, but dammit, Ty, I'm no good at politics. It goes against my grain."

"You'll do okay. Trent might've done okay, too, if he hadn't hired Slater for a deputy, but Slater's poisoned the well for Trent because nobody trusts the deputy."

"Getting rid of Slater'll be my first act as sheriff, and he knows it."

"We know it," Ty answered. "That's why you'll likely win."

A grin wormed its way across Vandiver's

lips. "Thanks, Ty, and give my regards to your pa. We best break up 'fore too many people see us and create more problems for you with Trent."

Vandiver turned away toward the dance ground and the gathering crowd, a lift in his step now. Ty lingered a moment, rolling himself a cigarette and bringing it to a light. He drew hard on the cigarette, exhaling a ribbon of smoke and studying the folks gathering for the dance. As he scanned the crowd, his gaze came to rest on a slender figure standing alone by a cottonwood. It was Dewey Slater.

As Ty stared, Slater pulled the pipe from his mouth and pointed the pipe menacingly at Ty, shaking it. It was a threat, as sure as Ty was standing there. Slater motioned long enough to be sure Ty understood the message, then shoved the pipe between his lips and strolled away from the tree and around the crowd.

The musicians sounded as if they were almost ready to start, and Ty figured he'd best find Wilma Jackson before every single male in Oldham County was lining up for a dance. He finished his cigarette and stepped toward the crowd.

He found Wilma seated on a quilt with Molly and Delia, under the shade of a cottonwood tree. A pair of admiring ranch hands stood at the edge of the quilt. Though Molly was quiet, Wilma was animated, both in playing with Delia and in talking with the cowboys, but her face positively lit up when she saw Ty approaching. "I'm with him!" She pointed at Ty, and the two men nodded jealously and slipped away, searching for other prospective dance partners.

"I'm glad you're back. I've turned down a dozen offers to dance. Even had one from that vicious Deputy Slater." With her hand, she smoothed out a place on the quilt for Ty.

The sun was a fading candle on the western horizon when the musicians began a waltz. By tradition, the first dance was restrained, reserved for older couples whose courting days were long past, or the young couples whose courting days were recent, with young ones to show for it — young ones who would have to be put to bed early. The second dance, and the remainder, would be open to everyone lucky enough to have a partner.

Ty knelt on the quilt beside Wilma and took Delia's arms as if he were dancing with his niece and her doll. Swaying back and forth, Delia giggled, then squealed when Ty tickled her ribs. Delia slipped from Ty's fingers, then danced alone with Kay-Lee. Ty slid beside Wilma, his hand finding hers. Her fingers tightened around his. They watched the dancers gliding by, both of them occasionally glancing at Molly, who stared at the festivities wistfully. Ty released Wilma's hand and put his arm around her shoulder, drawing her closer to him. She rested her head against him and he could smell the fragrance of her auburn hair and her perfume.

When the music ended, the dancers and spectators laughed and clapped their approval. Immediately, several unmarried couples scurried onto the tarps. A murmur of excitement rippled through the crowd when the second song began, and the tarps flurried with motion and color as the young couples danced across them in inviting arms.

"Aren't you two gonna dance?" Molly asked. "Even if Trent were here, I'm too tired."

"There's plenty of time, Molly," Ty answered, knowing Molly was embarrassed by her husband's absence. "This is only the second dance, and it could last until dawn."

"Aren't you glad Momma made you dance with me when we were kids, now that you've got someone you'd really like to dance with?" Molly tried to tease away her embarrassment.

Ty flushed. He remembered how his mother had taught him and Molly to dance, and how he had hated that forced closeness with his sister. He had never understood his mother's wisdom. Until now, with Wilma at his side!

By the time Trent returned, the darkness had enveloped the land and shafts of yellowed lanternlight illuminated the dance area and perimeter. Already, several cowboys in new boots were standing around, gritting their teeth against certain blisters and screwing up their courage to ask another girl to dance, despite the damage their stiff boots would do. For some, it took a nip from the whiskey flasks they had stowed in saddlebags or from the jugs that had mysteriously appeared in several wagons around the dance.

Trent nodded at Ty, but in the lanternlight, Ty could neither see his eyes nor gauge his sincerity. As Trent helped Molly up, Wilma shooed Delia toward Ty. "You get a good night's rest and we'll get you home tomorrow."

"Come on, Delia, it's time for you and Momma to go to bed," Trent said, as he took Molly's hand. He said nothing more, and man, woman and child disappeared into the darkness.

"I pray for the day this election is over," Wilma said, as they walked away.

"But let's not rush tonight," Ty replied. "Shall we dance?"

"Yes, Mr. Stoddard."

"My pleasure, Miss Jackson."

The two stepped to the tarp. Ty took her soft hand in his and placed his other at her waist, her hand rising to his shoulder. They waited a moment to time the music, then glided into the stream of dancers. It had been so long since he had danced with Molly, Ty feared for a moment he might have forgotten. But it came back to him as naturally as riding a horse. They danced and laughed and talked through a half dozen songs, then sat out a melody to get a dipper of water from the water barrel. Then they stepped to the music until they lost track of the time and the number of dances. Through them all, they moved as one in each other's arms.

Well after midnight, they sat out a couple of dances, resting on benches by the water barrel, their heads beaded with sweat. They were giddy with pleasure and both were laughing, when they heard an unwelcome voice.

"Evening, Miss Jackson!"

It was Dewey Slater. He spoke to Wilma but he stared at Ty, his eyes beady like those of a snake about to strike. The laughter died in Wilma's throat just as another waltz began.

"I'd favor the next dance with you, Miss Jackson." Slater's eyes were riveted on Ty.

"I'm with Mr. Stoddard tonight."

"He don't care," Slater answered.

"Yes, I do!" Ty rose slowly from his seat, his hands wide of his waist so there would be no question that he was unarmed.

"Seems you've got no choice, Stoddard. Either you let me dance with Miss Jackson or I'll whip your tail."

"He's trying to provoke you, Ty. Don't let him," Wilma cried, pushing herself up from the bench.

Ty lifted his hand to his hat and handed it to Wilma. He took a deep breath, figuring he might smell alcohol on Slater's breath. He didn't. Slater was sober, and this was a planned provocation.

"Take off your gun, Slater. Let's settle a few things right now — like the rumors you've been spreading about me and my family," Ty said.

"Ask the man hanging from the cottonwood tree in the canyon if it was a rumor?"

Slater answered.

How could Slater know? Ty's brain reeled. The deputy hadn't been at the hanging. Only ranchers and Trent Jackson. Trent? Could he have broken his vow and told Slater?

Slater's hands moved slowly to his gunbelt, his fingers unbuckling it and handing it to one of the men in the gathering crowd. Behind them the music stopped in the middle of a song. "Let's have no trouble," called one of the musicians.

"Please, Ty, don't," Wilma whispered.

"Your badge, too!" Ty's voice was hard as granite, the challenge in his words even harder. "This is a grudge between you and me. The law has nothing to do with it."

The deputy unpinned his badge and slipped it into his pocket, nodding all the while. "However you want it, Stoddard. We'll just see how tough you are against a man whose hands aren't tied behind him."

Anger flashed in Ty's eyes and his fist exploded at Slater's nose, blood splattering down the deputy's shirt. Slater staggered a step, then caught his balance. Dazed, the deputy slapped his right hand against his hip, as if he figured to come up with his sidearm. His hand came away empty, and it seemed to clear Slater's muddled brain. He

225

lifted his fists and stepped toward Ty.

Circling away from the deputy, Ty remembered that a wounded animal is the most dangerous. More than his nose, Slater's pride had been injured.

Slater swung once with his right fist.

Ty dodged what was a feint and took a solid left to the jaw, jarring his teeth. The whole right side of his face spurted with pain. By reflex as much as plan, Ty's balled right hand plowed into Slater's stomach right beneath the breastbone.

The deputy gasped for breath, doubling over, then butted his head against Ty's stomach like an enraged ram. Unprepared for the blow, Ty careened wildly backward, with Slater driving him over the vacated bench and into a crowd of spectators.

Onlookers scattered like a covey of quail as the two men rolled on the ground, pressing for any advantage. They slammed into the water barrel and clawed to get up. Ty was on his hands and knees by the barrel, but Slater was quicker and had risen to his knees. The deputy's fist shot for Ty's head, but struck the barrel where it had been. Slater screamed from equal parts of anger and agony.

Ty leaped to his feet as Slater shook off the pounding pain in his hand. Ty clasped his two hands together and staggered to Slater. Raising both hands over his head, Ty brought them down with a crushing blow to Slater's head. The deputy absorbed the blow and quivered a moment. Ty lifted his hands again and brought them down, but the deputy collapsed beneath him and Ty's clubbed fists missed. The momentum of his arms unbalanced him and he stumbled forward, tripping over Slater and collapsing to the ground.

Earth came up suddenly and hard to meet him, and he saw a flash of light and lost touch with himself and the world around him. For an instant, he thought he heard applause and shouting, though he could not figure why. But that noise was replaced by a soothing one in his ear. Like a distant whisper, Wilma Jackson was talking to him, encouraging him, doctoring him. For all the pain throbbing through his aching body, this was the best medicine, and Wilma Jackson, the best physician.

Several folks helped him up and he stood on wobbly legs for a moment, staring at his vanquished foe. With Wilma on one side and someone else on the other, he stumbled past the water barrel just as someone tossed a dipper of water in the unconscious Slater's face.

"You shouldn't have done that, Ty," Wilma said. Her voice was punctuated with worry.

"I fear my dancing's over for the night." Ty's throat was moist with blood but dry for water. "Get me water and help me to the stable."

"You can't go home tonight, not like this."

"I'll sleep it off there, ride home tomorrow. You explain to Trent that his deputy provoked the fight."

How Wilma answered, Ty could not be sure. The next thing he remember was a cup of water at his lips and a bed of straw at the stable. He collapsed in it and slept soundly. At times, he felt that Wilma was seated beside him, her hand stroking his hair and dabbing blood from his face, and at times he felt alone in the whole world, as if Wilma had left him. When he finally shook the mud from his mind, the barn was growing hot from a Sunday sun. From down the street he heard hymn singing, and realized it was late in the morning.

Pa would be expecting him and worrying if he were late. Ty worked his way to his feet, each step taking conscious thought to handle. His body ached from a thousand places, and his mind couldn't make sense of it all. Somehow, he finally managed to gather his belongings, put on his gunbelt and new hat, and saddle his horse.

When he rode out of the stable into the bright sun, his eyes were blinded by the light, and he pulled the brim of his hat low over his eyes and rode toward the Diamond S, vaguely aware that some people on the street were pointing at him.

The ride took forever, each step of his roan seeming to jar his entire body with reminders of the fight. He knew by the time he got to the ranch, his father would be back from his Sunday morning ride. He hoped his father would have something cooked for lunch to fill that cavern in his stomach.

As he rode up to the corral, he smiled at his father's saddled horse. Then panic set in. Something was wrong, but his addled mind still couldn't put it together. His father's piebald was lathered with sweat and standing on the outside of the corral not the inside.

Ty jumped from his saddle and stumbled toward his father's horse, one hand grabbing the reins, the second landing on the saddle horn. That hand came away sticky and red. Ty's eyes gradually came to focus on his hand, then the pommel. Both were stained with blood. Ty knew his father was dead.

PART TWO

Chapter 15

Ty Stoddard wore his best clothes, the ones he had buried his father in four months ago. He had pushed himself hard since then, working the ranch. Always in the back of his mind lingered the thought that one day he would identify his father's killer and dispatch him to hell. The bushwhacker had shot Pa Stoddard in the back during his Sunday ride and left him to bleed to death by the river where once he and his wife had walked, talking of their future. Now, their future was Ty's, like the Diamond S.

Up ahead he saw the Jackson place and people gathering for a lunch on this, the last Saturday before the election. This was also Jackson's last gasp to win votes. Ty did not care for the politics or the social, just Wilma Jackson. She was why he had ridden over from the Diamond S.

Too, this would be his first time to see his new nephew. Delia had a little brother now, and Ty wondered how she was handling her mother's divided attention. Likely she was a miniature mother herself.

Ty rode past a dozen men on his way to the corral, giving them curt nods instead of a cordial smile. Ty never looked at a man without wondering if he were his father's killer. Likely that man was the same one who had tried to kill him. It was a sorry state when folks suspected their neighbors. Just two weeks ago, a man had been lynched in northern Oldham County, but neither Ty nor the regulators had been involved in that. Rumors floated around that some folks were solving personal grievances so that the regulators would be blamed.

Ty spotted Trent Jackson in a circle of men, smiling like a banker with two sets of books. Damn, if law and order wasn't falling to pieces in Oldham County, and yet he stood preaching about why he deserved votes. Trent had failed miserably as sheriff, and no social could ever change that or, Ty hoped, win the election. Some gossip even said Trent Jackson was behind the rustling. After hearing what had been said about himself, Ty discounted those stories. Some folks had quietly suggested Dewey Slater as the source of trouble. Ty found that more likely, though it said very little for Trent

Jackson that he kept the deputy. Ty shrugged. There were so many possibilities and so little proof.

At the corral, Ty dismounted and had barely tied the reins of his roan before he heard Molly's call. Spinning around, he beheld Molly, as trim and lithe as she had been before her pregnancy. From the blanket in her arms came another squeal, and then a bawl. Molly extended the baby to him.

"Hello, Molly. He's got good lungs." Ty took the boy and rocked him a moment, but the baby screamed. Ty felt as helpless as a mute coyote at howling time. "Fine-looking boy, Molly, but you best take him back before I break him."

Molly smiled. "I named him for Pa." Her eyes watered. "He's the future, Ty. There's been too much bad the past year, and I'm looking to the future which begins after the election."

Wilma approached cautiously. Her green eyes, brimming with concern, peeked out from behind the edges of her yellow bonnet. Within reach of him, she stopped and stared, biting at her bottom lip, as if uncertain what to say.

Ty took off his hat. Her hesitancy was contagious and he failed at words. Twice he had seen her since the fight with Dewey Slater, once at his Pa's funeral and once in town when he was riding out and she was coming in. He regretted now not staying, but that was when the responsibility of running the ranch and finding his father's killer had weighed hard upon his shoulders. He wished now he had taken the time to show her more attention and to visit her more.

"You've lost weight, Ty."

Ty's eyes avoided hers and he shuffled his boots.

Recognizing his discomfort, Molly excused herself. "I must find Delia."

"I've lost some, but have I lost you?" Ty lifted his head, studying her soft face for an answer. He offered her his hand. For a moment, his hand was suspended in the air midway between them; then hers reached to take it. In one fluid motion, he replaced his hat and pulled her toward him. She came willingly to him, her head falling naturally against his chest, his arms wrapping around her. They swayed against each other in silence, her breathing the only sound Ty cared to hear.

"Had you not come today, Ty, I don't know what I'd have done." Her voice was laden with worry and doubt, making Ty feel even worse. "With your father's death you've had a lot on your mind, but I've felt forgotten. All this time, and you never wrote or sent word along that you cared." Her words trailed off into despair and she pulled herself tighter against him.

"Have I lost you, Wilma?" Ty held his breath.

"Don't take me for granted again, Tyrus Stoddard."

Ty pulled his arm from around her and his hand went to her chin, lifting her face until he could see the tears falling in pairs down her pale cheeks. Softly, his lips touched hers. Wilma twisted away and rested her head on his chest again. "I worried so after the fight, staying with you in the stable."

It hadn't been a dream, Ty thought, but where had she been when he awoke?

"I had a dreadful fright after sunup. Dewey Slater came in, drunk, mumbling about getting even with you, but he saddled up and left. I followed him outside and watched him ride west out of town. I went to Harvey Worley's to see about bringing you some food and coffee, but when I got back, you were gone. Ever since your pa's burial, I've wondered if you were gone forever. You didn't seem to care."

Ty felt a knot in his throat. "I'll do better,

Wilma, I promise. I've missed you."

Wilma lifted her head and pecked Ty's cheek with a kiss. A laugh slipped from her throat as she eased herself out of his hug. "We keep doing this, folks will be talking about us instead of Trent's election."

"This damn election! At least it'll soon be over."

Her hand slipped naturally into his and they stood admiring the crowd that Trent's free food had attracted. "Trent thinks he's gonna win," Wilma said in a moment.

Ty shook his head. "Trent's blinded by his wants. Too many people, including a lot that are here, can't tolerate Slater and won't vote for Trent because of it. Has Slater bothered you since the dance?"

"He only wanted to provoke you, Ty. He's been scarce around here, coming out occasionally to see Trent, and I've been scarce in town. Shouldn't we join the crowd?"

"I'm with you, Miss Jackson," Ty answered.

They took a step away from the corral, but stopped in their tracks at a squealing voice behind them.

"Uncle Ty," giggled Delia.

Ty twisted around and caught a glimpse of Delia astride the gray pony, nervous among all the other bigger horses in the corral. Delia's hand held a tuft of mane and her legs were flapping against the animal's ribs.

"My horse Rainbow! Isn't he pretty?"

"Delia," Wilma scolded, "if you don't get down from there your momma'll spank you and I won't play any games with you."

Ty edged toward the corral, then stopped. The colt was skittish and might bolt away if he moved too suddenly. Delia giggled at the horse. "Can you move him to the fence, Delia?" Ty asked softly. "Let me pat him, Delia. Will you?"

"Yes!" Delia grabbed another tuft of mane with her free hand and tugged at the animal's neck. Begrudgingly, the animal inched toward the rail fence.

Holding his breath, Ty edged that way, raising his hands ever so slowly. His chest pressed against the fence rail and his arms reached over the top rail.

Delia stayed just out of reach, still tugging the reluctant animal closer, inch by inch. The pony missed a step and Delia's heels dug into the animal's side. The gray shook its head, Delia giggling as one hand lost its grip on the mane.

Ty stepped on the bottom rail, then onto the second. While the gray was distracted by Delia's grasp at another handful of mane, Ty lifted one leg over the top rail, then the other.

The horse came a step closer.

Ty's muscles tightened like the spring in a wound watch.

Tossing its head, the gray almost threw Delia. The giggle died in her throat as she lost her balance and began to slide off the horse, toward the fence.

Ty pounced from his perch.

The gray bolted, dashing out from under Delia.

Ty caught one hand and a flailing arm. His feet slipped as he hit the soft dirt and he stumbled forward, amid the spooked horses, nickering and tossing their heads as they scattered from his path. Ty jerked Delia to his chest and shielded her from a possible fall until he caught his balance. He felt his breath come out as hard as a bellows and realized Delia was giggling from the thrill. Ty shook his head and turned around for the fence. He had taken but a step when Wilma shouted angrily across the corral.

"Delia, don't you do that again. That horse'll hurt you one day." Wilma shook her finger at Delia.

"Rainbow likes me," she answered, her wide eyes as innocent as her words.

"We all do, honey; that's why we don't

like you playing on Rainbow, not without your father." Wilma held out her arms over the fence and grabbed Delia from Ty.

Delia giggled as Wilma pulled her over the fence. Wilma hugged Delia, tightly, shaking her head all the time, wondering when the child would mind. She was a good child, well-behaved and mindful, except when it came to Rainbow. Wilma wished Trent had never given the pony to her. "Next time I'll tell your momma!"

"I'll be good now," Delia said, patting Wilma's shoulder.

Wilma lowered Delia to the ground, swatting at her behind as she scampered away. "You go find some friends to play with, and stay away from the horses."

Delia skipped away, humming a song.

Crawling over the fence, Ty studied Wilma. Her hands were shaking. He jumped to the ground and put his arm around her. "Close call for that little girl."

"Ty, she loves that horse, but she's not old enough to ride, not without someone around to watch out for her. Why didn't Trent give her a puppy?"

"You ever tried to ride a puppy?" he asked, and Wilma's laugh brought a smile to his face. With his arm around her, Ty steered Wilma toward the crowd. "Maybe after we eat, the two of us can take a walk alone."

"I would like that, Tyrus Stoddard."

Trent Jackson was gladhanding a rancher and his wife when he spotted Ty. The sheriff's half-moon of a grin disappeared for a moment, then reappeared as if some slight cloud had blocked it for a moment. But the instant had been so imprecise that Ty wondered if Trent's smile had ever changed.

Ty could not comprehend how a man could still smile with so many rumors about him, like how the rustlers always missed Jackson's place, how his cows always calved twins, how his herd grew faster than anybody else's, how he was head of a gang of rustlers, how Slater was running the sheriff's office, how Jackson owed money yet seemed to be prosperous enough for all the socials he had thrown to buy votes, how the sheriff had ambushed his father-in-law to claim the Diamond S for himself and Molly. People forgot the ranch wasn't all Molly's as long as Ty was alive. Politics! Cheating at cards, robbing banks, and running whorehouses seemed honorable professions by comparison.

Trent Jackson broke away from the couple and strode toward Ty, his arm extended. "Glad you finally pulled yourself away from the Diamond S, Ty," the sheriff said, grabbing Ty's hand and shaking it like a water pump. "You seen my boy? Fine-looking kid! Shame he can't vote, but by the looks of this crowd," Jackson said, with a sweep of his arm, "I won't need his vote, but I hope I can count on yours, come election day."

Cocking his head, Ty looked at Trent with narrowed eyes. "It'll be a close election, Trent. A lot of folks would think the better of you if you cut Slater loose as deputy."

The grin evaporated from the sheriff's face. "He's a hard man, and a lot of folks don't understand that. I need a tough deputy, as much time as I must devote to the ranch."

Ty dug out his cigarette makings and began to construct a smoke. "What I'm saying, Trent, is Slater's not a good man."

Wilma tugged on Ty's arm. "I tried to tell him that, get him to let Slater go, but he won't do it."

Trent's eyes flashed with anger. "Lady, if you plan on staying in my house and eating my food, even at my invitation, I'll expect you to keep your opinions to yourself when I am discussing matters with other men." Wilma turned up her nose and stormed away.

"Slater was out of line at the dance, Ty.

243

We all know that, but a lot of folks get rowdy when they've ad a drink or two."

Ty flicked a match to light against the heel of his boot and touched the flame to the cigarette. "Slater wasn't drinking, Trent. I was close enough to smell his breath."

"You're as stubborn as your pa was, Ty."

"And as honest as he was, Trent. All my accounts are paid up in Tascosa. Are yours?"

The sheriff clenched his fists as his face reddened. "Why have you turned against me, Ty?"

"Dammit, Trent, it's Slater. Can't you get that through your skull? In the barbershop the day of the dance, Slater accused us Stoddards of not backing you. Only people that knew what Pa told you was him, you and me. Pa didn't tell anyone and I haven't." Ty's voice lowered and he looked around to see if anyone might be close enough to hear. "That leaves only you, Trent. How else would Slater know? He's also accused me of hanging Jake Shaw with the regulators. For a man that wasn't there, he seems to know a lot. Nobody else at the hanging would speak to him, save you, Trent. How do you explain all that?"

The sheriff spat in the dust at his feet. "You've listened to too many of Bob Vandiver's lies, Ty. I'm sorry you've taken to believing them."

Ty drew heavily on his cigarette, a cloud of smoke gradually escaping from his lips. "I don't know what to believe anymore, Trent. I do know this; I won't stand by you in the election if you stand by Slater."

"Damn shame family don't count for something, Ty." Trent spun around and stepped toward his guests. He stopped and spoke over his shoulder. "You're still welcome to stay to the meal. We killed two beeves to have enough for all."

Like a rooted tree, Ty stood watching Trent throw himself into the pool of visiting voters. He finished his cigarette, dropped it to the ground, then crushed it with the heel of his boot. He studied the crowd for Wilma, but he failed to spot her, and walked up to the house to sit in the porch shade. As he stepped up on the porch, he heard sobbing from inside. Wilma!

The door creaked as he pushed it open. Wilma stood in the front room, dabbing her eyes with a handkerchief. She seemed embarrassed at first; then she just shrugged and cried. "He's changed, Ty," she said amid the tears. "He trusts nobody. He wears his gun all the time, except when he milks the cow in the morning for Adam. He's changed."

"Politics!" Ty put his arms around her.

"It's not just politics, it's stubborn pride! You men've got too much of it. Many a day during the last four months, I've thought about leaving this place. Trent's stubborn and you seemed to forget me, Ty."

Her words struck Ty as hard as a cast-iron fist. He had come to expect Wilma to always be there. The thought that she might leave was troubling. With his finger, he lifted her chin from his shoulder and kissed her full on the mouth, the moistness of her tears mingling with the sweetness of her lips.

When their lips broke, he looked into her soft eyes. "Let's take a walk, Wilma — into the canyon, get away from the crowd."

Wilma dabbed at her eyes, pulled her bonnet from a peg, and tied it over her head. They stepped together onto the porch, Ty pulling the door shut. Before them, Trent Jackson stood on a barrel, addressing his visitors. His words carried on the gentle fall breeze. "The Jackson family is proud to welcome you to the ranch, proud to let you meet the newest member of our family, my son." The sheriff was enjoying his control over the crowd, planning his subtle plea for their votes. Ty glanced at Trent, who seemed more relaxed then he had in weeks. He enjoyed being the focus of attention.

"I know some of you are saying the timing of my son's birth was indeed a lucky stroke. After all, how can you vote against the father of a boy that handsome," Trent called. "Hold him up for them all to see, Molly."

Steering Wilma down the trail, Ty sighed. "Reckon Trent will deputize the baby when the election's over?"

The sheriff's voice trailed their every step. "But I tell you," Trent continued, "his birth came at the worst possible time, because there's no doubt he's too young to vote for his father in the election." The crowd laughed, and Trent seemed pleased with himself.

Wilma's pace picked up. "I'm tired of it all, Ty. So many lies, so many rumors."

They walked without words to the brim of the canyon, stood a moment paying homage to the grandeur of the breaks and the Canadian River, a silver ribbon which stretched to the horizon. A solitary hawk floated on the wind currents in the canyon, a creature without worry over a land without conscience. The grade was gentle where Ty escorted Wilma down the trail, and they walked until they found a canopy of shade under a juniper tree which had taken root between twin stones which resembled huge brown marbles embedded in the soil.

They took seats on the rocks and looked at each other. Wilma's eyes peeked out around the lace trim of her bonnet and Ty could see the pain in them. Her eyes explained more than her words ever could. The stress of the election and being caught in the turmoil between Trent and Molly was showing. Ty felt a closeness to her unlike that to any woman he had ever known. It was hard to define — more than just her good looks, more than her manner of fairplay, more than just her common sense. She was a woman worth marrying, but he wasn't quite sure how to say it. He stood up and fidgeted, circling the rock and tree a couple times, finally taking her soft hand in his and patting it with his fingers.

"You're nervous, Tyrus Stoddard. Are you in danger?"

Squeezing her hand, he shook his head. "Nothing that simple?" His mind raced with doubts about how he should ask her to marry him, if she would accept his proposal, if this were the proper time.

"In Oldham County, nothing's simple, I've learned," she answered the question herself.

"Wilma . . . ," he began, the word trailing off into silence. A movement had caught

Ty's eye, about a hundred yards on the other side of the trail. He squinted against the afternoon glare and the distance. It was a wolf fighting something, or at least kicking up dust. "Odd."

"What?" Wilma stared blankly at him, her lips spread.

Ty pointed to the animal.

Squeezing his hand, she stood up for a better view. "What is it?"

Shrugging, Ty stepped in that direction. The walk would give him a chance to consider how to propose to Wilma. Ty patted the revolver at his hip, in case the animal were rabid.

"Don't leave me, Ty," Wilma said, lifting her skirt as she crossed the trail and followed in Ty's wake.

Something seemed odd to Ty, and his long deliberate strides outpaced Wilma. Within fifty yards of the wolf, Ty pulled his gun and the animal stopped. Whatever it had been fighting was limp in the wolf's mouth. Ty lifted his revolver, trying to edge a little closer for a better shot. The wolf sensed the danger, for whatever he was holding fell from his mouth, and the animal trotted into the broken cover that littered the slope.

Reholstering his gun, Ty held up a moment, waiting for Wilma to catch up to him.

A patch of eroded topsoil gave way beneath Wilma's shoe and Ty grabbed her arm as she slipped. She caught her balance, paused for a moment, then advanced with Ty's hand gripping her arm. When he reached the spot where the wolf had been, Ty was confused for a moment. The ground was soft, and beneath the many wolfprints were bootprints. A cow's head, its tongue bloated and its eyes crawling with insects, was half buried in the soft ground, and nearby, where the wolf had dropped it, was a cowhide, stiff from drying out but still pink with meat in places. The scent of that meat had attracted the wolf. Whoever had buried the hide had been lazy or in a hurry, because it wasn't deep enough to throw off the wolf's sharp nose.

With the toe of his boot, Ty dug around the shallow depression from which the wolf had pulled the hide. His boot struck something hard, then slipped under the hard object, and Ty pried at it. Slowly, the sandy soil here slipped away and the horn of another head appeared. Ty shook his hand free of Wilma's arm and squatted in the depression, scooping away the sand and uncovering half of the cow's head and the corner of another hide. Two beeves slaughtered, the hides buried, not more than two days ago by the looks of things, Ty thought. How many beeves did Trent say he had cooked for his social?

Standing erect, he stepped over to the other hide, toed it with his boot and kicked it over. He caught his breath at what he saw. Burned into the hide was a brand. The Diamond S brand! At today's election social, Trent was feeding folks Diamond S beef. Quickly, Ty turned the hide over, wondering if Wilma had noticed the brand.

His jaw was tight when he turned to her. Wilma's eyes were wide with confusion. "I don't understand, Ty. It's like somebody was trying to hide something." Then a look of realization washed across her face, her hand flying to her mouth. "Oh, no!" Her pale skin whitened even more.

CHAPTER 16

Gray clouds blanketed the sky, muting the midday sun with the breath of the season's first cold spell. Leaving the barbershop, Ty lifted the collar on his coat and shivered. It was a somber day in Tascosa, election day.

Men, few bringing their wives and families for fear the weather might worsen, had ridden in from throughout the county to vote. Wagons lined the streets and horses crowded the hitching posts, but few people lingered outside because of the cold. It being election day, the saloons couldn't serve beer or whiskey until balloting had ceased. Nonetheless, most saloons stayed open and Shriff Trent Jackson had spent the day wandering from one watering hole to another making sure every bartender maintained proper respect for the democratic process.

Ty marched down the street, no real destination in mind, though he knew where he should be going: the courthouse to vote! He passed the Exchange Hotel where the major cattlemen had gathered with Bob Vandiver to await the vote count. Ty knew of no comparable gathering place for Trent's supporters, figuring that was indication enough of the ultimate outcome. And then, there was the matter of the two Diamond S hides Ty had uncovered in the canyon. Unlikely any rustler would've slaughtered beef that close to the sheriff's place, nor carried hides onto the place to bury them. Likely, Trent or his two hands — Tom Higgins or Bill Witherspoon — had killed the beef to feed the social. There was no answer to the question except the one Ty had trouble admitting. Trent was involved in some way in the rustling. Ty saw the sheriff down the street, coming out of the Equitable Saloon. Ty turned around in his tracks. He had put it off long enough, so he turned off Main Street and marched toward the courthouse to cast his ballot.

A couple of men emerged from the courthouse, talking in low voices which suddenly went silent. Both nodded curtly at Ty as he passed. He swung open the courthouse door and felt a blast of heat slap him in the face. The courthouse was always the hottest building in town. Of course, the commissioners were burning other people's money — taxes — instead of their own. Ty stomped his feet in disgust, wishing it were August, when all the tax money in the state couldn't buy relief from the heat. He let the door swing shut behind him.

At the end of the hall, the stairs led to the second floor and the county clerk's office, where voting was taking place. Ty unbuttoned his coat before ascending the stairs. He could hear the voices of several men and could smell the smoke of their strong cigars. Reaching the top of the stairs, he halted in his tracks. Leaning against the clerk's counter was Dewey Slater, his cold pipe stuck in the gap in his teeth.

Slater straightened up, his hand brushing against his holstered revolver, then advanced toward Ty with snakelike movements. "Came to vote against your brother-in-law, did you?"

"Men are voting against you, more than Trent. You're the bad apple, Slater, and you may've ruined him."

Slater sucked on the dead pipe, and it whistled. "If Trent loses, you won't have me to protect you. You could wind up like your pa." Slater sneered at Ty, then stepped past him to the stairs. "There's an odor up here now, and it isn't bad apples."

The deputy leisurely worked his way down the stairs, Ty watching as if Slater were a rabid dog. After the deputy disappeared into the sheriff's office, Ty turned across the room to a desk clerk wearing wire-rim glasses not much larger than his eyeballs, his forehead pimpling with tiny beads of sweat in the room's oppressive heat. "Glad to see you, Mr. Stoddard, and glad the deputy left. He's been harassing voters all day."

Ty signed a voting roster where the clerk pointed, then took a ballot and moved to an empty table in the back of the room. At an adjacent table, one of the clerks was helping an illiterate cowboy by reading him the ballot. Ty marked his choices in each of the races until he came to the sheriff's position. He pondered for a moment; then slowly, steadily, his pencil circled the name of Bob Vandiver. Poor Molly, he thought, if Trent wins. Or, if Trent loses. Even though he knew Vandiver was the right choice, he felt a traitor to Molly. She, after all, was family. Her children were blood kin, the next generation of the Diamond S progeny.

Slowly, he pushed himself away from the table, the ballot clamped in his hand. Passing the padlocked ballot box, he dropped the folded paper in with the others and marched down the stairs, pausing only long enough to look around for Slater and to button his coat before stepping outside.

The wind had picked up, kicking up dust along the street and banging into the clapboard buildings, which groaned and creaked under the assault. Had he not agreed to meet Wilma, Ty would've gone back to the Diamond S without a doubt in his mind that Vandiver would win the election. But finding the Diamond S hides on the Jackson place last week had delayed his proposal to Wilma. Tonight he planned to ask her to marry him when she came to town.

With the wind shoving at his back, Ty aimed for Harvey Worley's restaurant to kill some time before riding toward the Jackson place to meet the women as they rode in. Worley's door slammed shut as Ty slid inside. The place was busy, though it appeared most were biding time until the saloons started serving liquor again.

Worley, his apron stained from too much business, waved his arms at Ty, then pointed to an empty table in the corner. Ty nodded and took a chair. Worley made it around shortly with a cup of coffee and took Ty's order. When his food came, Ty toyed with it. He felt his nerves creeping over him and he tried to figure if it was from the election or his planned proposal. Undecided, he left money at his plate for the meal and slipped outside toward the stable, where he mounted his roan and headed toward the Jackson place. And Wilma!

Two miles out of town he spotted a wagon coming his way. He nudged the roan into a trot and soon recognized Wilma and Molly bundled up under quilts on the seat, their faces red from the chafing wind. Wilma's smile burned bright as he neared.

"I'd left town sooner, if I'd known you were early," Ty offered, turning his horse in to ride beside the wagon

Wilma shook off his apology. "We figured an early start best," she called over the wind, "in case the weather turned worse. We don't want these young'uns taking sick."

A crack between quilts widened and Delia's face emerged, red with cold. Molly, holding the baby beneath the quilts, nodded a greeting, but nothing more. It was hard to converse over the wind and the cold, so he rode back to Tascosa in silence. Ty left his horse at the stable, then climbed into the back of the wagon and rode to the courthouse. While Wilma helped Molly and the kids into the sheriff's office, Ty watered the team, then drove the wagon to the side of the courthouse and set the brake.

Wilma joined him shortly and they walked arm in arm toward the stores. What little daylight had broken through the dreary clouds was gradually diminishing. Wilma aimed Ty toward Tobe Burleson's store, saying she had a few things to purchase. That was as good a place as any to kill time, Ty thought, it lacking a couple of hours until the election results were totaled.

The weather being what it was, and with so few women in town, Burleson's was quiet for a Saturday afternoon. Ty eased into a chair by the crackling potbellied stove and held his hands up toward the heat. After unbuttoning his coat, Ty grabbed the copy of the Tascosa Pioneer that was draped over the arm of an adjacent chair. The four pages rustled as he shook out the folds of the newspaper and sank deeper into his chair to read. But the pages were covered with election news, filled with promises no politician could or would keep. He had had enough of politics, and he folded the paper and tossed it on the seat of the adjacent chair. Rocking gently on the hind legs of his chair, Ty enjoyed watching Wilma as she moved about the store, selecting some sewing needles and thread for mending her dresses, and some pink ribbon for Delia's hair.

Wilma giggled as she held up a baby's red

wool cap. "Just what the baby needs to stay warm on the trip home," she said to Ty. "Molly was figuring on another daughter, and he just doesn't look right in the heavy bonnet she has for him."

Ty smiled his approval, figuring the longer she shopped, the longer his reprieve before asking for her hand in matrimony. He smoked a cigarette, not from nerves, but just for the enjoyment it could bring a man idling away time. When two customers left, leaving only Wilma and Ty, Burleson came over and plopped into the chair beside Ty. Occasionally, Burleson would call out to Wilma what a good deal he had on the merchandise she had just picked from a table. Mostly, though, Burleson talked in whispers about the election and all the rumors he had been hearing. Ty just nodded occasionally so Burleson would not think he was being ignored, but Ty had little to offer. He felt the storekeeper was fishing for some answers about Trent's plans after the election. That was something Ty didn't even know himself. Ty was relieved when Wilma indicated she was done. Burleson pulled himself away from Ty and totaled a dollar and ten cents on Wilma's purchases.

After digging into her coin purse for the money to pay, Wilma slipped the thread, needles, ribbon, and cap into her coat pocket; she smiled at Ty. "The children will look cute in ribbon and cap."

It was still early, but with no place else to go, Ty took Wilma's arm and steered her out of Burleson's and toward Harvey Worley's eatery. Worley was cleaning a table by the window when Ty opened the door for Wilma. "Come back for more, have you, Mr. Stoddard?"

Ty pushed the door to, the glass pane rattling in the wind. "Came back because it's cold and I've no place else to go."

"Neither do a lot of other folks," Worley replied, with a sweep of his washrag toward the full tables. "If everyone was eating as much as they were talking, I'd be a rich man." Worley dusted two chairs beside the table he'd just finished cleaning, and offered them to Ty and Wilma. They unbundled and eased into the seats beside a drafty window opaque with condensation.

"Two coffees to warm us up, and put more wood in your stove, Harvey," Ty commanded.

"I run a restaurant, not a courthouse." Worley shrugged. "I can't afford as much wood and hauling as the county can. I can get you a cup of coffee, though."

After Worley returned with the steaming

coffee, Wilma reached across the table and took Ty's hands. "I said nothing about the hides to Molly. Should I?"

Ty shook his head. "You forget that. I'll discuss it with Trent after the election. There's something I've been wanting to ask you, though."

Wilma's hands squeezed tighter around his and her eyes seemed to light up. "Yes?"

Suddenly, Ty was nervous, not knowing quite what to say. "Did you have a nice ride into town?"

A cloud of disappointment shaded her face and her eyes were glazed with it.

"I mean," Ty sputtered, "we haven't known each other long, but I was wondering if it were long enough?"

"Long enough for what?"

"For me to ask you to marry me?"

Her features softened, like a flower opening its petals in the sunlight. Her eyes misted. Her lips parted as if to say something, but words seemed beyond her reach. She stared a moment longer and then she nodded, her hands squeezing his as a lone tear rolled down her cheek.

"Will you marry me, Wilma Jackson?"

Wilma released his hands and pulled a kerchief from her sleeve. Dabbing at her eye, she spoke, her voice a whisper. "Yes, Tyrus Stoddard, I will marry you."

Wilma's grip tightened on Ty's arm as each ballot was called out. The clerk's office was jammed but hushed as men listened to the growing count. With two of every three votes going for Vandiver, it was clear Trent Jackson had lost the election.

With Dewey Slater at his side, Trent stood glowering at the crowd, his fists clenched, his jaw thrust forward in defiance, his eyes narrow and mean. Few words had passed through his lips since the counting began, though occasionally he would lean over and whisper something to Slater, the deputy nodding and fiddling with his pipe. In the back corner sat Molly, the baby asleep in her arms, Delia leaning her head against her mother's leg. Molly was dazed, and occasionally Ty saw a tear rolling down her cheek, but he could not be certain whether it was a tear of joy or sorrow over the election. Trent would have his tail between his legs for a while, but he would get over it eventually.

"Molly looks so sad, and I've such good news to tell her about us," Wilma whispered to Ty, as the clerk called out another vote for Bob Vandiver. "She'll be pleased, I know she will. Maybe my leaving will help ease the tension between her and Trent. It embarrasses her so with me around."

"Think she'll be surprised?" Ty asked.

"No, sir," Wilma said emphatically. "She's said all along we'd get married. It'll likely surprise her we're getting married so soon."

Ty nodded, but he was more interested in watching Bob Vandiver. The next sheriff and several of the ranchers, their faces covered with smiles, stood near the tallying table. Already the county commissioners were gathering around him, offering their hands in congratulation, though eight weeks still remained before Trent Jackson's term expired. With each new vote he received, one or two ranchers would slap Vandiver on the back, celebrating the obvious outcome. As the operator of the Diamond S, Ty felt a kinship to them, but for Molly's sake he stood with Wilma toward the back, sweltering from the courthouse heat.

When the last ballot was tallied and the final total written on the chalk board, Trent Jackson lowered his head, staring at the floor, his shoulders stooped. A few men ambled down the stairs, likely headed for the saloons for a little liquid to warm their innards, but most lingered to congratulate Bob Vandiver. The sheriff-elect, though, pushed his way through them toward Trent Jackson.

Vandiver extended his hand to his defeated opponent. "No hard feelings, Trent?"

Jackson looked up from the floor, studied Vandiver's outstretched hand, then stared the victor hard in the eyes. Without a word, Jackson turned his back on Vandiver.

Vandiver's hand slowly fell to his side. "Sorry you feel that way, Trent, but I'm gonna play the hand you deal me." Vandiver turned to Dewey Slater. "One thing I'll state for everyone to hear," Vandiver continued. "When I take office, Slater'll be out of a job. You'll not be my deputy, and I'll encourage you to move along, out of the county."

Slater pulled the pipe from his mouth and pointed the stem like a gun at Vandiver's nose. "We'll see, Vandiver!" Slater turned away just as Jackson had done.

Vandiver's backers moved in like the tide around him, boisterous in their congratulations, all suggesting a celebration at the Equitable Saloon. Vandiver shook every hand extended to him, then moved toward the stairs with his backers. As he reached the stairs, he stopped and nodded to Ty. "I've nothing against you and the Diamond S, Ty. I know you've been caught in the middle on this." He offered his hand and Ty

264

grabbed it.

"Good luck, Bob; all any of us want is a little law and order," Ty replied, realizing Trent would likely be offended by his choice of words.

Vandiver and his entourage receded down the stairs, taking the celebration with them, leaving behind the clerk, a couple of county commissioners and a knot of Trent Jackson supporters. Molly was crying, and Delia tried to comfort her.

Half-heartedly, Jackson shook a few hands thrust in his direction, and nodded at the condolences his friends offered with hat in hand. The half dozen sympathizers ignored Dewey Slater, and shortly they left meekly.

Trent stood like a statue, his eyes vacant, his shoulders slumped, frustration wrinkling his face. Slowly, he lifted his hand to his chest, his fingers wrapping around his badge, lingering there for a moment, toying with the metal star. Then, he unhooked it and tossed it on the clerk's table. The whispers of the two county commissioners nearby stopped suddenly. Both men turned to Trent, questions on their lips.

"There's my badge! It's what the voters wanted, so they can have it early. We'll see how quick Bob Vandiver brings law and order to Oldham County." Trent stared at

Ty, as if the words "law and order" had stuck in his craw. He stepped toward the stairs, looking neither left nor right, acknowledging neither his wife nor his sister, the plod of each footfall echoing in the now quiet courthouse.

Molly sobbed now, and Wilma released Ty's arm and went to comfort her sister-in-law. Careful of the baby, Wilma helped Molly to her feet, grabbed the quilt Delia had been using, then picked her up. "We need to go with your father, Delia."

"Is he not sheriff no more?" she asked, wrinkling her nose.

"Not any more, darling!" Wilma answered.

"Good!" she replied, her voice rising with excitement. "Now maybe he will let me ride Rainbow more."

Wilma helped Molly to the stairs, then paused to smile at Ty. "I'll remember election day for a different reason, Tyrus Stoddard."

Ty nodded and watched them go down the stairs, wishing he were with Wilma and that Molly wouldn't have to endure the next few days with Trent Jackson. They were barely out of sight when Ty heard Dewey Slater boast to the commissioners.

"Guess I'm sheriff now!"

Both men, whitefaced, turned to one

another, as if their stares could give each other courage to say no.

Ty stepped toward Slater. "Take off your badge, Slater! When the sheriff resigns, his appointments are no good anymore. Isn't that right, gentlemen?"

Both commissioners nodded, tipped their hats and scurried for the stairs.

Ty and Slater stood staring at each other, like two cats waiting for the other to make a move. Slater sucked on his pipe, but the fire had died, and all he drew was a whistling noise.

Pulling his pipe from his mouth, he lifted his heel and tapped the bowl three times against it, then blew through the pipe three times.

Somewhere Ty had heard that noise before. His mind raced, and for a moment he could not place it.

Then Slater repeated the ritual. Tap-tap-tap. Whistle-whistle-whistle.

Now Ty remembered the sound. He'd heard it the day he had been ambushed chasing rustlers. Dewey Slater had shot him in the back.

CHAPTER 17

"Over there, Bob!" Ty stood in the saddle and pointed to the west. His muscles were taut with exhaustion and his voice tight with the strain of a hard day on the trail of rustlers. His coat felt frail against the cold wind seeping in from the north, and the sinking sun was taking with it what little heat it had offered all day.

Beside Ty, Bob Vandiver reined up his chestnut and gave a low whistle. Though pinned to Vandiver's thick coat was a sheriff's badge, it was meaningless in New Mexico Territory. The gun at his side and the carbine under his saddle were all the authority he had now. He lifted the binoculars that hung from a frayed leather strap around his neck and studied the broken land just ahead. "Three of them!" His words came out in a cloud of condensation from the cold.

"Slater with them?" Ty asked, his hand

rubbing the butt of his revolver. In the five days since election night, Ty had heard a thousand times in his mind the tap-tap-tap-whistle-whistle-whistle of Slater cleaning his pipe. The same noise that he remembered when he was ambushed. And burned into his mind was another, even more haunting image of himself slapping the horse out from under Jake Shaw, the kid twisting furiously for a breath of air, then slowly strangling until he was nothing more than a fleshy pendulum. Shaw had told the truth. Slater had set Shaw up. And Ty had murdered an innocent man and had done it with pleasure once he had seen his grandfather's watch in Shaw's hand. But Slater had been shrewd and Trent Jackson had been suckered in or, even more troubling, had been in on it.

Vandiver slowly lowered the binoculars. "Slater's not with them, but Trent's two hands are!"

"Bill Witherspoon and Tom Higgins?"

Vandiver grunted. "And one in a red sombrero I don't recognize."

Ty shook his head and slouched in his saddle, letting out the cloud of a deep breath. "Poor Molly," he said. "Trent's likely been in on it all along." Ty cursed the cold.

"Things are pointing that way," Vandiver

answered, pulling out his revolver and checking the load. He repeated the process with his carbine.

Now was not the time to sort it all out, Ty decided, pulling his revolver from his holster and spinning the full cylinder. Slipping the gun into its scabbard, he pulled the carbine from its boot. It was loaded and he was ready.

The men nudged their horses and, they started out at trot, gradually picking up to a canter. The distance between them and the rustlers closed quickly, the thieves preoccupied with herding twenty head of Diamond S cattle and likely thinking they were out of danger now that they were in New Mexico Territory. Drawing within a couple hundred yards of the rustlers, Ty saw one tilt his head back, then lower it and pass something to the man beside him. The two were drinking liquor to fight off the cold.

The third man, the one in the red sombrero, rode on the opposite side of the cattle, staring for a moment at the other two. Then he glanced back over his shoulder, spotting Ty and Vandiver, now within a hundred yards. "¡Vamos!" he yelled, and flailed his horse with a quirt. For an instant, the other two men seemed not to understand. The cattle stampeded. Then so did

Higgins and Witherspoon. Higgins dropped the bottle and grabbed his pistol. Twisting in the saddle, he pointed his gun at Ty. A puff of white smoke came out, and in its wake, Ty heard the report.

Ty spurred his roan and the animal lunged ahead, taking great strides, his hooves kicking up dirt. Managing the reins with his left hand, Ty jerked his carbine to his shoulder, aiming as best he could from his unsteady perch. His finger tightened on the trigger, but his roan skirted around a cactus and the carbine exploded before Ty was ready. "Damn," he cried, trying to lever the empty hull out of his carbine with just one hand. The carbine slipped, then almost fell before he grabbed it.

Nearby, Vandiver managed two shots at the riders, one of them, by its sound, striking flesh, though likely horseflesh. One horse stumbled, throwing Witherspoon forward onto the animal's neck. With flailing arms, he grasped for a handhold. The animal tossed his head back, fighting against the rider and trying to maintain its feet. The horse wailed and seemed to catch his balance for but an instant. Then its forelegs buckled and the animal crashed down upon its chest, the rider flying headlong into the ground, the rear of the horse following him over until both man and animal tumbled like a pair of rag dolls over the ground, the horse coming to rest on its rider.

Ty winced at the bloody heap as he dashed by, chasing Higgins. He and Vandiver were both gaining. Ty squeezed off a shot, intentionally high, figuring Higgins might give up. Instead, he twisted in his saddle, pointed his revolver at Ty and fired. Ty saw the gun-barrel and ducked, just as his roan darted around a bush. Ty heard the whiz of flying lead. "Give up, you son-a-bitch," Ty yelled, releasing another shot that went wide.

Higgins leaned forward in his saddle, slapping his frothing horse on the neck with his pistol. Ty spurred his roan and the horse reacted with a burst of speed that pulled him within twenty yards of the rustler. Ty released the reins over his saddle horn, giving the roan full freedom. The animal responded, closing the gap to within ten yards. Ty lifted his carbine to his shoulder. "Stop," he yelled. Higgins ignored the command. Ty's finger tightened around the trigger as his left hand steadied the carbine. He counted to three, aiming not where the rider was, but where he expected he would be. On three, he squeezed off a shot that found its target with a thunk.

Screaming a pink froth, Higgins threw up

his arms and lost the reins, then slumped over the saddle, riding maybe fifty yards before he slid out of the saddle and tumbled to the ground, his arms and legs twitching.

As Higgins fell, Vandiver yelled, "I'm after the other one." He slapped his reins against his chestnut's neck and veered off toward Red Sombrero, who had a half-mile lead. Ty waved him on, then grabbed his reins and eased the roan from a dead run to a trot, and then a walk. Circling his roan around, Ty put the animal into a lope toward Higgins, who was sprawled upon the ground, groaning. Shoving the carbine back into his saddle boot, Ty slid off his roan, grabbing his canteen as he hit the ground.

Higgins's breath came with rasping irregularity and pink foam bubbled out of his nostrils. His eyes blinked continuously, as if he were staring into a bright light beyond the horizon. Ty bent over him, pouring some water into his mouth. Higgins's eyes seemed to focus on Ty, and a crooked smile worked its way across his face.

"Cold," he gasped. "It's so cold."

Ty unbuttoned the rustler's coat to check the wound. By the time his fingers unfastened the second button, he could see the red and purple mush below, and he knew

Higgins would die. "Did Trent put you up to it?"

Higgins stared blankly ahead, his eyes vacant. They seemed to refocus for a moment on Ty.

"Did Slater have anything to do with the rustling?"

He nodded. "Yes," he whispered, then coughed a pink foam.

"Was Trent Jackson involved?" Ty shouted, as if Higgins were slipping away into a deep hole where he could not hear. Ty recognized desperation in his voice.

His eyes closing, Higgins relaxed.

"Was Trent Jackson involved?" Ty screamed and shook him hard. Higgins's eyes fluttered open and pleaded for Ty not to shake him again. "Was Trent Jackson involved?"

A perplexed look clouded the dying man's face, then a smile washed across it, his eyes widening, then closing slowly. Higgins seemed to nod, but Ty could not be sure. Then Higgins opened his mouth as if he were trying to say yes, but no words came out. Then his mouth fell open and he went limp.

Ty studied him a moment, then realized he was no longer looking at the face of a man, but at the face of death. He released the man's head and turned away, recorking his canteen and hooking it over his saddle-horn. His foot slid into the stirrup and he pulled himself atop the horse and headed back to Witherspoon. He rode for a quarter of a mile to reach the intertwined bodies of man and horse. Witherspoon had been crushed by the fall and, from the angle of his neck, Ty knew it was broken. Witherspoon had uttered his last word and had stolen his last cow.

To the west, the sun was halfway behind the horizon, and Bob Vandiver cast a long shadow as he returned, herding a half-dozen cattle before him. Ty's hand trembled, not so much because of what he had done, but because of what he had confirmed. Slater was involved, and almost certainly Trent Jackson. Damn him! Poor Molly! Ty shoved his hand into his coat and pulled out his cigarette fixings. Because of his quivering hands, he spilled more tobacco than was usual before he folded the paper over on itself and licked the edges. He shoved the spit-stained roll in his mouth and the tobacco pouch and papers back inside his coat. He fingered in his pocket for a match and finally extracted one, quickly flicking it aflame with his thumbnail and touching the point of his smoke. The cigarette flared at the tip and he inhaled. He finished the cigarette slowly before riding off to round up the scattered cattle with the Diamond S brand, not caring to ride within talking distance of Bob Vandiver until it was darker and the sheriff couldn't read his face so easily.

The last light was dying in the west when Ty and the sheriff rode together, Vandiver with eleven beeves, Ty with seven.

"Sombrero got away," Vandiver said.

"Slater was involved," Ty replied, staring at his saddlehorn so Vandiver couldn't see his face for the brim of his hat. Ty wished the next question would never come, but he knew Vandiver would ask it. That was his job! That had been Trent Jackson's job, too, but Trent had broken the trust of the voters who had put him in office.

"So Slater put them up to it," Vandiver mulled, then paused for a minute. "Anybody else involved?"

Ty just stared at the saddlehorn, holding his breath, making no movement that might be considered an answer. He could feel Vandiver's gaze hard upon him, boring into his soul where the answer could never be hidden. Ty nodded. "Higgins died before he answered, but I'm certain he nodded. I'm sure Trent is involved."

"You're as solid as your father was, Ty," Vandiver replied. "A lesser man would've lied!"

Ty lifted his head and stared at the dark shadow that was Vandiver. "I appreciate that, Bob. I'd like to handle this myself with Trent; that's what I pledged with the regulators."

Vandiver nodded. "I'll not make a move against Trent without letting you know. Now, I figure we're missing a couple head of cattle; we can wait until morning and look for them."

"Let's get a little closer to Texas and then bed down for the night. The Diamond S may have lost two beeves, but we'd lost twenty without you."

"Knowing Slater's hate for you, I just figured it was a matter of time before he tried to get more of your cattle. Too, I figured, he'd try to make me look bad my first few days as sheriff, so he could spread around that I was worse than he was at enforcing the law."

"Shame we aren't leaving his body out here for the buzzards like the other two," Ty answered as he rode his horse out to stop a couple of his cattle from leaving the small herd. Together he and Bob headed them toward Texas and home.

They put some distance between themselves and the two dead men, then picked out a campsite and bedded down the cattle. They unfurled their sleeping rolls and crawled in between the covers. "Wish I'd brought another blanket," Bob said.

Ty grunted as he pulled the covers tight around his neck. "I wish we'd got Sombrero. He was there when I was ambushed."

"Maybe just as well we didn't, Ty. Word'll get out that the other two were killed. That may help us more than anything else. I figure Sombrero's from around Fort Sumner. I hear tell Slater hides out there and it could be Sombrero's the link that's been providing cattle to fulfill contracts with the army and the Apache reservation."

"The spillover from New Mexico Territory will plague us until this country is cleaned up, Bob." Ty turned over in his bedroll. A man never realized how many blemishes flat ground had until he tried to sleep on it.

"Word'll get out there's been a change in the sheriff of Oldham County. They'll steer clear," Vandiver answered.

Ty settled into his blanket. A new sheriff would make a difference because the previous sheriff had violated his oath. And that sheriff was his brother-in-law. Tired though he was, Ty slept restlessly, plagued by Trent Jackson's legacy, worried about Molly's and her children's future. And then the question Ty feared to ask: How would all this affect Wilma and her feelings for him?

Dawn came much too early for Ty; his muscles ached and his bones seemed brittle when he pushed himself up from the cold ground. His legs were wobbly as a newborn calf's. And the cold seeped through his clothes and bit into every fiber of his body until his fingers were so stiff he could barely roll up his bedding and saddle his roan.

Vandiver was squatted over a pot of coffee, waiting for it to boil from the meager heat of a cowchip fire. "Restless night? A little coffee'll warm you up shortly."

Tying his bedroll down on the back of his saddle, Ty nodded, then fished in his saddlebags for his tin cup. Just beyond their camp the eighteen head of cattle stirred, bellowing as they rose from the ground and wandering around, nibbling on tufts of grass and sniffing at the air for the smell of the nearest water. The coffee finally boiled and Vandiver filled Ty's tin, then his own. They drank silently, one cup, then a second, before Vandiver dumped out the grounds and gave the pot a chance to cool before strapping it behind his saddle.

A sliver of sun was just peeking over the eastern horizon when Ty and Vandiver mounted and began herding the cattle back toward Texas and the Diamond S. It was a day's ride with plenty of time to think, more time than Ty wanted. All the rumors, all the gossip about Trent Jackson had been true. It galled Ty that Trent had tossed it all off as campaign slander. Hard as it might be on Molly, Ty knew he must run Trent out of Oldham County. Or kill him! He was not the type Oldham County needed.

It was dusk by the time Ty and Vandiver reached Diamond S land. Vandiver headed back to town and Ty drove the cattle up the Canadian. It was dark by the time he reached the house. After tending his horse at the barn, Ty went through the kitchen door, built a fire and heated bath water. After filling a tub, Ty peeled off layers of trail dust. Once done, he dried, put on clean long johns, threw more wood in the stove to warm the house as much as possible, then headed to bed. He slept soundly, awaking in the morning refreshed. He dressed and strolled to the front of the house, stepping through the front door and out onto the porch. He studied the clear sky for a clue as to how long the cold spell would last, and figured the worst was over.

Turning around, he stopped at the door. There, tacked on the facing, was a folded note, his name written on the outside in Wilma's hand. He jerked the note loose and unfolded it. The message hit him like a thunderbolt.

"Terrible news," read the note. "Delia was killed in accident. Come soon as you can. Wilma."

CHAPTER 18

In the evening sun, the rough cross cast a long shadow over the Jackson place. As soon as he topped the ridge from the canyon trail, Ty picked out the cross and the fresh mound of dirt beyond the house. Molly must be devastated, Ty thought, so many problems with Trent, and now Delia dead and buried. Ty stared, not wanting to go on, because he didn't know what to say if he did. But why Delia?

As he waited, powerless to force himself to ride on, Ty saw Trent emerging from the barn with a pail in his hand, likely milk for the baby. Trent circled away from the barn to the fresh grave and stood, his head bowed. Ty dismounted and led his roan toward the grave. Trent seemed oblivious to his approach, and Ty was almost beside him before Trent lifted his head. Tears rolled down Trent's cheeks and Ty felt ashamed that he had intruded on a father's grief.

"I'm sorry, Trent. I came when I heard."

Trent said nothing, hate mingled with the grief in his eyes.

"How'd it happen?" Ty asked.

Trent spat at Ty's feet, then brushed past him toward the house, spilling a cupful of milk on the grave.

As he tied his horse, Ty studied Trent, noting his brother-in-law was minus a sidearm. Trent disappeared into the house for a minute, then came outside again, this time with his holster and revolver strapped around his waist. Trent angled straight from the house to the barn, where he disappeared for several minutes, then came out astride his horse. He galloped away toward the canyon trail.

Wilma poked her head out the kitchen door, staring toward Trent, then moved to close the door but stopped. "Ty?" she called, then dashed out the door, her arms outstretched.

He rushed to meet her and took her in his arms, kissing her cheeks and tasting the saltiness of her tears.

"It was so terrible, Ty. Rainbow kicked Delia. I found her. Molly's taken to bed. Trent's been without hired hands the last couple of days. And we couldn't find you and didn't know where you were."

Stroking her red hair, Ty comforted her. "It'll be okay, Wilma." He knew the words were hollow, and that nothing could ever bring back Delia.

"And Trent and Molly are blaming each other. Trent took that horse out and shot it, a dozen times or more, like a madman. Ty, I can't stand much more of it."

"It won't be long now and you'll be with me at the Diamond S. I'll put you up in the hotel in Tascosa if it'll make it easier on you."

Wilma grew indignant, and Ty recoiled at her sudden change. "I'll not leave Molly, now. She needs me."

His arm around her waist, her head resting on his shoulder, they walked toward the house. At the back door, Ty could hear the baby crying and Molly humming to soothe him, but her voice was listless and defeated.

"She doesn't know you're here, Ty." Wilma closed the door.

Wilma stepped toward Molly's room, but Ty grabbed her. He shook his head and walked around her to the door, knocking softly on the facing. "Molly, it's Ty," he said meekly, and walked in.

Immediately, Molly began to cry. She was sitting up in her bed, her eyes bloodshot, her cheeks red and chapped, her face drawn and sad. The baby wailed in her arms.

"I came as soon as I got word, Molly. I'm terribly sorry."

Molly placed the baby in her lap and reached up for Ty. He bent over and hugged her and she returned the hug, tight and long, as if Ty were the only man she could hug that way now. "First Momma, then Pa, and now Delia," she sobbed. "You being shot. Trent mad about the election and crazy over Delia's death. Everything's going to hell, Ty."

He couldn't answer. Nothing made sense out of Delia's death. Ty sighed. He still had to confront Trent. Molly might have more sorrow to deal with before things settled down.

"We buried her when no one could find you, Ty. I feared something terrible might have happened to you."

Ty released Molly. "I was in the territory after rustlers. I came as soon as I found out."

Molly grabbed his hand. "I knew you would. She was so pretty when we buried her, Ty, in her Sunday dress, her arms wrapped around Kay-Lee, almost like a smile on her face. She's in . . . God's arms now." Molly broke down again, sobbing loudly. "With Momma and Pa to look after her."

Never had Ty felt so helpless. He patted Molly on the shoulder and retreated from the bed. Wilma stood in the door, helplessness in her eyes. Why Delia? Why a child who had harmed no one? Moving into the kitchen, Ty shrugged away his questions. There was no answer, just bad luck.

Ty plopped into a kitchen chair, propped his elbows on the table and rested his forehead in the palms of his hands.

Wilma walked up behind him, her hands rubbing his shoulders, softly. She hummed an old hymn, her voice as soft and soothing as her touch. Running her hand along his cheek, Wilma turned silent for a moment, the only sound the baby whimpering in the next room. "Maybe one day we can have a daughter, name her 'Delia,' " Wilma offered.

Ty nodded half-heartedly. It was a pleasant thought, sharing a child with Wilma, but that seemed so far into the future, when the present was confronting Trent Jackson.

"You must be tired. Can I fix you something to eat?"

Ty shook his head.

"Something's bothering you, Ty, something more than just Delia." Her hand fell away from his face and there was alarm in her voice. "Is it us? You giving up on marrying me, Ty, is that what's galling you?"

Ty shoved himself up from the table. "No!" His voice came out louder, more emphatic than he wanted. He could see the shock on Wilma's face. Before she could ask him something else, he grabbed her and pulled her to him, his lips finding hers. He felt the softness of her hair brushing the edges of his face and he lingered in the sweetness of her breath. At first she seemed startled, then confused. For a moment she fought against him, rebelling at his impulse. Then she softened and clung to him, sharing the moment with abandoned propriety. Ty loosened his grasp around her, his hands slipping to her arms. He broke from her lips and pushed her away gently, his eyes looking deep into hers. "Marrying you is the one thought, Wilma Jackson, that has pleased me these last few troubled days."

Wilma sighed. "So much happening, so much of it bad."

Ty frowned, then started to speak.

Wilma waved away any comment. "And you aren't staying?"

"I'm staying, Wilma, but in the barn. I want to talk to Trent, alone. It's men's business."

She lowered her head and folded her arms

across her breast. "It's trouble between you and Trent, isn't it?"

Ty exhaled a deep breath. "Nothing's easy any more, Wilma. Many things have changed. The thing that hasn't is that I love you and plan to marry you in two weeks. If that's not enough, let me know now, because there are things I have to do. Alone!"

Wilma had the eyes of a scolded puppy. She shrugged. "I wish you'd share your burden with me." Her words were loaded with resignation that her wish would not, could not, come true.

"I'll bed down in the barn, catch Trent when he comes back . . ."

"If he comes back," Wilma interrupted. "He's been staying away several nights, even the cold ones."

"I doubt Trent'll like my company after we talk, so I'll be leaving early in the morning."

"Will you . . . ," Wilma started.

Ty's finger touched her lips. "No more questions. I stand by my promise to marry you. Come wedding day, I'll meet you at the courthouse at one o'clock." He leaned over and kissed her gently on the cheek, then turned for the kitchen door.

"Be careful, Ty! Whatever happens, I love you!" Her words trailed him out into the cold. He shivered as he closed the kitchen door and headed for his horse and the barn. He untied the horse and led him through the gate and into the barn. Inside, he quickly uncinched the saddle, removed the reins and hung them on a stall wall, then tended to the animal's needs. From the feed bin he carried a scoop of grain and dumped it into the feed trough. His eyes had adjusted to the darkness enough that he found a bucket and marched outside to the water trough, breaking the layer of ice over the water and filling the bucket for the roan to drink. Finally, Ty tied the roan into a stall.

With his horse cared for, Ty edged his way in the barn's dimness to the back corner where a carpet of hay bordered a feed bin. Tossing his bedroll on the mat of hay, Ty unfurled it and sat down to wait in the darkness.

The time limped by and Ty grew drowsy with the wait. He had almost nodded off after two hours when he heard the roan whinny. Ty snapped to attention and slid his revolver out of his holster, just in case. The barn door creaked open and, against a starlit sky, Ty could see Trent striding ahead, his saddle in both hands. The roan neighed and Trent dropped the saddle, his hand going to his gun. Ty heard the click of the hammer cocked for firing. Ty lifted his own pistol, pointing it at Trent. His brother-in-law was still waving his pistol around when Ty spoke. "Trent, it's Ty."

"You fool," Trent cursed. "Good way to get killed. Where are you?"

"Put up your gun, Trent. I can see you, but you can't be sure where I am. When you put up your gun, we'll talk."

Trent hesitated.

"My gun's aimed at your gut, Trent. When yours goes back in the holster, so does mine." Ty heard Trent ease the hammer down on his revolver and saw him slide it back in his holster. Ty lowered his own gun.

"What the hell you doing out in the barn, Ty?"

"I had to talk to you, Trent, and I figured you might not come home for the night if you thought I was still here. You didn't seem so glad to see me when I came up."

For a moment, Trent didn't answer. By his silence, Ty knew he had pegged Trent on the head. But he wished he could see Trent's eyes so he could read them. When Trent spoke again, his words came out hard and insincere.

"You caught me at a bad time, surprising me at Delia's grave."

"I've got more surprises for you, Trent."

Trent hesitated before answering, as if the wheels of his mind were spinning for an explanation, turning over what Ty might know. "It's been a bad month, Ty — the election and then Delia. It can't get much worse."

"Maybe not, Trent, but Tom Higgins and Bill Witherspoon are dead." Ty let the sentence hang in the air like a noose, wondering if Trent would slip it around his neck.

Only silence answered — no surprise, no remorse, no emotion whatever. Now Ty knew for certain the rumors about Trent were not rumors. The dying Tom Higgins had not wasted his last breath with a lie.

"What are you getting at, Ty?"

Ty spat out his disgust. "Bob Vandiver and I killed them, Trent. They were herding Diamond S cattle into New Mexico Territory."

"Damn 'em." Trent struck his palm with his fist. "So they were the ones that were stealing cattle, here under my nose all the time."

Ty lifted his gun slowly toward Trent again. If Trent tried anything, it would be on reflex after Ty's next statement. "I'm not buying it, Trent. Before Tom died, he told me a few things, things like you and Dewey

Slater being in on it all along."

"He was lying, Ty." The shadow that was Trent braced itself as if he was about to draw his pistol. His arm moved slowly toward his side, then froze at the click of Ty cocking his pistol hammer.

"Been a lot of lying going on, Trent, and you've been the one responsible. There are other questions I've got, but won't ask, because if I found out you killed Pa, I'd kill you now."

"Lies, Ty; it's all lies." There was resignation in his voice. "It's all untrue."

"Shut up, Trent; you've done too much talking for your own good. Now, you're gonna listen."

"You don't have proof, Ty!"

Ty rose slowly to his feet and stepped toward Trent, hoping for a better view of his eyes. His gun was levelled at Trent's gut. "I got more proof on you than I did on the man I hanged. His blood weighs more on my conscience than your blood ever would, Trent. The beef you fed the folks before the election. Diamond S beef, not yours. I found the hides buried in the canyon."

"You put that gun in your holster now, Ty, and we'll settle it for sure. Gimme an even break."

"Like you gave Jake Shaw?"

Trent didn't answer.

Ty cleared his throat and spat on the barn floor. "If it weren't for Molly, I'd kill you right now, Trent Jackson. In two weeks, I'm marrying your sister, Trent. I don't want you at the wedding; I don't want you in Oldham County; I don't want you in the Panhandle."

"You're not running me out, Ty! Molly wouldn't go, anyway, not with my new son."

"Understand me, Trent. I'm not saying you and Molly are to leave. Just you. Molly stays. You just get up one morning, Trent, and you ride away. Forever. Or one night, you just forget to come home. Ever."

"I'm not running away." There was defiance in his voice, and anger. "I've worked too hard to build up this place."

"Nobody'd begrudge you, Trent, if it were honest work, but it wasn't. You turned this county on end with your crooked ways, making neighbor suspicious of neighbor, and all the time saying you were doing everything you could. Word's getting around, and most folks hate you for it. You're a dead man if you don't get out of Texas, Trent. If I don't kill you, others will. I should, by God. I vowed with Pa to the other regulators that I'd take care of my own men if they were the rustlers. I figure kin's included in that."

Trent bent over and picked up the saddle he had dropped at Ty's first sound. Turning back toward the barn door, he called back over his shoulder. "When you come for me, Ty, you best come shooting. Your likes'll never scare me away." He shoved his way through the door and into the corral, catching his horse, saddling him quickly and riding away into the darkness.

The horse's hooves had pounded into the distance before Ty lowered his gun and collapsed on his bedroll. Poor Molly! Soon, he drifted off into a fitful sleep that finally ended about an hour before sunrise. Not wanting to run into Molly or Wilma before he rode out, he gathered up his bedding and readied his horse for the ride to the Diamond S.

Leading his horse out of the barn, Ty was startled at the door to see lamplight seeping out of the kitchen window, and to smell woodsmoke. He pulled open the corral gate and led the roan out. He didn't feel much like seeing Molly. He had his foot in the stirrup when the kitchen door swung open.

"Ty," came a soft voice, Wilma's voice. "Ty, don't leave." There was an urgency in her voice, but she approached him cautiously.

His foot fell from the stirrup and he twisted around toward her. She held her hand high, awkwardly in front of her, as she advanced toward him. Then he smelled the aroma of coffee.

"I brought you this," she said, extending the tin cup. "I'd hoped you would stay for breakfast, but when Trent rode away last night, I figured you'd be leaving early."

Ty took the hot cup from her hand and sipped at the steaming liquid. He saw Wilma shiver in the cool morning air.

"Bad blood between you and Trent, isn't there, Ty?"

The coffee was good and it warmed up his insides. Wilma was caught in the middle, too, he realized, as he contemplated a reply. Poor Wilma! In love with a man who had threatened to kill her brother.

"Bad blood, isn't there?"

Ty swallowed his coffee hard. "I won't be welcome here anymore, Wilma."

"Trent's in trouble, isn't he? He's let the election ruin his life. He did something stupid, Ty, didn't he?"

"Could be."

"You've gotta tell me, Ty. Please?"

"He's your brother, Wilma."

"You're to be my husband, Ty."

Taking another sip of coffee, Ty shook his

head. Why were there always complications? Why couldn't she just accept his word that it would be better if she didn't know? It was something that had to be settled between men. A woman would only muddy the waters. "It's between me and Trent, Wilma." He offered her the empty cup. "Some things are a man's business, and not even his woman should know."

"Nor his wife, too? If you'll not trust me with your secrets, how can I trust you as a husband, Ty?"

"You think Trent shares everything he knows with Molly? I'll bet not," Ty spat out. He shoved the coffee cup at her.

"And that's why they're having troubles now, Ty."

Ty jerked himself atop his roan. "That's their problem, Wilma."

"And this is ours." Her voice quivered with emotion as she grabbed his coffee tin. "I'll not marry a man that won't trust me with his confidence."

Ty jerked his hat down tight and stared at Wilma with burning eyes. "I'll be at the courthouse at one on our wedding day. If you're there, we'll get hitched. If not . . ." He let the words hang heavy in the air, slapped the roan's flank and gave it free rein.

For a moment, he thought he heard a sob over the pounding hooves.

CHAPTER 19

In the hazy light of dawn, the blackened cottonwood tree down the trail appeared like a corpse suspended by an unseen rope from an amber sky, like the body of Jake Shaw come back to haunt him. Ty patted his revolver and then his pocket watch, another reminder of Jake Shaw. His roan twitched his head, his ears flicking back as if he had heard something. Ty pulled back on the reins and the gelding stopped. He listened and heard nothing, except his own breath and the horse's breath. Dawn slipped ghostlike across the land.

Ty twisted around in his saddle and stared back over his shoulder, toward the Jackson place, toward Wilma. In his mind, he could still hear her crying, as if she were mourning a love that had died, but nothing followed him in the canyon except the dawn muscling the night aside. Ty settled back into his saddle and glanced at the tree, its cadaverous mask gradually sliding away with the light. It was under that tree, with a storm rumbling in the distance, that Trent had organized the regulators. Under that tree had sprouted a malevolent seed that had killed an innocent Jake Shaw and likely his own father. Under that tree, Trent had betrayed all the big ranchers. And under that tree, Ty had sat before knowing Wilma Jackson. He had ridden from there ahead of the rain and surprised her and himself at Molly's clothesline. It all seemed recent, and yet so long ago.

"Damn you, Trent Jackson; you betrayed us all," Ty spat out. His frustration was wider than the gash in the tree. "Damn you, Trent Jackson. You betrayed Molly most of all."

Slapping his reins against the neck of his roan, Ty headed down the canyon, toward the deep shadows which still clung like death to the jagged crypts that were the canyon walls. Several times he glanced back over his shoulder, because he couldn't shake the idea that some threat was trailing him. Or was it just caution — the caution that comes after you are backshot once, the caution from realizing your brother-in-law is a thief, possibly even a murderer. It seemed as if the whole world was cautious. Not a bird sang, not a varmint moved, not a cow stirred, not even at the riverside where trails had been worn by thousands of milling hooves as the cattle came down for water.

The roan's steady stride could lull a man to sleep, especially one who had slept in a barn. By good light, Ty was nodding in the saddle, tired of so much trouble, when all he really wanted was to run the Diamond S as well as his father had. The sun peeked into the canyon now, and Ty enjoyed the soothing warmth that countered the chilled breeze coursing along the river.

On the wind's cold breath, Ty sniffed a faint aroma. At first it teased, then tickled his nose. A realization gradually pried its way into Ty's senses, and he suddenly shook the lethargy out of his head and scanned the canyon around him. It was narrower here, and the river squeezed the trail up against the sloping canyon wall peppered with boulders and rock. That faint aroma? The roan nickered. That faint aroma? Ty saw the flick of the roan's ears. The horse had heard something. That faint aroma was tobacco. Pipe tobacco! Dewey Slater?

Ty pitched forward in his saddle, reaching for his Winchester rifle. Just as his hand touched the wooden stock, he heard the zing of a bullet whiz by his head. A second shot echoed through the canyon, spooking the roan. Ty lost his balance for a moment as he jerked his carbine out of its saddle boot. Grabbing the saddle horn, he righted himself for an instant, then twisted out of the saddle and hit the ground on his feet just as the animal bolted for safety.

Dirt thrown up by a bullet at his feet splashed against his boots. Ty darted for the nearest boulder, diving behind it just as another bullet whined by him, then struck rock and ricocheted with a wail. Ty rolled over, squeezing off a shot at the rocks above him. Ty wriggled in his rocky den until he reached a spot offering a sheltered view of the canyon wall above him. There were a thousand places for Slater to hide. Slater could be there forever and Ty still not spot him.

As he studied the rocks, looking for his assailant, Ty felt a burning sensation in his shoulder, reminding him of the last time Dewey Slater had taken a backshot at him. Ty saw no movement. Slater could wait him out forever, unless Ty could get him to give his position away.

"Slater," Ty yelled, "you got me once, but not again."

The words echoed through the canyon. The only answer came in the whisper of the cold breeze.

"You're a sonuvabitch, Slater. Your days are numbered in Oldham County," Ty yelled.

Still, the only answer was an echo and then the silence. Slater wasn't going to fall for it.

"You killed Pa, didn't you? And Phipps and Baker? You sonuvabitch."

No answer, no movement, no clue to Slater's hiding place. Nothing!

Ty studied the canyon above him as best he could without exposing himself further. Ty had to draw Slater's fire long enough to spot him. Otherwise, he might be here all day or, for that matter, forever, if Slater's aim improved. He looked at the hiding places beside and behind him. If Ty had smelled the tobacco smoke, then Slater must not be too far away.

Taking a deep breath, Ty crawled on his hands and knees, then crouched, cradling the Winchester in his arms. He yelled, then dashed away from his hiding spot, watching the canyon above him. A shot exploded from the canyon wall and ricocheted off a rock as Ty passed. Chips of flying rock stung his back and spurred him ahead. A second shot plowed into the ground at his feet, but as it did, Ty spotted a puff of smoke by a crooked juniper tree with a wall of rocks around it.

Ty tripped and tumbled forward. Briefly exposed, he clambered toward a rock, losing his hat but managing to hold onto his rifle, just as another bullet ripped into the ground where he had been. Ty tasted dirt and his lips were dry. He lunged forward, behind a larger boulder, and drew himself into a crouch. Hugging the rock, he slowly worked around it until he could just see the juniper tree. Suddenly, he leaped up and squeezed off two shots at a flash of movement beside the tree. One shot was low, careening off a rock and whining down the canyon. The other thudded into the juniper tree, a small branch tumbling down behind the rock.

Figuring Slater wary of exposing himself for a moment, Ty darted across a small clearing and then jumped among a jumble of boulders. Ty crawled between two of them, grinning at the natural gunport he found looking up toward the juniper tree. He slid his rifle into the opening and wedged a stone into the crevice to steady his aim. Slowly, he sighted in on the tree, anticipating where Slater might show himself next.

For several minutes, the world was silent,

and Ty's finger trembled on the trigger. Suddenly, Slater popped up, his rifle trained on where Ty had been rather than where he was. Ty adjusted his aim slightly as Slater fired into the wrong rocks. Ty's finger pulled softly on the trigger. The rifle kicked into his shoulder and the retort rang in his ears. Slater screamed. The carbine slipped from his hands and clattered down the slope as Slater swatted at his hand, then disappeared.

Dammit. Ty had winged him, at best. Levering the still-smoking hull out of his Winchester, Ty studied the juniper and waited. With the carbine out of Slater's reach, Ty figured his chances for taking the former deputy had improved. Ty eased away from the sheltering rocks and climbed cautiously up the slope. Once, twice, three times, he advanced without Slater showing himself. Perhaps Slater was wounded worse than Ty figured.

Ty reached ten yards of open ground, studied the stillness around the juniper, then dashed into the clearing, just as Slater bolted up. Ty squeezed off an awkward shot from his rifle. Slater lifted his right arm, his revolver following Ty's course. The gun exploded and instantly Ty felt the kick of a mule in his stomach. He gasped for air and stumbled forward to the nearest rocks. His side throbbed. His hands dropped his rifle and grabbed at his stomach. His right hand slid down his stomach, expecting the soft, mushy feel of a bleeding gut wound. Instead, his hand rubbed over something as stiff as a bone. Ty gritted his teeth and glanced at his wound, expecting the worst. But there was no blood, and only a black hole in his coat. Patting at the wound, he felt a hard clump of metal in his vest. His watch? His grandfather's watch? Slater's bullet had hit the watch. Ty tugged at the watch chain and the watch came out reluctantly, its jagged edges catching in the vest pocket. His grandfather's watch was ruined, its springs and gears crushed and dripping from around a flat lead slug.

Except for the soreness and what would likely become a big bruise, Ty knew he was okay. He glanced at the juniper tree, observing no movement, then looked at his weapon behind him on the open ground. Ty jerked his pistol from its holster, crouched for a moment, then sprinted toward the rifle, firing a shot at the tree. Despite the ache in his side, he grabbed the rifle and dragged it by the barrel back to cover. Squeezing between a couple of rocks for a sheltered vantage point, he watched the juniper. Time passed on its hands and knees and the canyon seemed calm. Overhead a hawk circled and Ty caught the cooing of doves and the hackling call of a jay. From the distance, he thought he heard the sound of pounding hooves. He looked down the canyon from where he had come. In the distance, the galloping horse looked like Slater's, though he was too far away to be sure and the stakes were too high to let his guard down.

Ty studied the juniper. Nothing! Then he took in the terrain, plotting the route with the most cover to reach that den. From the cartridges in his belt, he reloaded his pistol and rifle. He shoved his pistol back in the holster, then darted from hiding spot to hiding spot. The only noise was the sound of his footfall and heavy breathing. In minutes, he was within twenty feet of the juniper and within reach of Slater's carbine. His nerves taut, Ty leaped forward, jumping from rock to rock until he stood by the juniper, looking down into Slater's den.

Slater was gone! Ty cursed. Slater had ridden off, down the canyon toward Jackson's place. Ty looked over Slater's lair, observing on the ground scattered cartridges, an empty whiskey bottle and the ash from Slater's pipe. And a single spot of blood! Ty had no more than nicked Slater. He cursed.

Slater's perch was thirty-five yards from the trail, close enough that he should have plugged Ty without any trouble. Ty toed at the empty whiskey bottle. Likely the whiskey Slater had consumed to fend off the cold had affected his aim.

Ty couldn't shake from his mind that Slater had ridden away toward Jackson's place. Even if Slater didn't go to Trent's, Slater's positioning seemed more than coincidence. Ty's mind slipped back to last night and his confrontation with Trent Jackson. The one-time sheriff had ridden away in the darkness and had not returned by dawn. Had Trent alerted Slater that Ty might be riding back home down the canyon today? The possibility seemed too real, the coincidence too great, for there not to be some credence to the thought.

"Damn Trent Jackson," Ty said aloud, booting the whiskey bottle into the rock. The bottle shattered much as Molly's world was shattering around her. A daughter just days in the grave and a scoundrel for a husband.

Ty spat at the glass shards, then walked around the rocks, heading back down the canyon slope, stopping to retrieve Slater's carbine. He carried both weapons under his arm, looking for signs of his roan as he walked. The ambush had spooked him, and no telling how far he might have gone. Ty whistled, shrilly, in the vain hope his horse might hear his call and return. Ty knew he was afoot. Reaching the trail, Ty pointed Slater's carbine skyward and fired four rounds until the carbine clicked empty. If anyone were nearby, perhaps they might respond to the gunshots. Only the cold wind answered his shots, and Ty headed toward the Diamond S afoot.

The sun was a low flame in the sky, providing warmth in the open but not enough in the shade. It gradually climbed, reaching its peak, then began to descend. Ty plodded along steadily, like the sun, wishing he had taken more than a cup of coffee before he left the Jackson place. It was late afternoon when Ty spotted two riders trailing a horse ahead on the trail. He quickly scampered for cover and checked the load in his carbine, just in case.

As the riders drew closer, Ty recognized one as Bob Vandiver and the other as one of his hands. Ty stepped out from behind a willow bush and whistled at them. Their heads lifted and turned in his direction. He waved and they pushed their mounts into a lope, Ty's roan trailing along behind.

The men rode over, nodding their heads

and holding back their grins. "Decided to take a little walk, did you?" Vandiver asked.

Ty nodded. "Good way to learn the land, fellows."

Both men laughed, until Vandiver pointed at Ty's coat. "Bullet hole?"

Ty nodded again, stepping around to his roan and slipping his rifle in its boot.

"Damn, you're tougher than we thought, taking a gutshot like that," the sheriff said.

"Watch saved me," Ty said, strapping Slater's carbine to the saddle, then mounting up and turning toward the Diamond S.

"Know who did it?" Vandiver asked.

Ty nodded. "Dewey Slater! I got his carbine, but he got away." Ty offered it to Vandiver.

"Just confirms what we've suspected all along," Vandiver said, waving the carbine away.

They rode the rest of the way in silence, reaching the Diamond S a couple of hours before dusk. Ty dismounted and told his cowhand to tend to his roan for him. Then he invited the sheriff up to the house for a bite and some coffee.

"Damn shame Slater got away, Ty; it'd saved me some work!"

"Shame you rode out this way for nothing."

Vandiver shook his head. "I had business to talk with you about." His voice was cold and serious. "I told you, Ty, I'd not lift a hand against Trent without first letting you know. I've got the final proof that Trent's been involved in all this rustling."

Ty gave a low whistle. "I've kept wishing it wasn't so, for Molly's sake. Poor Molly!"

CHAPTER 20

The dry slats on the porch moaned as Ty opened the door for Bob Vandiver and motioned him inside. The house was cold, and Ty headed for the kitchen to make a pot of coffee. As Ty lit a lamp, the sheriff threw his hat down on the table and straddled a chair, propping his elbows on the chairback and holding his head between his hands. "Wish it weren't so, Ty."

Opening the black stove door with a clang, Ty stacked wood and kindling inside, then pulled a match from his cigarette tin and struck it against the stove. The flame took to the kindling with a dance and a crackle. Ty held his hands up to the stove door, the warmth thawing out the stiffness in his fingers. He fiddled with the coffeepot, filling it from the water bucket by the door and dumping a couple of scoops of coffee in it. After dropping the pot on the stove, he worked on a cigarette and stood there inhaling the tobacco smoke, all the while wondering where it had gone wrong with Trent Jackson. The cigarette was down to a nub between his thumb and forefinger before Ty turned around and stared at the sheriff. "It's been a bad year, Bob."

Stroking his chin, the sheriff nodded. "Especially hard on you Stoddards."

Ty stared at the sheriff and Vandiver never flinched. "I'm not disputing you, Bob, but what's your proof on Trent?"

"Walt Storm came across one of Jackson's cattle on the Lightning Bolt spread. The yearling had broken his leg somehow, and Storm shot him, gutted him and carried the carcass home for meat. The original brand had been blotted, and when he skinned it, he found the hide had been a Lightning Bolt animal, rebranded with Jackson's brand. Storm hasn't sold cattle to Trent."

"Fact is, Bob, somebody else could've done it, Dewey Slater or the two hands we killed."

Vandiver nodded. "There's more."

Ty coaxed the last breath from his cigarette, opened the stove firebox door and tossed the remains into the hot flame, which consumed it as quickly as Vandiver's story was burning the remnants of his faded hope that somehow Trent Jackson might be vindicated.

"Walt's not bashful, and he rode over to Trent's place to confront him with it, in case it was one of his men. Walt rode down the canyon and spotted a man by the river, acting suspicious. He drew up into the canyon and watched."

"Trent?" Ty asked.

Vandiver nodded slowly. "Yes, sir, Trent Jackson himself, burying something."

Ty remembered the Diamond S hides he and Wilma had found. "Hides?"

Vandiver did not have to answer. Ty could read the truth in the sheriff's eyes.

"Two hides — another Lightning Bolt animal and one of mine, a Double Deuce! I've got the hides back at the jail if you care to see them."

With a wave of his hand and a shake of his head, Ty accepted the sheriff's word as truth.

"Everybody's been losing cattle, Ty — everybody but Trent. His herds haven't been touched by rustlers."

"I talked at gunpoint with Trent last night, Bob, told him to get out of Oldham County, to leave Molly and the baby here."

The sheriff shrugged. "I was elected to do a job, Ty, and I can't allow him that opportunity, not with so much pointing against him. I'll arrest and jail him, see that he gets a trial. That's more than he did for that kid we hung on his place."

Ty's wadded fist hit his palm. "That's been weighing heavy on me, too, Bob."

"I'm riding there from here to take him in, Ty."

"No, Bob, don't go alone. Trent won't be taken by a single man. Get the regulators together and I'll ride with you. We'll meet in town tomorrow after dark and ride out before dawn."

"We're not nightriders anymore, Ty."

"Trent's always armed, except when he milks the cow for the baby in the morning and evening. We catch him then, we may keep someone from getting hurt."

"No tricks, Ty. I'm holding you to your word. If you tried to warn him, I'd take poorly to it," Bob said, pushing himself out of his chair.

Ty's jaw tightened. "He'd likely kill me if I tried."

"Sorry it's come to that, Ty." Vandiver picked up his hat and pulled it down tight. "I best ride on and get the word out. I'll take you up on that cup of coffee when it's over. Meet you at the courthouse tomorrow night." Vandiver marched away.

The sheriff carried his badge well, Ty thought. Shame Trent hadn't! Ty engineered another cigarette and then watched it go up in smoke. Like the cigarette, his energy was long consumed, and he just stared blankly at the stove, enjoying its heat but little else. Maybe Trent would just ride away tomorrow, get out of Oldham County forever, abandon Molly and his new son so his transgressions would not stain them. That would be easier on Molly than seeing her husband convicted as a thief.

The coffee finally boiled and Ty fetched a tin cup and the pot and plopped them on the table. He finished one, then a second, and finally a third cup, the coffee settling like stiff medicine in his stomach. He lifted the lid on the dutch oven sitting on the stove and found a couple of leftover biscuits from a previous meal. The biscuits were heavy as rocks, but he gnawed on them anyway. Unpalatable as they were, they beat trying to fix something for himself. He wondered if his meals would always be this poor. Would Wilma still want to marry him after he helped arrest her brother? He wasn't even sure she would marry him now, not after their last exchange. Damn the luck!

The biscuits sat on his stomach about as easily as Trent's problems sat on his mind, and he dragged himself to bed, his muscles aching with exhaustion, his mind mulling over questions that only time could answer. Sleep came slowly and ended early, but he just lay in bed under three quilts, watching the room lighten with the dawn, knowing that in twenty-four hours he would be waiting for Trent to milk the cows, waiting with the others to take Trent. And worrying how Molly would react and, even more, how Wilma would handle it.

The day crawled by and Ty couldn't keep his mind on what minor chores he tried around the place. As dusk arrived, he was relieved finally to saddle his roan and mount up. The breeze was stiff and he shivered as he rode into its face. He pulled the kerchief Molly had bought for him around his neck while he recovered in hers and Trent's bed. That now seemed like a different life. Delia and Pa were alive then, and the baby was just a hope. And nobody suspected Trent of doing anything but stretching himself too thin to give his wife and family the best that he could. And Jake Shaw was still alive instead of hanging from a tree by Ty's hand. And Phipps and Baker were still alive and waiting their pay from Trent.

Ahead of him, Tascosa was bejeweled with a strand of lights and perfumed with woodsmoke. Ty rode around town, coming up behind the courthouse. A half-dozen horses were tied to the hitching post in front, and lamplight seeped out around the closed shutters in the sheriff's office. Ty dropped from the saddle and tied his horse beside the others. Stamping his feet, he stared around him with the uneasy feeling that everyone must know the plan, but the street was empty. He turned and walked through the gate and up the courthouse steps unnoticed. The muffled voices he heard from the sheriff's office went silent as he pushed open the courthouse door.

The courthouse was as hot as usual and Ty unbuttoned his coat in the dim hallway light. Only so many things a man had control over in this life, and how the commissioners burned so much wood was not one of them. Just as Ty reached the door, it parted enough for Vandiver to stick out his head, then opened all the way. Ty was blinded by the bright light from three lamps. When his eyes adjusted, he found himself staring into the barrels of three revolvers and a couple of carbines. The regulators were there, all grim-faced as they lowered their guns.

Ty nodded around the room. He felt their hard stares boring into him. A couple shifted in their chairs and slid their feet across a wooden floor polished slick from wear.

"And you're a man of your word, just like your pa," Vandiver said, as he moved over to a chair by the black bars of the jail.

"I'll go along with that," interjected Zack Miller, his bullwhip tucked under his arm. Miller was now the last of the original Oldham County pioneers.

Red Stewart edged toward Ty. "Fact is, Tyrus, we know you're in a tight, Molly being Trent's wife and you being sweet on Trent's sister."

Ty felt his face grow flush.

"Nobody'd fault you," Stewart said, "for throwing in your cards on this hand."

Man to man, the others nodded, the Mason Brothers, Stan Ballard, Mart Bigsby and Walt Storm. Ty saw that what he had mistaken as suspicion in their eyes was concern, men offering him a way out of his spot, a way out without malice. But Ty had given his word to them and to Trent Jackson, who had betrayed them all. Ty couldn't back away now, not with his pa dead, likely killed with Trent's knowledge. Along with the other regulators, he had vowed to take care of his own, if it came to that. He must abide by his word, even if it meant turning his sister against him, even if it meant losing Wilma.

Taking off his hat, Ty rolled the brim in his hand for a moment, not knowing what to say to the men's gesture. "You're good men. Come morning, I'll ride out with good men."

"We figured as much, Ty," Vandiver said, "but wanted to give you the chance. We aim to leave town a couple of hours before dawn, ride down the canyon and come up on Trent's place from the canyon side. Half of us'll take Trent and the rest of us'll follow the river about four miles east. There's an old shack back up in the rough country where Dewey Slater may be hid out. Which group you want to ride with, Ty?"

Ty stood up straight and spoke with a firm voice. "Trent's bunch."

Vandiver nodded. "Men, there's no way we're gonna talk him out of it. So, let's get some rest and meet here in front of the courthouse, come three-thirty. You fellows leave here in ones and twos and don't attract any attention. Nobody is to visit any saloons or do any drinking tonight," Vandiver said, staring at Red Stewart.

Stewart stroked his red beard and swore silently.

"You fellows understand that?" All answered or nodded except Stewart. "Red?" Vandiver called across the room.

Stewart held up his hand and swatted at the air, as if he were trying to make Vandiver's command go away. "I heard you, but if I freeze to death tonight because I don't have a little firewater in my gut, I'll come back and haunt you."

"Hell, Red," Vandiver answered, "you've haunted and pestered us for years, and you ain't even dead yet."

The men laughed with Red and began to grab their coats and slip out the door in pairs. Vandiver nodded toward Ty. "You got a place to stay tonight, Ty?" the sheriff asked, when the last of the others closed the door.

"I figured there'd be a room at the hotel. If not, I'll stay at the stable."

Vandiver pointed to the cot. "That's where I'll sleep, though it's not as good as my other bed." The sheriff pointed to the jail cell. "You're welcome to it. The mattress is new straw."

"Just as well," Ty answered. "I've never spent a night in jail before." Then a sinking feeling came over him. Maybe the men didn't want him riding with them tomorrow. Maybe Vandiver planned to lock him in during the night. "You wouldn't lock me up during the night to keep me from riding with you?"

Vandiver angled his head at Ty, his brow furrowed, his nose wrinkled. "What?"

"Keep me penned up and from riding with you?"

A strange grin crept like a ghost across his face. "Hadn't thought about it, Ty."

Seeing the surprise in Vandiver's eyes, Ty shrugged and waved his concern away. "Dammit, Bob, I'll be glad when this is all done. Worst thing about this rustling and killing is it's made everybody suspicious."

"Forget it," the sheriff said. "Maybe we're about to get some of this settled."

They talked a bit more while they readied their beds; then Vandiver blew out the lamps and they settled in for the night, the sheriff on the cot and Ty on the jail bed, the bed where Trent would spend tomorrow night. By his snoring, Ty knew Vandiver had had no trouble getting to sleep, but he took longer before he settled into the haze that was rest.

He forgot where he was, and when he heard a noise across the room, he shot up from his bed.

"You okay? It's time to ride."

Ty recognized Vandiver's voice and felt foolish. "Yeah!" He shook his head, then rubbed at his eyes and pushed his way out of bed.

Silently, both men pulled on their boots, then gathered their coats and guns. The bitter cold slapped them fully awake when they marched outside to their horses. Other regulators were approaching the courthouse and Ty and Vandiver mounted and turned their horses to meet the others.

Vandiver counted men. All were present. With a wave of his arm, they rode silently down Court Street toward the gentle slopes which led to the river. The cold air bit at their cheeks and dried out their lips and slipped under their coats and became a stiffness in their fingers. Eventually they came to the trail that led to Jackson's place. Half followed the sheriff up that trail, the rest heading for Slater's supposed hideout on down the canyon. As they neared the canyon rim, Ty nudged his roan up with the sheriff's mount.

"Cold one!" Vandiver shivered.

Ty nodded. "If we ride up before he heads to milk the cow, we may have a fight on our hands. I'll walk up to the rim and spy him out. Once I see him enter the barn, I'll wave my hat and the rest of you come up at a walk. We'll have time to catch him before he gets back to the house."

Vandiver looked toward the sky, which was paling pink around the fringes, and nodded. "Maybe forty-five minutes before dawn. Our timing's right. Now, if Trent just plays along."

When they came within fifty yards of the top, Vandiver motioned for the riders to halt. Ty slid out of his saddle and stamped his feet as he handed his reins to Vandiver. He studied the men around him, realizing for the first time that he hadn't paid attention to who had ridden with Vandiver and who had gone on for Slater. With him now were Zack Miller, the bullwhip coiled around his shoulder, Red Stewart, and Walt Storm.

Ty slapped his arms against his chest to beat off the cold, but only sunrise and a strong sun would help now. He plodded up the trail, stopping at the rim and hiding behind a pile of rocks. Settling onto the cold ground, he heard his teeth chatter while his whole body convulsed with shivers. Several horses trotted around the corral, a good sign that Trent was in the house, which brooded in the darkness, sullen and still. For a half hour, Ty saw nothing but the earth's gradual preparations for a new day.

Then he saw a glow in the kitchen window as someone lit a lamp, and moments later smoke began to rise from the stovepipe. The aroma of burning wood gradually reached Ty's nose, and he was jealous of the heat it was giving to someone while he shivered under the fading stars. After a time long enough for someone to boil a pot of coffee and swallow a couple of cups of the brew, the back door of the house swung open, then shut hard, and Ty saw Trent Jackson emerge, a milk pail in one hand, his other hand in the pocket of his heavy coat. Trent stepped off the back porch and angled away from the barn, stopping at the cross where Delia was buried. Trent took off his hat and bowed his head, standing motionless for a full minute. Then he replaced his hat and headed for the barn, a stoop in his shoulders that Ty hadn't noticed when he came out of the house. After Trent disappeared in the barn, Ty stood up and waved his hat.

Vandiver and the others advanced. They all paused while Ty accepted the reins to his roan and mounted. Zack Miller was slipping the bullwhip off his shoulder as Ty settled into his saddle.

"Ride in quiet and easy," Vandiver commanded. "He shouldn't be armed, but be careful."

Ty nodded that he was ready and the men nudged their horses ahead. The men rode two, abreast until they reached the flat land that fanned out toward the Jackson buildings and the rest of the Panhandle. They spread out and moved quietly toward the barn, drawing up on their reins and waiting wordlessly. Ty glanced over his shoulder at the house, but saw no signs of activity by the women. Turning away from the house, his gaze fell upon Delia's grave and he felt a lump of regret in his throat, regret that it had come to this — Delia dead and her father a crook and cheat. The creaking of the barn door snapped Ty's senses back to reality.

The barn door parted enough for Trent Jackson to scurry out, a pail of milk in his hand. He was moving quickly to get back to the warmth of the house, and at first he did not see the riders. As he dropped the latch on the barn door and turned to the house, he froze as if the cold wind had caught up with him for good. Beneath the dark brim of his hat, his eyes widened with surprise, then narrowed with anger as he looked at the men.

"Morning, Trent," Vandiver said, "we've come to arrest you."

Trent stood motionless, only his eyes moving, their arc going face to face around the posse. For a moment, the silence was broken only by the wind which whistled around the corner of the barn. Trent cocked his head and spoke with a challenge in his voice. "Arrest me for what?"

"Stealing cattle we can prove, Trent, and I figure there's a killing or two you were involved in," Vandiver answered. "You can come along peacefully or we can settle things here."

Trent's gaze moved from Vandiver to Ty. Trent licked his lips. "You put them up to this, Ty?"

"Everyone's figured you out, Trent. You should've cleared out long before now."

"Put down your pail of milk, Trent, and unbutton your coat," Vandiver ordered. "If you're wearing a gunbelt, we'll have to ask you to drop it."

Slowly, Trent squatted until the pail touched ground, the handle clinking against the side as he released it. Slowly, his hands moved to his coat and his fingers loosened the buttons and spread his coat. Trent wasn't wearing his gunbelt. Ty let out a breath of relief.

"Fine, Trent; we'll saddle up your horse and take you to town."

Trent nodded and rebuttoned his coat with his reddened fingers. He clasped his frigid hands together and blew into them, trying to return some of the warmth that the milking had taken out of him. He clapped his hands together several times, then slid them into his coat pocket, as he stamped his feet and shook his shoulders against the cold.

Red Stewart dismounted and gave his reins to Ty while he stepped over to the corral to saddle a horse for Trent Jackson.

Ty studied Trent, who mirrored his hard gaze.

Trent scowled at him. "You put 'em up to this, didn't you?"

"What's it matter, Trent? You always thought you were smarter than the rest of us, but you got caught. You've caused enough misery on Oldham County, on your family, on the Stoddards."

"You Stoddards; hell, you think you own the county."

"Maybe so, Trent, but at least we didn't try to steal it from our neighbors like you."

A perverse smile spread across Trent's lips like a stain. His coat quivered as his right hand came slowly from his coat. The smile evaporated as his hand cleared the coat pocket and his eyes flamed with hate. A pistol appeared in his hand. It swung in a deadly arc toward Ty.

Ty froze as the pistol pointed at his face.

He was staring into the bore, a tiny opening that seemed to gape all the way to eternity. Ty could see Trent's thumb pulling back the hammer, yet he seemed paralyzed to do anything. Ty saw Trent's trigger finger tighten. Ty gritted his teeth against impending death. The air snapped with a crack; then there came a blast of gunfire. Ty sat mesmerized as Trent's gun flew from his hand; he heard the whiz of a bullet overhead. The gun tumbled to Trent's feet. Instantly, Jackson fell to his feet, upending the milk pail. Just as Trent's hand touched the gun, the air snapped again and Zack Miller's bullwhip jerked the pistol out of Trent's grasp.

CHAPTER 21

Around Ty, all was commotion. Horses bucked and kicked. Vandiver was yelling at Trent not to move. Zack Miller cracked his whip again. Trent screamed and grabbed his ear. A rivulet of blood appeared between Trent's fingers. Ty's roan danced skittishly among the other animals. Ty jerked his revolver and cocked the hammer as he reined the roan in.

"Gimme my gun," Jackson yelled. "I'll not get a fair chance if you take me in."

"A fair chance like you gave Jake Shaw," Ty yelled. "You knew Slater had set him up and you let us hang him anyway."

Behind him, a scream pierced the air and Ty twisted in his saddle, swinging his pistol around in a deadly arc. He grimaced at Molly, running from the house in her nightclothes. Behind her, Wilma stood at the kitchen door. She was crying.

"Leave my husband be," Molly screamed;

then she stopped in her tracks, confused at what she saw and stunned to see Ty a part of it. "Ty? What's happening?"

"Gimme a gun, you cowards," Jackson pleaded, slumping to his knees. "Let me have my chance now."

"Trent," Molly cried, "what's going on?" She ran to his side and wiped at the blood dripping from the facial cut, squatting beside him and holding his head against her shoulder. Realizing she was standing in a spot of mud, she looked from Trent to the pail and back at her husband. "The milk?" She began to sob. "Don't let them take you, Trent." She glanced from Trent to the other faces surrounding her with drawn guns. Her tearful gaze settled on Ty and she shivered. "What has gone wrong, Ty, what?" Her voice rang with desperation, her pleading rang hopeless. "Ty, what is it?"

Her words knifed into him. His awkwardness lumped in his throat and he just stared, feeling so foolish with his gun in his hand while Trent, in Molly's arms, seemed so helpless on his knees in a puddle of milk.

"What is it, Ty? You owe me an answer!"

Ty coughed and the lump seemed only to lodge deeper in his throat. He coughed again and his words came out in a rasp. "Trent's in a bit of difficulty."

"Why?" she demanded amid tears and sobs. "Why?"

"Stealing cattle," Ty blurted out. "Stealing cattle and maybe worse, Molly! Your husband's a cattle thief."

"No! No!" she screamed, the desperation rising. "It's not true, it's not true! Tell them, Trent, it's not true! It's not, is it, Trent?"

Trent stared blankly ahead. "They wouldn't believe me ever. Just remember, Molly, I love you and I've done nothing more than try to provide for you and the kids — I mean the baby."

Molly sobbed as Trent turned his lips to her cheek and kissed her gently. Slowly, Trent eased himself away from her and stood up, then helped her to her feet. "Get back inside, Molly, before you catch a chill. The baby still needs you."

Molly rose, her color drained from fear, and stared listlessly ahead as she stepped toward the house.

"We'll get this cleared up, Molly, we will," Trent called. The defeat in his voice betrayed him, but Molly, still stunned from events, seemed not to notice as she retraced her steps to the house. Wilma rushed out to help her up the porch and inside. Shutting the door behind Molly, Wilma stepped tentatively toward Ty.

Releasing the hammer on his pistol, Ty slid the revolver back in his holster as Wilma approached awkwardly. He tried his best to smile, but he couldn't bring himself to, not under the circumstances. Wilma dabbed at her eyes and seemed not to have it in herself to smile. Near Ty's roan, she reached out for Ty's hand. She held it against her tear-moistened cheek and patted it softly. "I knew it would be hard, Ty, but not this hard, not on Molly, not after so much pain for her these last few months."

Ty pulled his hand from hers and stroked her auburn hair, still mussed from a night's sleep. "I'm sorry for your brother, Wilma, and for you and Molly. Wish it weren't so, but there's too much for it all to be coincidence."

"Poor Trent!"

"And it's worse, Wilma. More than you need to know, but it's worse than just rustling."

She shook her head. "His life and Molly's are in ruins now, Ty, but what about ours, you and me? Are you still interested in me?" There was fear in her voice, and her head sagged as her eyes stared at the ground.

Ty dismounted and stepped to her. With his index finger, he lifted her chin, which was pimpled from the cold. "I've always been interested in you, Wilma. That didn't change when I rode away from you last time, but sometimes a man just can't tell all he knows, even to his woman or even to his wife. If you'll stand by me, I'll marry as we agreed."

Wilma stepped in to him, wrapping her arms around him and kissing him on the cheek and whispering, "I'll be there no matter what, Tyrus Bartholomew Stoddard."

Behind him, Ty heard Vandiver ordering Trent into the saddle. Red Stewart tied Trent's hands together, then lashed them to the saddle horn. "Funny, ain't it, Trent, that you organize the regulators, and the biggest rat we snag is you?"

"Enough said," Vandiver cut in.

Stewart twisted around and stared at the sheriff. "First you won't let me drink; now you're trying to keep me from talking. Haven't you heard of the U.S. Constitution?"

Vandiver laughed. "If the others caught Dewey Slater, Red, I'll buy drinks and let you jaw all night long."

Ty stroked Wilma's hair. "I must ride in with them, see this through to the end. I figure Molly'll want to stay in town for a while. I'll get you and her rooms at the Exchange Hotel until this is settled."

Quickly, he turned from Wilma and pulled himself into the saddle.

"I'll miss you, Ty," Wilma said, then ran to the house.

Vandiver pointed the way and Trent nudged his gelding toward Tascosa. Behind him lay his wife, his ranch, and his dreams, as empty now as the overturned milk pail. The regulators rode in silence, each man lost in his own thoughts, each staring at the back of the man who had betrayed them.

As they approached Tascosa, the news seemed to precede them. Folks on the street stopped and stared and those inside their warm buildings scurried out into the cold, eyeing the passing posse, pointing at the former sheriff, nodding their own thoughts to their neighbors. This spectacle embarrassed Ty. By marriage, Trent had done the Stoddard name wrong, and it angered Ty.

Ty felt his shame ease when the posse reached the courthouse and led Trent into jail. A sullen Jackson retreated into the cell corner and collapsed on the stool. Members of the posse lingered, waiting to hear how the others had managed with Dewey Slater. For more than an hour, Vandiver waited by the window, staring at the street. "They're back," Vandiver finally called, "all of them."

The men rushed outside, forsaking their coats.

Walt Storm answered the question before it could be asked. "He got away, Sheriff!"

Vandiver cursed.

"There was a fire in the fireplace and a pot of coffee boiling, but he was nowhere to be found. We searched the area good, but found nothing."

"Men, you best ride careful until Slater's found," Vandiver warned, then retreated into the courthouse, leaving the others to swap stories about Trent's capture and Slater's escape.

Ty mounted and rode away for the Exchange Hotel to arrange rooms for Molly and Wilma. That done, he walked over to Harvey Worley's restaurant, settled into a window table, and ate an early lunch alone, waving off any attempts at conversation by the proprietor. The food was palatable and rested easily in his famished stomach. As he was finishing up his meal, he saw a wagon pass by with Wilma and Molly, in her arms a bundle of quilts that would be the baby. Now his meal didn't rest so easily on his stomach. He dreaded facing Molly, dreaded telling her the truth about Trent.

After allowing time for the wagon to reach the hotel, Ty pushed himself away from the table and escaped outside into the cold, untied his horse, and led him down the street to the stables. Abe Polk, the smithy and liveryman, was hunkered near the stove in his office with three other men. Their conversation went dead when Ty marched inside.

"I put my roan in the back stable," Ty said, as he nodded his greetings around the room. He tossed a couple of coins from his pocket toward the proprietor. "That's for some extra grain." Polk nodded and stood up, hitching his overalls up and pushing his way through the cluster of chairs circling the hot stove. "Take care of it right now."

Ty followed him out into the stable, breezy with cold drafts of air that seemed to come straight from the north pole. "Lot of hard feelings about Trent Jackson," Polk said. "Everybody's saying he's a two-face thief, stealing cattle, not paying his bills in town, and some are saying he was involved in the killings of Phipps, Baker, and your father, Ty."

"Nobody's certain," Ty responded.

Polk whistled as he slit the top of a sack of grain and dished a couple of scoops into a feed trough. The roan attacked the food vigorously. "I've never seen the mood of Tascosa turn hostile so quick. A lot of rumors are flying about. Tonight'll be dangerous night."

"The law'll handle it," Ty answered, and turned away.

"The law can't handle a whole town," Polk replied.

Ty strode outside into the cold. He saw Molly's wagon tied outside the Exchange Hotel, but didn't feel like heading there, so he moved on down the street, turning into the Equitable Saloon and ignoring the stares as he took the back table. The barkeep was a barrel of a man who dispensed his whiskey straight and his advice only when asked. Just the type of man Ty felt like dealing with today.

The barkeep wandered over from behind the bar, carrying a bottle of liquor and a glass. "A little something to warm your innards?"

Ty nodded and the barman placed the bottle and glass on the table in front of him. Ty unbuttoned his coat and dug into his vest for cigarette fixings. He took his time building a smoke, then enjoying it. When he was done, he uncorked the bottle and poured himself a healthy glass, sipping on it occasionally, but mostly just staring off into space, thinking it all through, the events of the last few weeks.

Come dusk, the bottle was half empty and Ty still hadn't figured things out, knew he never would as long as he kept looking for the answer at the bottom of a bottle. As he was about to pour himself another glass, he saw a rider race by on the street, shouting for the sheriff. What could it be now? He shrugged, then finished pouring his glass. Letting each swallow settle before taking the next, Ty had just taken a second sip from his latest glass when the saloon door burst open and a man with wild eyes shot in.

"You folks heard Dewey Slater's coming to town to bust out Trent Jackson? Could be trouble!"

"What?" boomed the barkeep, his hands on his hips.

"Fellow just rode into town seen Dewey Slater and a couple dozen men coming this way."

A murmur went through the saloon's patrons.

"Slater couldn't find a dozen men in Oldham County to ride with him even if he paid them," the barkeep announced, turning to the bar and wiping a shine on it. "Are you sober, mister?"

"Damn right, I'm sober. I'm just passing on what I heard." The man spun around and went to look for a more receptive saloon.

Ty shoved himself away from the table and left money for the damage he'd done the bottle. His appetite was building and he had had liquor enough, so he headed toward Harvey Worley's for a little supper. There, he would decide whether to ride back home for the night or stay in town. If Dewey Slater were to ride into Tascosa tonight, Ty wanted to be around to take a shot or two at him.

Down the street, Ty saw a knot of men gathered outside another saloon, gesturing and arguing among themselves. A fight, Ty guessed, and stepped off the plank sidewalk onto the street, pausing a moment to steady himself at the hitching post. He could go to the hotel, probably get a room, but he didn't want to run into Molly tonight. Maybe tomorrow, but not tonight. Maybe he should have gone home this afternoon instead of spending it in the saloon. He might just sleep in the stable tonight if he could convince Polk to let him sleep in the office by the stove. He strode down the street toward Harvey Worley's, figuring he would at least fill his stomach before retiring.

As he pushed his way into the restaurant, he saw Bob Vandiver finishing off his meal at a window table. Twice, the sheriff leaned his head against the window, looking down the street at the gathering crowd. Ty weaved among the tables toward Vandiver's place. For a moment, the sheriff ignored Ty as he stared out the window. Glancing back to the table, he saw Ty and nodded. "Have a chair, Ty. It's gonna be a long night."

Ty slid into a chair, dropped his hat on the table and propped his elbows beside it. "Been a long day, Bob!"

"I wish it were over, Ty. Trouble's boiling. A lot of bad blood's rising against Trent Jackson. And word's around that Slater's riding into town to save Trent." Vandiver took a swipe at a puddle of gravy with his bread, then glanced outside.

"I reckon people got a right to be riled," Ty said, as Harvey Worley walked up. "Gimme what Bob's got, and plenty of coffee."

Worley moved on to another table.

"Maybe they've got a right to be riled, Ty, but they don't have a right to take things into their own hands. Trent's got a right to a fair trail. Some men gathered down by the saloon don't feel the same way."

Ty thought back to Jake Shaw, hanged in the canyon without a trial. An innocent man, hanged. Ty knew Trent was guilty, but he figured there'd be a lot of men in that crowd by the saloon that had about as much evidence on Trent as he had had on Jake Shaw. Bad medicine, a mob.

Vandiver sighed. "I figure Trent deserves to be hanged, Ty; that's the straight truth about how I feel, but, dammit, I took an oath to uphold the law. I can't let them take the law into their own hands or make me break my oath."

"You'll manage, Bob."

Vandiver picked up his tin of coffee and studied it for a good while. He took a sip, then shook his head. "I'll manage, Ty. I just hope I don't have to kill any of my friends to do it." The sheriff unfolded himself from the table and picked his hat off the adjacent chair. He seemed to speak as much to himself as to Ty. "I don't want to kill any of my neighbors." Vandiver marched to the door and out into the street. From the window, Ty could see him standing and staring toward the gang of men down the street. Vandiver's words seemed burned in Ty's brain. Unlike Trent, Vandiver was a man who took his oath seriously, and now he was facing a deadly dilemma. Dammit, how things never seemed to work out fairly for men who deserved it.

Harvey Worley showed up with a plate of hot food and shoved it in front of Ty.

"Coffee'll be here in a minute." Worley picked up Vandiver's plate, utensils and cup. "I'll be damned," Worley said. "Bob forgot to pay for his meal."

"I'll pay," Ty said, shoving his hand in his pocket and pulling out enough coins to cover both meals. "This'll do for both of us, and keep the difference, Harvey. Bob's got a lot on his mind tonight."

The dishes clattered as Harvey shifted them in his hand to take the money. "I've never seen the town like this, Ty. I expect trouble."

Ty shook his head and attacked his food, not out of hunger as much as frustration. Events had a way of building their own momentum, something that couldn't be changed. And Trent, the cause of it all, was sitting in jail out of reach of the summary justice that he had allowed to take Jake Shaw's life. Damn! And Trent likely knew that Slater killed Phipps and Baker. And he had done nothing about it. Slater likely killed Ty's own father, and Trent did nothing about it. Even when Ty took the bullet in the back, Trent found him and brought him in for dead. He had to know Slater had ambushed him, and yet the sheriff had done nothing about it. The food was as salty and bitter as the memories. Worley brought coffee, filled a tin for Ty, and left the pot.

Outside, the sky was darkening like the mood of the mob at the end of the street. The men's threats drifted in the air. There would be trouble if the mob started for the courthouse, because Vandiver was a man of his word, a man who believed an oath was a sacred vow. Ty remembered an oath of his own, made under a cottonwood tree, the day the regulators were formed. By his word, he had sworn to take care of the rustlers if they were his own people. Trent was his own people, whether he liked it or not. And now the mob down the street would force Bob Vandiver to pay for Ty's broken vow. Ty gulped down another swallow of coffee.

"Dammit," he said, and slammed his coffee cup into the table. He could feel the stares of the other customers boring into him. He kicked his chair over as he stood up. He grabbed his hat, then barged out the door into the street, stopping a moment to stare at the mob, still liquoring up outside the saloon, still talking big.

Ty marched toward the courthouse, spotting the movement of a shutter behind one of the barred windows in the sheriff's office. Vandiver was watching the street, waiting for the mob to screw up its courage. Ty

343

climbed the steps and grabbed the court-house doorhandle. The door didn't budge. The sheriff had barred it. Ty pounded on the door. "Bob, Bob Vandiver. It's Ty Stod-dard." As he stopped pounding on the door, he heard the sheriff's office door swing open.

"Who is it?" Bob called through the door. "I've got a shotgun, so don't try anything."

"It's Ty Stoddard."

"Back out by the fence, Ty, so I can make sure it's you," Vandiver yelled.

Ty obliged and, in a moment, he saw a shutter move in the office and Bob's face il-luminated in a momentary triangle of light. Then Ty heard the door being unbarred.

Slowly, the door opened, a crack and then a gap, the neck of a double-barrel shotgun peeking out first, then Bob's head. "Come on in, Ty; I just had to be cautious."

Ty stepped easily toward the steps, then inside, making no sudden movements in case Bob was nervous. Ty didn't want Bob's finger slipping on the trigger. Ty stepped into the stifling heat that was the courthouse and helped Bob bar the door again. Then they stepped across the hall and into the sheriff's office, Bob shutting and barring that door as well.

"I came to help you," Ty said, and he

meant it.

The sheriff grabbed Ty's hand and shook it. "I appreciate that. I can't let them get him."

Ty nodded. "I knew you wouldn't." He unbuttoned his coat as Vandiver leaned his shotgun in the corner.

Trent stood silently behind him, his hands wrapped around the steel bars, his eyes jittery, his tongue licking his lips.

Quickly, Ty removed his coat and threw it over a chair. The orange and white kerchief, though loosely tied around his neck, seemed close and threatening. Ty's fingers tugged at the kerchief, then slid to his side and his pistol, tapping gently on the revolver butt.

Bob's shoulders slumped as he studied Ty. "Some of them are regulators, good men most of them, but I can't let them take Trent, even if he is a polecat." Bob glanced toward Trent. "How can a man betray so many friends?" It was a question that came out of Vandiver's own sincerity, a man who could not believe it could happen, and yet seemed to be toiling with whether abiding by his oath might be betraying his own friends, even killing them. Vandiver moved to his desk and fell into his chair, propping his elbows on the desk and resting his head in his hands. "I never figured it would come to this," he said.

"Me, neither," Ty answered, moving around the desk and behind Trent. Ty's fingers slipped the gun from its holster and held it by the barrel. He lifted his hand above the sheriff's head.

Vandiver saw the shadow of Ty's arm and twisted around.

That was when the butt of the pistol slammed into the sheriff's head. He fell to the floor like a sack of potatoes.

"Sorry, Bob," Ty said, swinging the pistol butt into his palm.

"Thanks, Ty," Trent called, his eyes suddenly animated and his lips grinning. "The keys are in the desk." Trent rattled the bars with anticipation. "I knew you'd come to save me."

Ty waved the gun toward Trent. "I didn't come to save you, Trent. I came to kill you!"

CHAPTER 22

Trent's face went pale and his hands trembled on the cell bars. Ty saw fear in Trent's eyes as he backed away from the bars until he ran out of room, his shoulders against the far wall.

Ty cocked his revolver and stepped toward the jail cell.

"Think of Molly and the baby; he needs a father," Trent pleaded. "Remember all I've given them."

"You gave them your name, Trent Jackson, and it's been a curse upon Oldham County, upon the Stoddards."

"And Wilma; you think she'd marry you, if you killed me?"

"I intend to find out, Trent. Now you answer some questions. Slater shot me, didn't he?"

"Yeah, but I didn't know until it was too late."

Ty could feel his anger building and his

finger tightening against the trigger. He advanced to the jail cell, sticking the gun through the bars at Trent's heart. "And Phipps and Baker?"

"He was a bad man." There was desperation in Trent's voice.

"Who killed Pa?"

"Slater; you gotta believe me, Ty."

"Maybe so, Trent, but you wanted Pa dead for not supporting your reelection. You wanted Pa dead and me dead so Molly'd get the ranch and you'd run the biggest spread in Oldham County."

"Dammit, Ty, you've let folks put too many things in your mind."

"Then explain the Diamond S hides I found buried down the canyon at your last barbecue."

Trent's face went ghostlike and he shook his head. "The hands did it — Witherspoon and Higgins. It don't matter whether you believe me or not; I deserve a trial by judge and jury."

"Like the trial you gave Jake Shaw? You and Slater set him up to get us off your tail, didn't you? Slater wasn't at Mobeetie, was he?"

"No," Trent replied, his shoulders slumping and his head drooping.

"You let me hang him. It was no more to

you than killing a rabid dog."

Trent lifted his head. "No, Ty, no," he yelled, and leaped for Ty's gun poking through the bars.

Ty snapped the trigger. The gun exploded. Trent staggered, blood streaming out his nostrils. His knees wobbled and he stumbled toward Ty. His breath was ragged and each gasp sounded like a bellows with a hole in it. The gun went off again in Ty's hand, and again, both bullets ripping into Trent's torso. He collapsed on the floor, his hand reaching out and touching a steel bar, then sliding away onto Ty's boot.

"Why?" Trent gasped, and then fell limp in a puddle of blood. For a moment the only movement was a pink foam bubbling out of Trent's nose. Then even that stopped.

And for an instant, the whole world was still, as if listening to figure what had happened and where. A shrill scream then broke that silence, and came again and again, incredibly close, it seemed, like a wailing ghost. Ty had to escape quickly!

Vandiver was moaning behind him. Ty spun around. The sheriff was groggy on the floor. Ty shoved his pistol in its holster. Grabbing his coat, he jammed his arms into the sleeves.

Someone was pounding on the courthouse

door. And that scream! Ty ran to the office door and unbarred it. It swung open and he stepped into the hall. Someone was outside the door, screaming. Ty's palm fell to his pistol. But it sounded like a woman. He released the revolver butt. If he stepped outside, he might be recognized. His kerchief! He pulled it up over his nose, like a bandit, and his hat down low over his eyes. His hands fell to the door and unlatched it, jerking the door open. As he jumped outside, he collided with a slight figure, a woman.

It was Molly!

Ty cursed to himself, then caught Molly as she stumbled.

She looked him square in the eye. Her own eyes were flooded with tears and panic.

Ty released her.

She stepped back, staring in horror at him, sniffing the odor of spent gunpowder. There was a moment of silence.

Ty felt naked before her. Instinctively, his hand went to his kerchief and tugged it higher up his nose. Instantly, Ty realized that had been a mistake.

Molly's jaw dropped and her mouth gaped open. By the orange and white checks, she had recognized the kerchief, the one she had given him while he recuperated in her own bed, the bed she had shared with her husband, the husband he had just killed. "No," she called softly, then loudly, as she erupted in a scream.

Ty dashed toward the street. Seeing the mob running toward the courthouse, he jumped over the fence.

"Trent! Trent!" Molly's shrill cries carried through the cold night air. "Please be okay!" Then a final cry of horror was followed by sops. "No! No! No!"

With darkness his ally, Ty ran around the courthouse and down the street, startling a cat by the walk. Behind him now, he heard the deep-voiced shouts of the mob, suddenly indignant that someone had robbed them of their prey.

"Stop!" a man yelled behind him. A gunshot sliced through the air.

Ty cut behind a building and dashed by an outhouse. "What's going on?" a gruff voice called out.

Ty stumbled toward safety, each breath burning from the cold and the exertion. All around him dogs barked and howled. The curious emerged from their dwellings, carrying lamps and guns. Amid the confusion, Ty felt all eyes focused on him. He slowed and found himself behind the Exchange Hotel. Even over his gasping breath and his pounding heart, he heard the cry of a baby. Gradually, he caught his breath, but the baby still cried. Then Ty heard a gentle voice, a familiar voice, singing to the infant. It was Wilma. Ty turned to an adjacent window; through a crack in the lace curtains he could see Wilma on the bed, cradling Molly's son.

Ty wondered if she could marry him after what he had done.

The excitement and noise were concentrated at the courthouse now, though a few men were still running through the streets, looking for the killer. Ty pulled the mask from his face and adjusted it around on his neck as he watched Wilma. It was a sorry thing he had done, Ty knew, but he figured Dewey Slater's finger was on the trigger with his when he killed Trent Jackson. Trent hadn't been a bad man until he took on Slater as deputy. And then, Trent and Oldham County had changed.

Ty pried himself away from the window. He wanted to stay, but felt a twinge of guilt that he was violating Wilma's privacy. He wanted to marry her, but he had another job to finish. One more act to rectify his conscience. He had to kill Dewey Slater!

Slater was no fool, and Oldham County had seen the last of him. If the rumors were true, as events had proven many of them to be about Trent and Slater, the murdering deputy might head to Fort Sumner in New Mexico Territory. Ty blew out his breath, wondering if the chain of violence would ever end.

Behind him, the baby had turned quiet and Ty twisted to glance through the window at Wilma, but she had risen from the bed and was out of sight. As he stepped away from the window, he wondered if he had seen the last of Wilma Jackson.

What folks were out on the street were gathered at the courthouse, like vultures waiting for carrion. Ty crossed the street and aimed for the stable. A lamp was lit in Abe Polk's office, but Polk was gone, giving Ty an opportunity to ride away unobserved. Ty worked his way back into the stable, finding his roan and his tack and quickly saddling the animal. Ty led the animal out the back door, then out the stock pen gate and behind the buildings for fifty yards. He mounted up and aimed his horse for the canyon.

Fort Sumner was more than a hundred miles southwest of Tascosa. Without pressing his horse and without riding straight through, it would be a hard two-day ride, though three days would save his horse. It was only ten days until he had agreed to marry Wilma at the courthouse. It didn't leave him much time.

Ty followed the canyon west until he reached the Diamond S, then stopped at the ranch house for provisions and a couple of boxes of ammunition. He changed horses, too. Though it pained him to leave an animal as good as the roan behind, he cut a chestnut from the corral and led him into the barn where he swapped the saddle. The chestnut was a big animal more than seventeen hands high, not as fast as the roan, but possessing great strength and endurance. Too, Dewey Slater might recognize the roan. After throwing a bedroll and warbag of provisions over the back of the horse, Ty led him out of the barn. As Ty shoved a boot in his stirrup and pulled himself in the saddle, he realized how tired he was, how much he'd like to spend the night in his bed before heading out. But the sheriff could send men out to arrest him, and Ty needed to get close to New Mexico Territory in case he had to run for it. He would rest tomorrow. He aimed his chestnut to the west and twisted around in the saddle for a final glance at the home place. It all became Molly's if he did not return. Ty nudged the chestnut toward New Mexico Territory and rode away into the cold night.

It took three days for Ty to get to Fort Sumner, and he timed his arrival at dusk. That gave him a few days, maybe five at most, to find Dewey Slater and then return to Tascosa in time to marry Wilma, if she showed up.

Fort Sumner was a sleepy community on the banks of the Pecos River. The squat adobe buildings melded into the earth from which they came. Once a fort, the U.S. Army had abandoned it years before and now a couple hundred folks called it home. A trio of saloons offered the best entertainment and practically the only barrel whiskey for miles around. So Fort Sumner stayed busy with cowboys and the vagabonds who tried to fleece them of their measly wages. The population was mixed between Hispanics and whites, and they seemed to get along pretty well, certainly better than the two races did back in Texas.

His first night in town, Ty visited all three saloons, paying for a jigger of whiskey in each and sitting in a back corner watching saloon patrons, hoping he'd see Dewey Slater walk in, but never getting a clue if he were even on the trail of the deputy. The

Hispanics mostly ignored him and the whites eyed him with suspicion. Likely most figured he was the law, and they made a wide trail around him. Ty was tired and impatient.

Late that night, when patrons began to stumble away in greater numbers than they walked in, Ty slipped out into the cold and rode his chestnut down near the river to a copse of willows where he could pitch his bedroll and the chestnut could graze on the dried grass left over from a wet summer. The world was a bubble of cold, and Ty shivered as he slid into the bedroll and the doubled wool blanket, but he was exhausted and tumbled quickly into sleep.

The second day in Fort Sumner was no more successful than the first, as he roamed between the saloons, drinking enough whiskey so he didn't look too suspicious, but never drinking enough to impair his judgment. He had made that mistake before killing Trent Jackson. By midnight, he had thrown another day away without success. Leaving the last saloon, Ty moved down the river to a bend carved out by floodwaters. He pitched his bed under the high bank's exposed shoulder, which broke the chill of winter's biting breath. He spent the third night there, as well, and come the fourth day, Ty knew he must leave Fort Sumner before dark to return to Tascosa in time for his wedding. With hard riding, he could make it faster, but time was quickly running out, and Ty had seen no sign of Slater. Even if he returned to Tascosa in time, Ty wondered if Wilma would be there.

The fourth day was fruitless as well. Come dusk, Ty sighed as he tightened the cinch on his saddle for the trip back to Tascosa. He was about to mount when a movement caught his eye down the street. A man was coming out of a store. He was a squat figure with a poncho hanging over his shoulders and a red sombrero hiding his face. Ty remembered the sombrero. He had seen it the day Dewey Slater had shot him in the back and the day Ty and Bob Vandiver had killed the two rustlers.

Sombrero was carrying a bag of supplies from the general store. He tied the sack on his bay, then climbed aboard and headed northwest out of town.

Ty waited a couple of minutes, then mounted, pacing the chestnut at a walk on Sombrero's trail. Outside of town, Ty waited until his prey was far enough ahead not to be worried about a man on his tail, then slapped his chestnut into a lope, trying to gain enough on Sombrero so that he could keep him in his sight in the dwindling light. Gradually, a shade was being drawn over the landscape, and Sombrero disappeared.

Ahead loomed twin buttes and plenty of space for Sombrero to hide. Ty feared he had been too cautious and let his quarry escape. He eased off on the chestnut, letting him slow to a walk. His eyes gradually adjusted to the darkness and he could make out the spooky shapes of cholla and ocotillo pointing toward the sky. And he caught a couple of pinpoints of light, winking at him from between the two buttes. He aimed the chestnut in that direction, his eyes fixed on the dots of light that gradually grew into windows in a small cabin. Against the dark of the night sky, Ty could just make out a smoky serpent crawling out of the chimney. He smelled the scent of burning wood. Sombrero had not been there long enough to build a fire. Perhaps Slater was here after all.

About half a mile from the cabin, he pointed his chestnut toward the nearest butte, looking for a place to stake the animal and leave him well out of sight. After the squat adobe cabin disappeared around the edge of the butte, Ty dismounted and found a spot among scattered sandstone boulders that would screen the horse from other directions. He found his stake pin and pounded it into the ground with a stone. Then he cross-hobbled his horse, just to make sure the chestnut didn't get far if he did pull the stake pin free.

Ty opened his saddlebags and retrieved his ammunition, tucking the two boxes inside his coat. He opened his warbag and grabbed a handful of jerky and hard biscuits for his pocket. He unstrapped his extra blanket, threw it over his shoulder, and grabbed his canteen and Winchester. He stroked the chestnut's neck, then strode away toward the cabin.

He moved quietly among the rocks at the base of the butte. Though they impeded his progress, they screened his advance and would provide him cover when the shooting started. Ty figured he might slip up to the window, peer in and check whether Slater was with Sombrero. Then Ty heard a dog barking as the cabin door opened. Now, for the first time, he was glad the cold wind was blowing in his face, downwind from the cabin and the dog which might sound the alarm. Ty knew now he must wait for dawn. He must be sure Slater was inside. Sombrero's horse was tied in front of the cabin with another. In the darkness, Ty couldn't be sure if it was Slater's horse or not.

Coming within about thirty yards of the cabin, Ty figured he had best not risk alarming the dog, so he settled in among a pile of rocks and began the long wait. He pulled the cartridge boxes from his coat and opened them up on the ground for quick retrieval. He spread the blanket over his shoulder and cradled his carbine. Staring at the cabin until it seemed to shimmer before him, Ty nibbled on the jerky and hard biscuits as he waited. And shivered.

Occasionally, Ty would hear the dog bark from inside or see movement behind one of the windows, but he could never distinguish either of the two men inside. Gradually, the aroma of woodsmoke lessened as the fire died down in the fireplace. And the light from the lamp seemed to be dying as it grew dimmer and dimmer, then finally flickered out. Then the cabin was in darkness and all was still except for the horses stamping in front of the cabin. No sense in staring at the cabin all night, Ty decided, or he might not be as sharp in the morning when he needed to have steady hands and a sharp eye.

Ty leaned against a rock, checked the safety on the carbine and drew the blanket around him. It took a while, but he finally got to sleep, waking periodically to check the sky and the cabin. When the world began to pinken around the edge, he sat up straight, shook his head to clear it, and began to rub the muscles in his arms of their stiffness. He fished a slice of jerky and a hard biscuit out of his pocket and began to gnaw on them. The salty meat made him reach for his canteen, but the water was frozen. The cabin before him was dark and motionless.

"Come on, Slater," he whispered to himself. Ty craved a smoke, but knew better than to flare a match for fear of giving himself away.

The cabin remained dark come morning, but the world lighted up around it like the grin on Ty's face. The second horse outside the cabin was Slater's dun. The wait would be worth it, now. Slater and Sombrero were not early risers, and it was maybe two hours, though it seemed longer, before Ty detected any activity in the cabin. A thread of smoke began to weave its way out of the chimney. Ty checked the load on his carbine and rested it on a rock, his steely eyes staring down the sight at the door.

The door creaked open. Ty's still finger touched the cold trigger. Sombrero stepped outside, hatless, but wearing his poncho. Just like Slater to let sombrero come out first in case there was trouble. Sombrero went out beyond the house to attend nature's call, then ambled back in, stretching his arms and yawning. The smoke out of the chimney was thickening and the door swung open. Ty flinched, the rifle scraping against the rock. Slater appeared in the door a moment, standing motionless as if he might have heard the noise; then he slipped outside, the dog with him, and followed Sombrero's trail to relieve himself.

Ty sighted in on Slater's back as he felt the warm heat of the morning sun when it cleared the edge of the butte behind him and bathed Ty in its light. Slater turned around, his hands fumbling with his britches, as he returned. Ty trained his gun on Slater, his finger touching the cold trigger again. The dog growled.

Before Ty could shoot, Slater's head jerked and his hand grabbed for his pistol. Ty squeezed off a shot, but as he did so, Slater dropped to the ground, squeezing off a shot of his own. The bullet plunked into the rock behind Ty. Ty jerked the rifle behind the rock, catching a glint of sunlight on his barrel. The sun or the dog had given his position away.

Slater fired again, the bullet ricocheting over Ty's head. Slater jumped up from the

362

ground and dashed toward the cabin. Ty leaped up between the rocks and loosed a couple shots, each missing.

Out of the cabin jumped Sombrero, carrying a carbine at hip level. Ty swung his carbine around and fired simultaneously with Sombrero. Ty felt his hat fly from his head. His own shot thudded into the cabin wall. Sombrero was a bigger target than Slater, who was scrambling to untie his bucking mount from the hitching rack. Ty aimed at Sombrero's heart. His rifle kicked into his shoulder when he touched the trigger. Sombrero screamed as blood splotched his chest. He looked down in disbelief and tumbled backward into the doorway.

Slater held the reins of his dun, but the animal was bucking too much for him to get a foot in the stirrup. He squeezed off a wild shot at Ty, then another aimless shot.

Ty ejected the hull that had killed Sombrero, then dropped his hand to the cartridge box to reload his Winchester.

Slater used the dun to screen himself from Ty.

"Coward!" Ty yelled. He aimed at Slater, but could never clear a good shot for the animal.

Then the horse reared on its hind feet and kicked at Slater, knocking his pistol over by

Sombrero. The horse jerked the reins free and bolted for freedom.

Slater dove for the pistol and grabbed it. He jumped toward Sombrero's terrified horse, shooting once at Ty. Slater jerked the reins free, then leaped for the saddle, grabbing the pommel with his left hand and pulling his leg over the seat. The horse dashed by Ty, the loose and bouncing stirrups terrifying the animal as much as the gunfire. Slater fired again; the bullet plunked into the rock in front of Ty, spitting gravel at him.

Ty felt the sting in his face. Slater was getting away, and Ty's own horse was too far away to give chase. Ty aimed at the horse, squeezing off one, two, three shots, the kerthunk of each telling Ty he had struck the animal. Yet the animal galloped out of terror another twenty yards; then its step faltered. The animal pitched forward onto its knees; then its rear legs shoved ahead and the animal tumbled ahead, throwing Slater clear. Slater spun through the air and hit the ground hard. He lay motionless.

Satisfaction coursed through Ty's veins as he ejected a spent shell from his Winchester and reloaded from the box on the ground. He gathered the boxes and shoved them back in his coat, all the time watching

Slater. He had not moved. Likely, he had broken his neck in the fall. Ty took time to throw his blanket over his shoulders, loop his canteen strap over his arm, and jump around a couple of rocks to pick up the hat that Sombrero had shot off his head. He brushed off his hat and looked at the hole in the brim. A couple of inches to the left and he would've been dead.

But that was could've beens. Now, he had done what he came to New Mexico Territory to do. If only for a moment before he died, Slater had known what it was like to be ambushed, to depart this earth with less than a fair chance. Ty ambled out to check the motionless Slater.

Ty approached Slater cautiously, the only movement coming from the cold breeze rippling his coat. The terror that Slater must have felt was reflected by the pistol still in his hand. He had held it so tightly that even in the nasty fall the pistol had not fallen from his grasp. Ty remembered the pain when he had been ambushed, the burning agony of being kicked in the ribs, the haunting sound of the tapping and whistling.

Instinctively, Ty drew back his boot and kicked Slater in the ribs.

There was a groan. Slater's eyes flickered open.

Before Ty could make sense of it, he saw Slater's hand lift off the ground. He was staring into the barrel of Slater's revolver. A wicked smile curled at Slater's lips. He pulled the trigger.

Ty saw the hammer slide back, then fall forward. He flinched against the expected explosion. He heard an empty click. He saw the smile on Slater's face turn to a horrified contortion at the sound of his empty gun. Ty lifted the barrel of his carbine until it was inches from Slater's chest. He pulled the trigger again and again until the gun answered only with a click of its own.

CHAPTER 23

Ty pushed the chestnut as hard as he could without running it into the ground and leaving himself afoot. He had made up considerable time, but he would still be three hours later than he had promised Wilma, if she had even showed up. How could she, if she knew he had killed Trent?

Ty followed the Canadian River, bypassing a stop at his ranch to swap horses. The chestnut's stamina was still good and the roan's better speed would make only a few minutes difference anyway.

The trail curved away from the river and toward Tascosa. Ty felt anticipation like butterflies in his stomach. Even if Wilma were there, Ty might be jailed in Trent's death and unable to marry her until after a trial, if even then. The chestnut finally topped the canyon trail and Ty's eyes fixed on the courthouse. Ty ignored the stares of the few people around.

"It's Ty Stoddard," someone yelled, but Ty didn't turn to look. He stared at the courthouse, reining up hard by the fence and jumping to the ground, not even pausing to tie the reins. He bolted through the gate and up the vacant steps. Wilma would be inside, he told himself. He was biting his lip as he shoved open the door, the door where he had encountered Molly after killing her husband.

The hallway was empty.

Ty felt his shoulders sag and his breath escape in a rush. He stood stunned. She had left him! But had he betrayed her? He would likely never know. Now it mattered little how Trent's killing was rectified by the courts. He turned toward the open sheriff's door and realized for the first time that Bob Vandiver was staring at him from his desk. Ty walked into his office and closed the iron door.

"I'm here to turn myself in, Bob." Ty unbuttoned his coat and lifted his revolver with his thumb and forefinger, placing the revolver on the desk.

Vandiver pushed his chair back and stood up.

Ty could see the bruise on the side of the sheriff's head from when he had slugged him. Ty winced at the memory, but something else was nagging at him. "Was Wilma Jackson here earlier today?"

Vandiver shook his head. "I've been here all day and I never saw her."

Ty slipped into a chair and slumped over, putting his head in his hands. "I killed Dewey Slater at Fort Sumner. Killed the one that escaped from you and me in the territory. I've become quite a killer since I slugged you alongside the head, Bob."

"They were bad men, all of them, Ty." The sheriff picked up Ty's revolver and handed it to him. "Go on home, Ty."

Ty looked up at Bob. "You know I slugged you; you know I killed Trent."

Vandiver nodded. "When I came to, I was groggy. I mentioned your name. Because of that, some suspect you did it. But after a night in bed, I was thinking straight. I told the justice of the peace that Trent had grabbed me as I passed his cell, that he grabbed my neck and pounded my head into the bars, but I was able to pull my gun and shoot him before I passed out. It's a poor story, Ty, but it'll hold."

"But why, Bob? You swore to uphold the law."

Vandiver shoved the pistol back into Ty's holster. "You were keeping your vow to the regulators about taking care of your own.

You kept me from killing some of my neighbors, which I'd done had they tried to lynch him. The killing, the suspicion — it's all got to stop somewhere, Ty. This is the place. You ended it. Nobody'll know, except you and me."

"And Molly." Ty sighed. "She recognized me as I escaped."

Vandiver cursed. "Far as the sheriff and the law are concerned, you had no part in it, Ty. How you work it out with your sister's up to you. She took it hard, it coming so close on the heels of Delia's death and your father's. She's Stoddard stock, Ty, so she'll manage. Fact, I was by there yesterday and she had hired a couple of hands to work the place."

Ty got up from his chair and stared Vandiver full in the eye. "What about Wilma? Was she around?"

Vandiver shook his head. "Wilma'd left. Molly didn't say where she'd gone, just that she'd gone a day or so back."

"I'm obliged to you, Bob, for all you've done." Ty shook Vandiver's hand. "It's good to have a neighbor like you for a sheriff." Ty released the sheriff's hand and turned for the door.

"You take care, Ty. Oldham County needs more folks like you Stoddard stock."

Vandiver said something else, but Ty didn't listen. He was devastated by Wilma's departure. Somehow, he had figured she would stay, Wilma not being one of fickle emotions. But that must have been just wishful thinking on his part. Ty marched out of the courthouse and past a knot of the curious who asked a few questions, then backed away when Ty turned his glaring eyes toward them. He mounted the chestnut and rode away toward the Diamond S.

He gave the animal free rein. His muscles ached and it almost hurt to think, Ty was so tired. The ride had taken a lot out of him, but not as much as knowing that Wilma had not shown up at the courthouse. So many questions had remained about his killing Trent Jackson, but Bob Vandiver had resolved those so neatly that Ty would never go to court. And while he should be pleased, that seemed like such a little victory compared to the loss of Wilma.

The chestnut gradually peeled the miles away and Ty found himself staring at the Diamond S headquarters. In the distance, he could see his roan prancing around the corral. It was good to be home, he thought, as he rode up to the barn and dismounted. Glancing over his shoulder at the house, he saw a plume of smoke trailing out of the kitchen vent. Likely the hands had kept a fire burning so the water barrel wouldn't freeze in the kitchen during his absence. Ty led the chestnut into the barn and quickly unsaddled him, fed him plenty of grain and broke the layer of ice atop the watering trough.

Picking up his carbine, bedroll, blanket, and saddlebags, Ty emerged from the barn. It was good to know that the rustling problems were over, but without Wilma, there was no one to share that satisfaction with.

As he stepped upon the plank porch, a rattle at the door startled him. He flinched as the door slowly swung open. There stood Wilma, her eyes glistening.

Ty dropped his load and stepped to her. She came out into the cold to meet him, tears streaming down her cheek.

"I feared you were dead," she cried.

"I figured you had left," he answered, then kissed her on the lips, pulling her tight against him. He smelled the sweetness of her hair and her skin and realized how awful he must smell. Even so, she seemed to dig deeper into his arms, resting her cheek against his shoulder. "In Tascosa I heard you'd left Molly's place; I figured you'd left for good."

"And leave the man I love? I came here because I thought you'd stop here before you kept our date at the courthouse." Her voice was pierced with hurt.

"But I know some bad things've been rumored about me and Trent."

"I've heard, Tyrus Bartholomew Stoddard, that you killed Trent. I've heard Trent was a rustler and a murderer. Maybe it is so, but I chose not to believe it about two men that have meant so much to me. I've lost Trent. I don't want to lose you. If it is true, I can't change it, Ty, because it's past. I'm through looking toward the past. I want to look toward the future."

"With me?" Ty asked.

"With you, Tyrus Bartholomew Stoddard," she said, then kissed him on the lips.

Together, they stepped inside the warm house, the door closing behind them on the cold world.

ABOUT THE AUTHOR

Preston Lewis is the Spur Award-winning author of 30 western, juvenile and historical novels. In addition to his two Western Writers of America Spurs, he is recipient of the 2018 Will Rogers Gold Medallion for Western Humor for *Bluster's Last Stand,* the fourth volume in his comic western series *The Memoirs of H.H. Lomax.* Two other books in that series — *The Redemption of Jesse James* and *Mix-Up at the O.K. Corral* — were Spur finalists. His comic western *The Fleecing of Fort Griffin* received an Elmer Kelton Award from the West Texas Historical Association for best creative work on the region.

Lewis is a past president of both WWA and the WTHA. He resides in San Angelo, Texas, with his wife Harriet. He holds bachelor's and master's degrees in journalism from Baylor and Ohio State universi-

ties, and a master's degree in history from
Angelo State University.